Also by Jennifer L. Schiff

A Shell of a Problem

Something Fishy

A Sanibel Island Mystery

Jennifer Lonoff Schiff

Shovel
& Pail
Press

This is a work of fiction. Names, characters, businesses, places, events, and incidents are either the products of the author's imagination or used in a fictitious manner. Any resemblance to actual persons, living or dead, or actual events, is purely coincidental.

SOMETHING FISHY: A SANIBEL ISLAND MYSTERY
by Jennifer Lonoff Schiff

Book Two in the Sanibel Island Mystery series

https://www.SanibelIslandMysteries.com

© 2018 by Jennifer Lonoff Schiff

Cover design by Kristin Bryant

Formatting by Polgarus Studio

ISBN: 978-0-692-07855-6

Library of Congress Control Number: 2018903433

Many men go fishing all of their lives
without knowing that it is not fish they are after.
—Henry David Thoreau

Guests, like fish, begin to smell after three days.
—Benjamin Franklin

PROLOGUE

Art was a closer. Closing deals was what he was known for. But closing the deal on this promotion? It had been harder than he had thought it would be. All because of Rick. Rick was younger than Art, more devious than Art, and had been totally sucking up to their boss, the vice president of Sales, for weeks. But Art had a plan. The annual sales conference was taking place in a couple of weeks, in mid-June, on Sanibel Island, Florida, and Art was going to arrange a private charter fishing trip for his boss, who had been telling everyone about the wonderful fishing trips he had gone on with his grandfather on Sanibel, back when he was a boy. That should impress him, Art thought.

Art knew nothing about fishing, but he wasn't concerned. He figured he could learn what he needed to know by watching a few fishing videos. He also had an ace in the hole, a secret weapon: his ex-wife, Guinivere, who now lived and worked on Sanibel. She was a reporter and had a knack for ferreting out information, like who the best charter fishing captains were, and she could arrange the whole thing. She had always been good at arranging things.

Art hadn't actually communicated with Guin in months, but he was confident he could get her to help him. He was the company's top salesperson for three years in a row for a reason. And he knew how to get what he wanted. And right now, he wanted that promotion—and to get his ex-wife back.

Art knew he had been stupid to take up with their hairdresser, Debbie, a college dropout who was nearly half his age and obsessed with reality TV shows, which Art abhorred. But she was so hot, and always made him feel so smart and attractive when he saw her, unlike Guin the last year or so of their marriage. And then he had impulsively asked her if she wanted to get a drink with him sometime, and she had said yes, even though she knew he was married to one of her clients. Of course, one drink led to another, and before he knew it, they were sleeping together, though there was very little sleeping involved.

He knew he should have broken things off. But whenever he saw Debbie—who had the body of a Playboy playmate and full, sensual lips—his libido took over. Afterward, he would feel guilty, until he went home and Guin started nagging him about something or other. Though, if he was being honest with himself, Guin probably had reason to complain. He hadn't been around a lot the last year or so of their marriage, due to his hectic travel schedule. And when he wasn't traveling for work, he worked from home, or on his golf game, or on Debbie.

It was only recently, after Debbie had gone back to Dallas to be with her mom, who was suffering from breast cancer, that Art realized he had thrown away a good thing. And he was determined to woo Guin back, and not just because being with her would help get him that promotion. (His boss, Alan Fielding, and Alan's wife, Emily, had adored Guin, and Art had a feeling his stock had gone down somewhat with the divorce.) He missed Guin. And if winning her back also meant he got that promotion, that would be a win-win.

He pictured himself and Guin having dinner with Alan

and Emily after a day of tarpon fishing and smiled. It was the perfect plan. He would impress his boss, get that big promotion, and get his ex back to boot.

CHAPTER 1

"No."

"But Guin—"

"I said 'no,' Art."

Guin paced around her bedroom in her nightshirt, a large old concert tee, holding her phone to her ear.

"Please, Guin, just hear me out."

"What part of 'no' did you not understand, Arthur?"

"Fine. What about a cup of coffee? Surely you can take thirty minutes from your busy schedule to have a cup of coffee with your husband?"

"Ex-husband."

"Ex-husband."

Guin sighed. When she saw her ex-husband's cell phone number flash up on her phone, she knew she shouldn't have picked up. And she hadn't the first three times he'd called. But it was late, and she was tired, and she figured if she spoke with him, maybe he'd go away. She was wrong.

"Guin, I'm sorry. I was an idiot. I know that now. I should have never let you go. I was a fool to hook up with Debbie. I clearly wasn't thinking—"

"You got that right."

Art wanted to say something in his defense, but he realized now was not the time. If he wanted to win Guin back, he knew he needed to apologize, even if he felt she had been wrong, too.

"Anyway, I broke up with Debbie—"

Guin raised an eyebrow. She highly doubted that. She knew Debbie, and that every man whose hair she cut (or colored) was secretly, or not-so-secretly, in love with her, and had been frankly stunned that Debbie had hooked up with Art, a man technically old enough to be her father. Granted, Art was very attractive (even in his mid-forties), and suave (when he wanted to be), and rich, or well off. No doubt he had dazzled or charmed Debbie, who hailed from a small town near Dallas and had never gone to university, or really anywhere, other than Texas or Connecticut, and Florida for spring break. He had certainly dazzled or charmed Guin when she had been not much older than Debbie.

Guin sighed. "So, she left you, did she?"

Again, Art wanted to protest, to defend himself. She hadn't so much left him as gone back home to help take care of her mother—and they had both agreed it was probably for the best. Dating a hot, younger woman had been fun at first (or the sex certainly had), but he had quickly grown bored.

"Her mom has cancer."

"Oh, I'm sorry to hear that," said Guin, who actually did feel sorry for Debbie and her mom. Cancer was a horrible disease, and Guin knew how close Debbie was to her mom.

"I miss you, Guin," said Art, and at that moment, he truly did.

Guin sighed, again. "Fine. I'll meet you for breakfast at the Over Easy Café."

"Excellent," said Art, quietly breathing a sigh of relief.

He knew if he could just get Guin alone, spend some time with her, he could woo her back.

"Thank you. I promise you won't regret it."

Guin was already regretting it, but she was tired, and a little part of her missed Art. What harm could there be in meeting him for breakfast?

"I'd better not," she said. "When did you say the conference was?"

"In a couple of weeks. Mid-June. I'm flying down a day early. Figured we could meet for breakfast that first morning, before the conference officially starts."

"Fine, send me a meeting request—I know how much you love them—with the time and the date, and I'll respond."

"Will do. Should I send it to your Gmail account?"

"That's fine," Guin said, wishing for the call to be over already.

"Just one other thing…" said Art.

Guin rolled her eyes. Of course, Art wanted something. Typical.

"Do you know of a good charter boat fishing captain? I need to arrange a trip for a bunch of the guys, and you probably know everyone, Sanibel being such a small place."

Guin sighed. Sure, she knew of several guys who did charter fishing trips. But she didn't know anyone personally, not being into fishing herself. But her colleague, Craig Jeffers, who covered fishing for the local paper, the *San-Cap Sun-Times* (*San-Cap* being short for *Sanibel-Captiva*), and her contact at the Sanibel Police Department, Detective William "Bill" O'Loughlin, who was an avid fisherman, no doubt did.

"What type of fishing are you planning on doing?"

"The conference is the second weekend of June, and I hear it's peak tarpon season," said Art, who had been reading up on the local fishing scene.

"Okay" said Guin. "Send me a couple of dates, and let me know how many people, and I'll get back to you in a couple of days."

"Thanks Guin. You're the best."

Guin made a face.

"I haven't done anything yet. Just send me an email, and I'll see what I can do."

"Aye aye!" said Art, a bit too cheerily in Guin's opinion. She rolled her eyes.

"Goodnight Art," she said, then ended the call.

Guin turned off her phone and put it in the drawer of her nightstand. She looked down at her bed, where her two cats, Flora and Fauna, were already fast asleep, and longed to join them. She shoved them aside and made space for herself under the covers. Then she turned off the light and closed her eyes, but she felt unsettled. She tossed and turned, unable to get comfortable. Finally, she turned the light back on. She looked at the clock. It was 10:25.

She got out of bed, much to the annoyance of the cats, and started to pace the bedroom.

"Why now?" she asked the cats, who gazed up at her. "Why did he have to call now, just when I thought I had gotten over him?"

The cats blinked and then closed their eyes and went back to sleep.

"You two are no help," she said.

She reached into the drawer and took out her phone, debating whether to turn it back on and text her friend, Shelly, though it was past Shelly's bedtime. Well, if she's asleep, her phone will be off, Guin reasoned as she turned on her phone.

She waited for the phone to go through its startup sequence, entered her code, then sent Shelly a text.

"You up?" she typed. "If so, CALL ME."

She sat back down on the bed and stared at the phone. A few seconds later, it started buzzing.

"What's up?" said Shelly, yawning.

"You're up," said Guin, surprised to hear from her friend.

"Apparently," replied Shelly. "So, what's so important you had to text me after ten?"

"My ex just called," said Guin, standing up again and pacing around the bedroom. "Actually, he's been calling me for days. But I just spoke to him. He's coming to Sanibel."

"Oh boy."

"You're telling me," said Guin.

"How does Ris feel about that?" asked Shelly. Ris was Harrison Hartwick, Dr. Harrison Hartwick, known by the female population of Southwest Florida as Harry Heartthrob, or Dr. Heartthrob. A noted marine biologist, professor at Florida Gulf Coast University, and acting science director at the Bailey-Matthews National Shell Museum on Sanibel, Harrison Hartwick had also been voted one of the sexiest men in Southwest Florida. And he was Guin's beau.

"I haven't told him yet," said Guin. "I just got off the phone with Art a few minutes ago—and immediately texted you."

"So, you going to see him when he comes to Sanibel?"

"I agreed to meet him at the Over Easy Café for breakfast. I figured that would be safe."

"Oooh, you want me and Steve to join you? Not join you, but, you know, sit a couple tables away and keep an eye on you?"

Steve was Shelly's husband.

"Tempting," said Guin. "But I think I can handle Art."

"You still have feelings for him?" asked Shelly.

"I don't know. I didn't think so. But he was very apologetic on the phone, and he sounded pretty sincere, and…"

Guin hiccupped, or perhaps it was something else.

"You okay?"

"No. Yes. I don't know. I guess I'm feeling a bit emotional. I haven't been getting enough sleep, and it's that time of the month, and I wasn't expecting to have to deal with Art. I'll probably be fine in the morning," said Guin, though she doubted it. Why did Art have to call?

"Okay, but if you want to talk, just call, or text me," said Shelly. "So, we still going shelling and then to Over Easy Sunday morning? It's been ages."

"Absolutely!" said Guin. "I wouldn't miss it."

Before Ris had entered the picture, Guin and Shelly had a standing Sunday brunch date. But recently Guin had been spending her weekends with Ris, often at his place in Fort Myers Beach.

"So, you're not spending the weekend with Ris?"

"No. We're getting together tomorrow night," Guin said. "He has some conference this weekend. So I'm all yours."

"Excellent," said Shelly. "Hey, I know we're getting together Sunday, but we're having a big barbeque Saturday. You're welcome to come, if you're feeling lonely. The kids are having some of their friends over, and we're having a few of the old folks," said Shelly, laughing. (By 'old folks' she meant people her and Steve's age, in their forties, which neither she nor Guin considered to be that old, though Shelly's college-age kids did.)

"Thanks, Shelly. Can I let you know tomorrow?"

"Sure."

Shelly yawned, which made Guin yawn, too.

"Well, I guess I should let you get to bed," said Guin. "Thanks for calling me so late."

"Anytime," said Shelly, letting out another yawn.

"Goodnight, Shell."

"Goodnight, Guin."

Guin ended the call, turned off her phone (again), and placed it back in the drawer. Then she got under the covers and turned off the light. This time, she fell asleep.

CHAPTER 2

Guin got up Thursday morning feeling much better, until she remembered she had promised Art she would help him line up a charter fishing boat captain to take him and a bunch of his sales buddies tarpon fishing around Sanibel in a couple of weeks. Ugh. And she had agreed to meet Art for breakfast while he was in town. Double ugh. Though a part of her secretly wanted to see her ex, if only to show him how great she was doing, and looking, without him. (She refused to admit to herself that part of her also missed him.)

She stretched, then got out of bed and headed to the kitchen to make herself some coffee. The cats padded down the hall after her, Fauna mewing loudly as they entered the kitchen.

"Yeah, yeah, yeah," I hear you, Guin said, addressing the two hungry felines. "Let me get my coffee going. Then I'll feed you."

She bustled about the kitchen preparing her coffee. As she waited for the grounds to soak up the hot water in the French press, she went into the pantry to retrieve the cat food, the cats on her heels.

"Back away from the cat lady and no one gets hurt," she said aloud to the cats, who were rubbing up against her legs.

She walked over to their bowls and poured in some dry cat food. Flora immediately began to eat, while Fauna looked down at the bowl, then up at Guin.

"Sorry, dude, that's what there is. Take it or leave it."

They locked eyes, but Guin stood her ground. A few seconds later, Fauna, like Flora, was scarfing down kibble.

"Good girl," said Guin, emptying their water bowl and refilling it with fresh water.

The cats taken care of, she finished fixing her coffee, then took the mug to her small dining table and stared out past the lanai onto the ninth green.

Since leaving New England nearly a year ago, Guin had been renting a furnished two-bedroom, two-bath condo in a golf community near the J. N. "Ding" Darling National Wildlife Refuge on Sanibel. One of her favorite things about the condo was the view. The living area looked out onto the ninth green, which had far more birds walking it than golfers. And Guin enjoyed sitting at her little dining table, or on the lanai, noting the different species. There were so many different types of birds: ibises, great egrets, woodpeckers, roseate spoonbills... She had acquired several birding books so she could properly identify the various birds she saw, both out her window and when she was on her daily beach walk.

Guin took another sip of coffee and continued to stare outside. She went to turn on her phone, only to realize that she had left it in the bedroom. She retrieved it, entered her password, and waited for her new messages to appear.

There was a text from Ris, an early riser, confirming their dinner date for that evening. She would be meeting him at the Beach House, their go-to place in Fort Myers Beach, which was owned by friends of Shelly and Steve's.

There was also a text from Shelly, checking to see if she was doing better, with an invitation to text or call her if she wanted to talk. Guin smiled.

Next, she checked her email. As a reporter for the local

paper, she was constantly receiving story ideas—and emailing with people about articles she was working on. While the print edition of the paper only came out on Friday, the paper's online edition posted new stories daily. So she was almost always either writing or researching a piece.

Mostly, Guin covered local events and did profiles of local businesses and business leaders. But ever since she had helped solve the case of the missing Golden Junonia, a rare shell that had been stolen during the preview for the annual Shell Show, and then helped uncover the killer of noted real estate developer Gregor Matenopoulos, the chief suspect, she had been tasked with writing about local crime, too. Not that there was a lot of crime on Sanibel.

Indeed, on Sanibel, the most common crimes involved littering, not properly disposing of lawn clippings or vegetation, and going over 35 mph (the island speed limit). Occasionally, there were more high-profile crimes, such as burglaries, carjackings, and murders, but these were extremely rare. Which was fine by Guin. She was perfectly happy covering the latest restaurant or store opening and events like National Seashell Day. (It was the first National Seashell Day that had initially brought Guin to Sanibel, on a freelance assignment. But that one assignment had changed Guin's life, resulting in her selling her house in Connecticut and moving to Sanibel a couple of months later.)

Guin continued to check her email. Most of it was junk, or unimportant. Her stomach rumbled. "Right. Food," she said aloud. She got up and went into the kitchen. She opened the fridge and peered inside. "Toast and eggs, or cereal?" Feeling lazy, she took out the container of milk. Then she grabbed the box of Cheerios from the pantry and fixed herself a bowl of cereal, which she took back into the living area. As she ate, she scrolled through Instagram.

Among the new photos was a picture of her colleague,

Craig Jeffers, holding an enormous fish. She "liked" it and then sent Craig a text. "Can you recommend a charter fishing captain who could take a bunch of landlubbers out tarpon fishing in a couple of weeks?" she typed.

A minute later Craig replied. "You want to call me?"

Might as well get this over with, Guin thought.

She waited as Craig's mobile rang.

"So, you're interested in tarpon fishing?"

"Not me," Guin clarified. "I was asked by a guy I know if I knew of someone. He's going to be attending a sales conference here in a couple of weeks, and he wants to impress his boss, whose grandfather used to take him tarpon fishing around here as a kid."

"A guy?" asked Craig.

Guin sighed. "Okay, technically my ex. He's up for some big promotion, and he thought that a charter fishing trip would tip the scales in his favor with the VP of Sales."

"Your ex, eh?"

"I know. I know. Can you help me or not?" asked Guin, who instantly regretted being so snippy.

"I know a lot of guys. Just a matter of finding the right one. You mentioned the VP of Sales. So, are these a bunch of sales guys?"

"I would assume so," said Guin.

"And have they gone tarpon fishing before?"

"Doubtful," said Guin.

"But they probably don't want to admit they know nothing about fishing."

"Probably," said Guin.

"Drinkers?"

"You filling out a questionnaire?"

Craig laughed. "No, but I want to match your ex up with the right guy. Unless you don't care."

Guin thought for a moment. Did she care? Part of her

wouldn't have minded Art being made a fool of. But then that wouldn't reflect well on her. And she prided herself on her ability to arrange things so that everyone involved was satisfied, even if she didn't particularly care for the people involved.

"Okay, ask away. Though I really don't know much about Art's current coworkers. I know some of them, or some of the ones he worked with a couple years ago. And yeah, they were all big drinkers. So I guess they'll probably want to bring some booze, unless that's not allowed. I can ask him."

"That's okay," said Craig. "I get the idea. So how many guys are we talking about?"

"I don't know. Art didn't say. Is there a limit?"

"Well, most of the guys I know won't take more than six guys tarpon fishing. And a lot of them won't take more than four."

"I'll let Art know. Anything else?"

"Not that I can think of," said Craig.

"So do you have a recommendation for me?"

"I actually have two, depending on which way you want to go."

"Okay, shoot," said Guin.

"Well, my personal pick is Al Boudreaux. He knows the area better than anyone. Been doing charter boat trips around Sanibel and Captiva for over 30 years. Takes guys out tarpon fishing all the time. Also does eco and shelling tours."

"He sounds great. Is there a catch?"

"He's one of those guys who will typically only take a max of four guys. And he's really into the environment. Hates it when he sees people littering or polluting the water, and some guys don't like being lectured. But for my money, Al is the best. And he does allow guys to drink when they're fishing, in moderation."

"Sounds like my kind of guy," said Guin. "So, who's your other pick?"

"Big Ben Johnson. He's more the freewheeling type, a real guy's guy, if you know what I mean."

"I'm not sure I do."

"Ben's a good fisherman, but a bit of a braggart and doesn't always obey all the rules. Knows how to tell a good story, though. If your ex's lot is on the rowdy side and cares more about having a good story to tell their buddies than about actually fishing, then Captain Ben's probably your guy, or your ex's."

"Well, I know who I'd rather go out fishing with," said Guin.

"I've known Al Boudreaux for years. Great guy."

"But maybe not the right guy for Art and his buddies. Do both of them have websites?"

"You want me to email you the information?" asked Craig.

"That would be great. Thanks," said Guin.

"No problem. Anything else I can help you out with?"

"Nope, I'm good. Betty still have you on that high fiber diet?"

Craig's wife, Betty, was always after Craig to take better care of himself.

Craig chuckled. "She does. And let me tell you, I never want to see another bran muffin again."

Guin laughed. "Well, I love Betty's baking. If you ever want to get rid of some muffins, drop them off at my place, or leave them for me over at the office. I stop by there most Tuesdays."

"Will do, Guin."

They said their goodbyes and ended the call.

Guin looked down at her phone. It was nearly eight-thirty. A bit late for shelling, but a walk on the beach would help to relieve some of the stress she had been feeling since Art's call. She quickly washed her cereal bowl and went into the bedroom to get dressed.

A few minutes later, she was in her purple Mini Cooper, heading to Blind Pass beach.

CHAPTER 3

Late May was a quiet time on Sanibel, or relatively quiet. There were still tourists who came to visit, but all the snowbirds had left, and Guin loved having the beach mostly to herself.

She walked along the shoreline, looking for shells, but her thoughts kept wandering back to the night before. Why did Art have to call now, just when she thought she was over him? Was he truly sorry for jilting her, or was it just a ruse to get her to help him impress his boss? He sounded as though he missed her, but she had been tired.

She stared out at the sea, watching some brown pelicans dive for fish. Then she continued her walk, examining shells as she went. Sanibel was famous for its seashells. Due to the island's shape and position in the Gulf of Mexico, it attracted many shells and shell seekers to its shores. And most days you could see dozens of types of shells on its beaches, from the quite common arks, clams, oysters, coquinas, Florida fighting conchs, lightning whelks, pen shells, lettered olives, and banded tulips, to the rarer alphabet and Florida cones and Scotch bonnets, to the rarest of them all, the junonia. Guin particularly liked the brightly colored scallops, which came in dazzling shades of orange, purple, and pink, as well as apple and lace murexes and worm shells, which resembled large worms.

Since moving down to Sanibel the previous summer, she had become an avid sheller, amassing buckets of shells. Nearly every morning, she'd scour the beach for new shells. She'd bring them home and let them soak in dishwashing liquid for hours, then dry them off and coat them with a little mineral oil. Then, when they were dry, she'd arrange them in glass vases or bowls, which she displayed around the condo. Her latest project was a large shell mirror.

There were not many shells to be had that morning, but it was a beautiful day, and she continued walking until she had nearly reached Bowman's Beach. Then she turned around and headed back toward her car, picking up a few more shells along the way.

It was nearly ten by the time Guin sat down at her computer. She opened her email and found a meeting request from Art, inviting her to breakfast at the Over Easy Café in a couple of weeks. She smiled despite herself. That reminded her: she should send him the links to the two charter fishing boat captains Craig had recommended.

She found the email from Craig and opened the links for Captain Al Boudreaux and Captain Ben Johnson, who everyone referred to as Big Ben. Looking at the photos on his website, she could see why. The man was a giant. He had probably played football in college. Next, she looked at Captain Al Boudreaux's website, which was filled with photos of families out fishing and women on shelling or eco tours. Hmm, thought Guin. She had a feeling she knew which captain Art would choose.

She clicked on "compose" and began the email to Art, summarizing what Craig had told her about each captain and including the links to their websites. "And be sure to book NOW," she added. "These guys get booked weeks in advance. And let me know which one you went with and how you liked the trip. Would be good to know for future reference." She quickly reviewed what she wrote and realized she had absent-mindedly typed "xo, Guin" at the bottom. She quickly deleted the "xo," then hit "send."

She spent the next couple of hours polishing her piece on Memorial Day weekend activities on Sanibel and Captiva. Then she sent it to the editor of the paper, Ginny Prescott, and took a quick lunch break. She got back to work, spending the rest of the afternoon transcribing an interview she had recently done with the owner of a new bakery. The owner, who was also the head baker, was French. He had fallen in love with Sanibel while on vacation there, and he felt that Sanibel could use a good French bakery and patisserie. Guin heartily agreed, especially after tasting his *pain au chocolat* and opera cake, and she wished him the best of luck. Though she wondered if it was wise to open Memorial Day weekend, instead of, say, December or January, which was the beginning of peak season. She also wondered how the delicate baked goods would stand up to the heat and humidity of summer on Sanibel. But Jean-Luc, the baker, was not concerned.

It was after four by the time she finished transcribing the interview and reviewed what she had typed. She got up and stretched, then walked out to the lanai, where she did a few more stretches. The cats had followed her out and decided to join in, stretching alongside her. Guin smiled and petted them. She bent her knees and took a deep breath in, then exhaled as she straightened. She repeated the exercise a few more times, then headed back into the kitchen to get a glass of water. The cats followed her and waited expectantly.

"Sorry, guys, it's not dinner time yet."

Flora gently swatted her ankle.

"Hey!" Guin snapped. "I'll feed you before I go out."

The cats sat in the middle of the kitchen and stared up at her. Guin sighed, then took another sip of water. She looked at the clock. She still had over an hour until she had to leave to meet Ris at the Beach House. She thought about doing more work but quickly vetoed the idea. And she didn't feel like reading as she had been staring at words all day. Maybe some mindless TV. She turned on the television and was about to sit on the couch when she remembered she had left her phone in the other room and hadn't checked her messages in a while.

She went to her desk and pulled her phone out of the drawer, where she kept it while writing. There was a text from Shelly, instructing her to have fun tonight, with a winky face. Guin rolled her eyes. There was also a reply to her email to Art: "You're the best, Guin. Thank you. Looking forward to our breakfast." And he had signed it "xo, Art." Guin stared at the email. Part of her wanted to scream, but another part felt a slight tingle. Stop it, Guin! she scolded herself. You have a boyfriend. You do not want or need Arthur Jones back in your life.

She walked back into the living room and plopped down on the couch, then grabbed the remote and turned on the TV. She scrolled through the guide and clicked on HGTV. There was a *House Hunters* episode on that looked interesting. Some newly married couple with totally diametric tastes were looking for their first house together in Charleston. Guin sat back and watched, wondering, not for the first time, how such people managed to stay married.

Guin turned off the TV and walked back into her bedroom to change for her dinner with Ris. She had been seeing Ris for just over two months now, and, even though he always said she looked great, no matter what she wore, she still felt self-conscious around him. Everywhere they went, women would stare at or flirt with him. She couldn't blame them. Tall, with dark wavy hair with just a touch of gray, a chiseled jaw and gray-green eyes, and the cutest dimples when he smiled, which was often, and a lean but muscular physique, he looked more like a yoga instructor or a model for *Men's Health* than a college professor or lecturer on marine biology. What he saw in Guin, Guin didn't know, especially when she saw photos of his ex-wife and his former girlfriends. So Guin always took care to dress nicely and apply a little makeup whenever they went out in public together.

Shelly and Guin's friend Lenny, a retired middle school science teacher whom she often went shelling with, told her she had nothing to worry about, that she was just as attractive as those other women. But since Debbie and the divorce, Guin had questioned her looks and felt old, even though she was only 41 and people always said she looked much younger.

She opened her closet and peered in. The Beach House wasn't fancy. In fact, a lot of people arrived on their boats, after a day out sightseeing or fishing, not bothering to change. But Guin was uncomfortable with the idea of showing up for dinner in shorts and a t-shirt.

She rummaged around in her closet, pulling out items and then putting them back. She finally decided on a pair of skinny white jeans and a low-cut blue top that brought out the blue in her eyes. Then she went into the bathroom and applied a little mascara and some lip gloss, the extent of her makeup regimen, except for formal occasions. She eyed her curly strawberry blonde hair, which was in need of a trim. It fell past her shoulders, and it had an annoying tendency to frizz. She held it up atop her head in a kind of French twist and sighed. Then she let it fall back over her shoulders. As she was staring into the mirror, she felt something brush against her leg. Fauna.

"What do you think, Fauna, up or down?"

Guin held her hair up again and looked down at the cat.

"Meow," said Fauna.

"I know, you want food."

Guin looked in the mirror and moved her head from side to side.

"Let's go with up," she said to the reflection in the mirror.

She reached into a drawer and pulled out a couple of barrettes and some bobby pins, fixing her hair until it (mostly) stayed up, with a couple of loose curls in front.

She made a face. "This will have to do," she said aloud. "Otherwise I'm going to be late."

She headed toward the kitchen, the cats trotting behind her.

"Okay, you two. Here you go," she said, pouring them each some food. "Be good while I'm gone. And Flora, no puking!"

Flora ignored her, trying to scarf down as much food as she could before Fauna could steal it.

Guin sighed (again). Then she grabbed her keys, put on a pair of strappy white sandals, which she kept with her other shoes in a closet right by the front door, and left.

CHAPTER 4

Guin arrived at the restaurant a few minutes late to find Ris by the bar, waiting for her, looking effortlessly chic as usual in a pair of jeans and a polo shirt. He bent down to give her a kiss on the cheek.

"Sorry I'm late," she said. "Busy day."

"No worries. I just got here, and our table isn't ready yet. Want a drink while we're waiting? I just ordered a beer."

The bartender came over.

"I'll have a Beach House margarita, please, no salt."

Guin had been debating whether to tell Ris about Art on her way over, and she still wasn't sure what to do. Maybe a few sips of a margarita would calm her nerves.

"Everything all right? You seem a bit distracted."

"Well, actually…"

The bartender deposited Guin's margarita and she took a sip.

"My ex called me."

"Oh?"

Guin looked up at Ris, to try to read his expression, but she couldn't. Ris seemed to have a good relationship with his ex, Victoria, with whom he had two children, twins who had just finished their freshman year at college. Maybe he wouldn't care that Guin's ex had contacted her and invited her out for breakfast.

"He's going to be on Sanibel, attending a sales conference, in a couple of weeks, and he asked if I knew any charter boat captains. He wants to organize a fishing trip to impress his boss. Apparently, he's up for some big promotion, and his boss is into fishing."

"Does he know you don't like fishing?"

"I don't think the topic ever came up. He just figured I'd know someone, and, as it happens, I do. Or, rather, I know someone who knows about fishing and charter boat captains—my colleague, Craig. He covers the tarpon tournament for the paper."

Guin took a couple more sips of her margarita. Well, that was easy, she thought. But then why did she still feel anxious?

"Anything else you want to tell me?" asked Ris, looking down at her. (He was a full head taller than Guin.)

"Why do you ask?"

"Well, whenever you are anxious, your cheeks flush, like they're doing now," he said, smiling at her. "And you're practically inhaling that margarita."

Guin looked down at her glass and noticed that it was half empty, and she could feel her cheeks flushing, one of the perils of being a strawberry blonde with fair skin.

"Art also asked me to have breakfast with him."

"Did you accept?"

"I did—but if you want me to cancel, I will."

Guin mentally kicked herself. It wasn't Ris's call. And she hated sounding insecure.

"It's fine. Good for you guys to clear the air."

Guin stared at Ris.

"You really don't mind that I'm seeing my ex?"

"Oh, I didn't say that," said Ris. "But I don't want to come off as the jealous boyfriend."

"You have absolutely nothing to be jealous of," stated

Guin. "I don't even want to see him, but it was the only way to get him to stop calling me."

Just then the hostess, Simone, came over to let them know their table was ready. As luck would have it, it was a corner table, overlooking the water.

"This is perfect!" said Guin, looking out at the boats.

Simone smiled at her and Ris, albeit mainly at Ris, thought Guin.

"Another round?" she asked, looking at their almost empty glasses.

"I'll have another High Five," said Ris.

"And I'll just have some water," said Guin.

"Very good," said Simone. "Your server will be right over with the menus."

An hour later, they were finishing their dessert, the Beach House's famous tres leches cake, and sipping decaf cappuccinos, when Ris reached over and put his hand on Guin's.

"Guin, there's something I've been wanting to ask you, to talk to you about."

"Oh?" said Guin, looking into his eyes.

"How would you feel about me giving you a key to my place?"

"A key?" said Guin.

"I know we've only been seeing each other just over two months, but I want you to know you're always welcome at my place."

Guin felt Ris's hand gently stroking hers.

"You don't have to give me a key to your place," she said, suddenly feeling awkward.

"I know, but I want to," he said, continuing to hold Guin's hand.

"Is this because I told you my ex is coming to town and wants to see me?"

Ris stilled his hand. "No," he said. "I was already thinking about it."

"Can I think about it?"

"What's there to think about?" he asked.

Was that a touch of annoyance Guin detected?

"Well, for me, it's a big decision. It's almost like you're asking me to live with you. And I'm not sure I'm ready for that."

Ris opened his mouth to say something, but Guin quickly put up a hand.

"Just give me a little bit of time to think about it, okay?"

"Until after you've seen your ex?" Ris replied, in a tone Guin didn't like. "It's just a key, Guin, not a commitment."

Guin blushed. She knew she was making a bigger deal of this than necessary. He hadn't actually asked her to come live with him. But she had been divorced barely a year, and now her ex was coming to Sanibel, and she didn't feel that now was the time, or the moment, to make a commitment.

"I know it's just a key, Ris. And I do appreciate the gesture. It's just..." She searched for the right words, but she couldn't find them.

"Okay," said Ris, once again placing a hand on top of hers. "I get it. You need a little time. The key is yours whenever you're ready."

He smiled at her, and Guin suddenly felt a little less anxious.

"Thank you," she said.

"Now if you're done with the tres leches cake and your coffee," he said, stroking her hand and smiling in that way that brought out his dimples, "let's get the check and continue this at my place."

"Sounds good to me," said Guin, returning his smile. Though for some reason, even as she looked at Ris, an image of Art popped into her head.

CHAPTER 5

Art was nervous. And he was rarely nervous. He hadn't seen his ex-wife in over a year, and he knew she was still angry with him. But his desire to see her outweighed his nervousness. And he liked a challenge. Thrived on it. If he couldn't win her over, maybe he didn't deserve to be head of U.S. sales.

He had made sure to thank her for hooking him up with a charter boat captain. As Guin had suspected, he had chosen Captain "Big Ben" Johnson. Art had visited his website and liked what he saw. And fortunately, Big Ben had an opening the day he wanted, which happened to be that afternoon. The only negative was that he had had to include Rick, his rival, in the fishing party. So there would now be five of them: Art; Rick; their boss, Alan; Justin Campbell, the head of sales for Canada; and Bob "Murph" Murphy, the local sales rep, who was based in Fort Myers.

Art had checked with Big Ben to make sure it was okay to have five people, privately hoping he would have to tell Rick he couldn't come. But Captain Ben had said no problem. They would just need to pay fifty dollars more, which Art had agreed to. (It would look bad if the boss found out that Art refused to pay a measly fifty bucks for Rick to be included.)

Art was sitting at the table at the Over Easy Café,

thinking about the afternoon's fishing expedition and how he could score points with his boss, when he felt a tap on his shoulder. Startled, he turned to see his ex standing over him, a smile on her face.

"Boo," said Guin. "Did I scare you?"

Art quickly got up. "No, no. I was just lost in thought."

He stood there, eyeing Guin. Damn, she looked good, even better than he remembered.

Guin noticed him staring and continued to smile.

"Here, have a seat," he said, catching himself and quickly moving around the table and pulling out the chair on the opposite side.

"Thank you," said Guin, sitting down. "Have you been here long?"

"No, I just got here a few minutes ago," he replied, sitting back down. "I left early, in case I got lost."

"It's kind of hard to get lost on Sanibel. If you're late, it's likely because of traffic on Periwinkle or San-Cap Road, especially in season. Though it's pretty quiet here this time of year, at least until National Seashell Day, later this month."

"You look great," said Art, gazing at Guin. He hadn't expected Guin to look so good or so relaxed, and it made him feel a bit less sure of himself.

"Thank you," Guin replied.

"Did you do something with your hair?"

Immediately after saying it, Art winced. How stupid to bring up her hair, after what he did. But Guin just smiled.

"You like it? I recently had it trimmed and some grays covered up by this marvelous man in Naples, Maurice. Maybe you'd like to see him while you're down here? Though I don't think he's your type. Though you are definitely his," she added, with a wicked smile.

Guin eyed Art's wavy, dark blond hair, which still looked

quite thick. How she used to love running her hands through it. She then gazed at his face, which, she had to admit, was still quite handsome. He had broken his nose playing football in college, but the doctors had done a good job fixing it, so there was only a slight bump, which Guin found endearing. Or did.

Art reached a hand across the table, laying it on top of Guin's. "I've missed you, Guin."

Guin removed her hand from underneath Art's, placing it on her lap.

"Let's get some menus and some coffee," she said, looking around for a server.

She eyed a waiter and signaled for him to come over.

"May we have a couple of menus, please—and some coffee?"

"Of course," said the young man. "I'll be right back with coffee and menus."

"Thanks," Guin said, giving the young man a big smile.

Art looked at Guin. "I mean it, Guin. I've missed you."

He waited for a response, but Guin did not reply.

"I know I behaved like a jackass," he tried.

"I'm sorry, were you expecting me to argue with you?" Guin replied, pursing her lips.

"No," said Art. "But maybe you missed me, too?"

Guin let out a snort. Then checked herself.

"What do you want, Art?"

"You." And at that moment, looking at her, he meant it.

Guin let out a peal of laughter, then continued to laugh until she felt tears coming out of her eyes.

"I'm serious," said Art, looking wounded.

"Sorry. Actually, I'm not sorry," said Guin, who could feel the pent-up anger and resentment bubbling up. "You treated me like shit for over a year. Then you had an affair with our hairdresser and left me, after I had just been laid off and could have really used some love and support. And you think that after that, and after barely communicating with me for over a year—not, mind you, that I wanted to hear from you, ever, after that—you expect me to melt at the sight of you, accept your apology, act like nothing ever happened, and get back together with you?"

That was exactly what Art had expected. Though hearing it put that way by Guin, a very angry Guin, made him realize that maybe he hadn't thought things through.

"I'm sorry, Guin. How can I get you to believe me?"

"You can't."

Just then the server came back with a pot of coffee and two menus, which he deposited on the table between them. "Coffee?"

"Please," said Guin, holding out her mug. Art nodded his head and the server poured coffee into his mug, too.

"And may I have some milk, please?" asked Guin.

"Coming right up," said the server.

"I mean it, Guin. I know I messed up, and I want to make it up to you. It's like fate brought me here."

"I thought it was a sales conference," said Guin, still annoyed.

"I've really missed you."

"If you've missed me so much, how come you waited until two weeks ago to call me?"

"You know I've been trying to reach you, but you wouldn't return my phone calls or emails."

To be fair, he had been trying to reach her for a while now, but she had refused to listen to his messages and had deleted all his emails without opening them. Until she stupidly answered the phone a couple of weeks before, in a moment of weakness.

Art recognized the look on Guin's face. It was the look she got when she was trying to work something out and was arguing with herself. That meant that maybe he still had a chance.

The server came back with the milk and took their order, then returned with their food a few minutes later. Guin immediately dug into her French toast.

"So, tell me about your life here on Sanibel," Art said, between bites. "It looks like a beautiful place from the little I've seen. I've read some of your articles, you know."

He smiled at Guin, and Guin couldn't help smiling back, despite herself. Curse you, Arthur Jones, she thought. Why do you have to be so frigging charming?

Guin then proceeded to tell Art about Sanibel, her job, and the friends she had made. She left out telling him about solving the case of the missing Golden Junonia and helping discover who murdered Gregor Matenopoulos, the Captiva developer who had been suspected of stealing the valuable shell, only to be found dead in his office a few days after the Golden Junonia had gone missing, with the shell nowhere to be found. She also didn't mention that she was seeing someone.

"Well, you sound very happy here," said Art, between bites of food. "So, you're not seeing anyone?"

Guin paused. Why hadn't she told Art about Ris? Was it because they had just had another argument about his key? Though she didn't quite understand herself why she was so reluctant to just take the key and put it on her keychain, even if she never used it. She certainly cared about Ris, and it wasn't as though accepting his key was tantamount to accepting a marriage proposal. Though in some ways it felt as though it was. She had been divorced barely a year, and she wasn't sure if she was ready to make another long-term commitment just yet. Then Art had to call her out of the blue and complicate things.

"A dollar for your thoughts?"

Guin crooked her mouth. "It's a penny."

"I factored in inflation. Plus, your thoughts are worth way more than a penny," he said, smiling at her.

Guin smiled back. Damn the man. He was doing it again.

Art's smile turned to a grin. So, she wasn't seeing anyone. He still had a chance.

"Actually, I am seeing someone," said Guin.

Art momentarily deflated, though he kept the smile plastered on his face.

"He's a marine biologist, a professor over at Florida Gulf Coast University. He's also the acting science director at the Bailey-Matthews National Shell Museum while the director is on sabbatical."

"A marine biologist, eh?" said Art, picturing a short, nerdy-looking guy in a wetsuit.

"Here's his Instagram," said Guin, passing her phone over to Art.

He took a look and immediately regretted it. Harrison Hartwick was no short, nerdy-looking scientist. And judging from the yoga pics he posted, he probably looked just fine in a wet suit. Art frowned and passed the phone back to Guin.

"Seems like quite a guy."

"Oh, he is," said Guin, that wicked smile appearing again.

Art ran a hand through his hair. This was going to be harder than he thought.

"So, uh, how long have you two been seeing each other?"

"A couple of months, but he just gave me the key to his place, so I'd say it's pretty serious."

Guin couldn't believe she said that. Just the other evening she had told Ris she needed more time, and now she was telling Art she had already accepted the damn thing. What was wrong with her?

"Well, um, that's great," said Art, momentarily at a loss for words.

"Thanks. We're pretty happy. And what about you?"

"What about me?" said Art.

"Are you seeing anyone?"

"I told you, I broke up with Debbie."

"I meant since then. As I recall, you don't like to be alone."

Art had dated a couple of women since Debbie left, but neither of them felt right. He meant it when he told Guin he missed her. And after seeing her again, looking so good and seeming so happy, he missed her even more.

"Come with me to the banquet Saturday night."

"What banquet?" asked Guin.

"The sales banquet. Everyone will be there. I know Alan and Emily would love to see you."

"I can't."

"Because of your *boyfriend*?"

Art made a face.

"No, not because of Ris," replied Guin. "He's away." Damn, why had she said that?

Art smiled. "Then come with me, Guin." He reached over and grabbed her hand, giving her a pleading look. "Please?"

Guin looked down. She knew she should pull her hand away, but for someone reason she felt unable to.

"I can't," she repeated, more quietly.

Art took his other hand and gently placed a finger underneath her chin, forcing her to look up at him. "Please, Guin. You'd be the most beautiful woman there."

"I doubt that," said Guin, removing her hand from Art's and his other hand from beneath her chin.

"There will be great food, and dancing. And I know how much you love to dance."

Guin smiled. She did love to dance, and Art was an excellent dancer.

"And you'd be doing me a huge favor."

Ah, so that was it. She knew Art wanted something. She eyed him skeptically.

"A favor?"

"Don't give me that look. I just meant that I wouldn't have to attend the party alone. Most of the guys brought along their wives or girlfriends."

"And you don't want to go stag."

"I don't, but that's because I'd much rather have you go with me."

Guin rolled her eyes. "Oh please."

Art leaned forward. "I mean it, Guin. I've missed you. I'd do anything to make things up to you. And the dinner should be fun. You have something better to do Saturday?"

Every brain cell screamed at Guin to tell Art she was busy. Instead she said "no."

"Good! Then come to the banquet with me."

"Fine," said Guin, already hating herself. "But you owe me."

Art smiled. This was his big chance, and he was determined not to blow it.

"I promise you won't regret it."

"I'm already regretting it," said Guin.

They had finished eating, and Guin signaled for the check, which Art insisted on paying. Then they got up to leave.

Art followed Guin to her purple Mini Cooper.

"You still have the Mini, I see."

Guin smiled. "I'd never sell her."

"I'll email you the details about the dinner when I get back to my room. Oh, and thanks again for the fishing recommendation. We're going out this afternoon."

"Have fun," said Guin. "Send me a picture."

They stood beside the Mini awkwardly.

"Goodbye, Art," said Guin, unlocking the door and opening it.

"Goodbye, Guin. See you Saturday." He closed the door after she got in and then walked to his rental, a smile on his face.

CHAPTER 6

"Thanks for arranging this outing," said Art's boss, Alan, as they climbed into the SUV to head to the marina. The marina was only about 10 minutes away from where the conference was taking place, at the San Ybel Resort & Spa.

"My pleasure," said Art, making sure Alan sat next to him. "I know how you love fishing, and my contact said Captain Ben is the best."

"Guys love Big Ben," Murph, the regional sales rep, chimed in from the back seat.

"Big Ben, like the clock?" asked Justin, the head of sales for Canada.

Murph chuckled. "I suppose so. He's a big guy, with a big personality, or so I've heard. Don't know how good he is at telling time though."

"A shame they don't actually let you keep the tarpon," said Rick.

"It's strictly catch and release here," explained Murph. "Besides, tarpon aren't good eating fish."

"Well, I am looking forward to our outing," said Alan. "I actually came to Sanibel as a kid, with my dad and granddad. We would go fishing and eat what we caught for dinner. Did some tarpon fishing, too. Of course, that was years ago. But from what I've seen, the island hasn't changed that much."

Art knew about those long-ago trips, and he fervently

hoped this trip lived up to Alan's memories of fishing with his father and grandfather.

A few minutes later they arrived at the marina.

"Big Ben said we could find his boat to the left of the Ships Store," said Art, addressing the rest of the party. He spied a structure in the distance and started heading toward it. The others followed him.

There were dozens of boats docked at the marina, and Art wasn't sure which one was Captain Ben's, so many of them looked alike. But he figured he could just go into the store and ask. Just as he approached the building, a large man in a polo shirt and khakis, with a bit of a gut, wearing a baseball cap, with a couple day's growth on his face, emerged.

"Excuse me," said Art. "Do you know where I can find Captain Ben Johnson?"

"You're looking at him," said the man.

Art extended his hand. "Art Jones. I booked a trip with you for this afternoon."

"Nice to meet you, Art Jones," replied Captain Ben, smiling. "You gentlemen ready to catch some tarpon?"

Captain Ben eyed the five of them. He could spot a group of city folks a mile away.

"Any of you gone tarpon fishing before?" he asked.

"I have, though it was many years ago," said Alan. "Used to go fishing around Sanibel with my dad and granddad."

"Well, the equipment's changed a bit, but I'm sure you'll have no problem. Anyone else?"

"I have," said Murph. "You actually took out a bunch of my buddies last year."

"They have a good time?" asked Captain Ben.

"They did, though they only caught a couple of fish."

"Not everyone can catch one. Pretty good they caught two. Glad they had a good time. So, you guys ready to head out? We'll be gone at least a few hours. Bathroom's over there, if you need it," said Captain Ben, pointing around the side of the store. "No bathroom on the boat," he added, "though I keep a jug for emergencies," he said, with a broad smile.

"May as well," said Justin, heading off toward the restrooms. Everyone except Rick, who hung back with Captain Ben, followed him.

A few minutes later, the five men had gathered around Captain Ben's boat. It was a Pathfinder bay boat, he explained, perfect for fishing in the shallow waters around Sanibel and Captiva.

"Now before you board her, I just want to go over some rules," said Ben. "Rule number one, I'm the boss. Whatever I say goes. Rule number two, have fun."

He then boarded the boat.

"That's it?" asked Justin, a bit perplexed. "What about safety? Are there any life vests aboard your vessel?"

"The water's pretty shallow where we're going, so you don't need 'em, but I got some under the seat over there," he said, pointing, "if it makes you feel better."

Justin eyed the boat. While he didn't see any life vests, he did notice a couple of very sharp-looking knives in an open box.

"What are those for?" he asked.

"Cutting line," replied Captain Ben.

"What's in the coolers?" Art asked, spying two coolers by the steering wheel.

"Bait's in that one," said Big Ben, pointing to the smaller cooler.

"What do you use?" asked Alan.

"Mostly threadfin herring," said Captain Ben, "but I also

got some crabs. You can use pinfish and ladyfish, too. Don't worry about the bait, though. It's all good. And I'll be the one baiting all the hooks."

"And what's in that larger cooler?" asked Murph.

"Beer," said Big Ben, smiling. "Your buddy, Rick here, asked me to make sure to bring along some Fat Tire."

"My favorite," said Alan. "You clearly have been paying attention, Richard."

Rick looked directly at Art and grinned while Art tried to refrain from scowling. Art had asked Big Ben about bringing beer, and he had said he had it covered. Clearly.

Captain Ben climbed on the boat. "All right then. You gents ready to go?"

"I sure am," said Murph, climbing in.

The rest of them followed suit. Captain Ben then cast off, and they were on their way.

CHAPTER 7

It had been a warm afternoon, and the men had gone through most of the beer in the cooler. There had been several tarpon sightings over the course of the afternoon. But as yet, no one had caught one. As a result, they had increased the pot for the man who reeled in the first tarpon. It now stood at $500, and everyone on board was eager to claim it.

They were cruising around Pine Island Sound, near Wulfert Keys and Ding Darling, when Alan called out that he spotted a bunch of tarpon nearby. Captain Ben confirmed the sighting and gently repositioned the boat. The men were all eager to get their lines in the water, but Captain Ben cautioned them to be patient.

"These suckers typically weigh over a hundred pounds, and they don't take kindly to being hooked," he reminded them. "I've seen tarpon jump several feet in the air, and if you're not careful, they'll cut your line. That's why I tell people to wait until after the second or third jump to take the reel out of the holder."

As he was talking, Captain Ben took down the poles, placing them one by one in the holders around the boat and then baiting them. When they were all baited, he cast each one.

The men had each claimed a pole at the start of the trip,

and each was eager to be the one to hook and reel in a tarpon. As they had already learned, hooking a tarpon was one thing. Reeling it in, and then being able to snap a photo of it, was quite another. And the only way to win the $500 was to actually get a photo of it.

As the afternoon wore on, and the men got increasingly inebriated, they became more competitive. While Alan was saying something to Big Ben, Rick moved close to Art, who was standing on the starboard side.

"Care to make a side bet that I get the tarpon, just like I'm going to get that promotion?"

"What makes you think *you* are going to get that promotion?" hissed Art.

"A little fishy told me," said Rick, looking over toward their boss, who was still conversing with Captain Ben.

Suddenly there was a commotion.

"I think I got one!" called out Alan, quickly moving over to his designated pole.

"Easy does it now," cautioned Big Ben, standing next to him. "Let's make sure he's hooked. Then you gotta slack the line."

"Hey, I think I got one, too!" called out Murph, whose pole was a couple feet away.

Art moved to join the men on the port side of the boat, but Rick put a hand on him to stop him. "You know, Arthur, if I were you, I'd start looking for another job."

"Awfully sure of yourself, aren't you?" said Art, trying to keep his voice low.

Rick gave him a smug smile.

"You going to come over here and help or what?" Murph called out.

There was a flurry of activity as both Alan and Murph attempted to reel in their fish, and Captain Ben tried to reposition the boat while helping them. It was quite a spectacle, watching the regal fish, known as the Silver King, thrash around and jump in the air. Alan and Murph were straining and sweating, all their attention focused on the tarpon as they tried to reel them in, changing angles as Captain Ben directed.

"Don't let 'em rest," called out Big Ben, taking turns helping the men reel in the fish. "Keep their head up! They're tiring out."

"They're not the only ones!" said Murph, whose arms were getting quite a workout.

"This is most exciting!" said Justin, who had entirely forgotten about his own pole and was watching the tarpon intently.

"I think I'm going to land him!" called out Alan.

Just then the fish appeared very close to the boat.

"He's a beauty!" said Captain Ben. "Someone got a camera? We're only going to have a minute to take a photo. Also, someone get me one of the knives."

Art said he'd get it and quickly made his way over to the box and grabbed one. Then he walked over to where Captain Ben was helping Alan reel in the fish and stood watching.

"You got the knife?" said Captain Ben, turning to Art.

"Right here," said Art, handing the knife to him. Captain Ben took the knife and looked down at it. "There's blood on it. You cut yourself?"

Art looked down at his hands. There was some blood on them, but he didn't recall cutting himself. No doubt it was from the knife. But where had it come from?

Captain Ben ordered Art to go grab a cloth from a drawer by the steering wheel, which he quickly did. Then Captain Ben quickly wiped the knife down.

"Okay, got your cameras ready?" called Captain Ben.

"May I do the honors?" said Justin.

"Whatever you like," said Captain Ben. "Just do it fast, as we can't hold onto him much longer."

Justin leaned over and snapped a photo of Alan and Captain Ben holding the fish off the side of the boat. Captain Ben then quickly cut the line, and they watched the fish fling itself away.

"Hey, a little help here, please!" called Murph, who was still trying to reel in his fish. Just then the tarpon reared up, jumping several feet in the air and snapping his line. "Damn! He got away!"

"Sorry, Murph," said Alan.

"Yeah, yeah, yeah," said Murph, rubbing his hands, which were quite sore. "You get a picture, Justin?"

"Sorry no," Justin replied. He looked around the boat. "I say, has anyone seen Rick?" he asked.

The men looked around. There was no sign of Rick.

"Where could he have gone?" asked Justin, scanning the water around the boat.

"He was drinking a lot," said Murph. "Wouldn't be surprised if he fell overboard."

"Do you think he drowned?" asked Justin.

"Doubtful," said Captain Ben. "The water around here is pretty shallow. Even if he did fall in, he should have been able to get back to the boat, no problem."

"Unless he was too drunk," said Murph. "Or was injured."

Captain Ben turned and looked at Art and the rest of the men on board followed suit.

"What?" asked Art. "Why are you all looking at me?"

Murph jerked his head toward the knife.

"The knife? I told you, I had no idea how blood got on it," said Art.

"I believe you were the last one to see Richard," said Justin. "I saw you two arguing about something."

"We were not arguing!" said Art, a little too loudly.

"What were you arguing about?" asked Alan.

"I swear, Alan, I didn't do anything to Rick!" said Art, his voice rising. "Look, Rick took me aside, and we had a little chat, but nothing happened. Don't you think you would have heard a scream or something if I stuck a knife in him? Come on, guys!"

"He's got a point," said Justin.

"We were all so absorbed with the tarpon. Rick could have gone overboard and we probably wouldn't have noticed," said Murph.

"True," said Alan. "Captain Ben, can you circle the area? If the water is as shallow as you say, we should be able to spot him, no?"

"Sure," said Ben. "Why not?" He didn't seem very concerned.

Murph glanced over at Art.

"What?" said Art, slightly annoyed. Leave it to Rick to ruin an otherwise good day. He had already shown Art up by arranging for the cooler of Fat Tire. It would be just like Rick to screw Art by faking his disappearance and having Art take the blame. But Art didn't want to say anything, for fear of riling his boss and having the others think he was being paranoid. But they didn't know Rick like he did.

"So, what were the two of you chatting about earlier?" asked Justin, as the boat slowly circled the area.

Art sighed. Best to be honest, he thought. "Rick was taunting me about the promotion."

Alan raised an eyebrow.

"Rick grabbed me and said he had the promotion in the bag, and that I should start looking for another job," Art continued.

"Did he now?" said Alan.

"He did. But I ignored him."

"Not very sporting of him," said Justin.

"No, but I swear to you, I didn't lay a hand on him," said Art.

"And that was the last you saw of him?" asked Alan.

"It was."

"Hey, what's that?" said Murph, spotting something in the water.

Captain Ben moved the boat closer and reached into the water. It was a baseball cap.

"That looks like Rick's cap," said Alan. "And there's blood on it."

CHAPTER 8

Art sat in the Sanibel Police Department, wondering how a day that started out so promising could end so badly. After finding the bloody baseball cap, Captain Ben had continued to search the area, looking for Rick. But there was no sign of him.

Then, at Alan's insistence, after they returned to the marina, they had radioed the Coast Guard and the police, who requested their presence at the Sanibel Police Department. They had obliged and had been sitting there ever since, answering questions. When had they last seen Rick? Had he had a lot to drink? Was he a good swimmer? Did anyone on the boat bear Rick a grudge?

Unfortunately, due to all the excitement, and drinking, no one really knew how much Rick had drunk or when he had gone overboard. Or if Rick was a good swimmer. Though they all agreed that Art had been the last one to see Rick, and Justin informed the officer that he had seen Art and Rick arguing.

When questioned about the knife, Art swore that he knew nothing about the blood on it, that he had barely looked at the knife, had just grabbed it and then handed it to Captain Ben. Still, it didn't look good for him. And he didn't like the way the officer who was conducting the interview, a Detective William O'Loughlin, was looking at him.

Something about the man unnerved Art a bit. He reminded Art of a boxer he once knew who always waited before pulling any punches, staring down his opponent as if trying to psych him out.

Art was tired of having to answer the same questions again and again. Why didn't O'Loughlin believe him? Art gritted his teeth and continued to answer the detective's questions. But he just wanted to go back to the hotel, take a nice hot shower, go to the bar, and have a drink.

Finally, it seemed as though the detective was done. Art waited for him to tell him he was free to go. I have nothing to worry about, Art said to himself. I bet Rick is going to show up later and tell everyone it was a big joke—a thought he relayed to the detective. However, the detective didn't seem to share Art's conviction.

"Dozens of guys must fall overboard," said Art, a bit nervously. "This must happen all the time."

"Not really," replied the detective, his face a mask.

"What about sharks? We saw some sharks when we were out. Maybe a shark got him."

The detective stared at Art, just as that boxer used to stare at his opponents, thought Art. It did not make him feel good.

"So, detective, we all done here? Am I free to go?" asked Art.

The detective was about to reply when there was a commotion down the hall. A minute later Guin burst into the detective's office, followed by a harried looking uniformed officer.

The detective eyed Guin.

"Sorry, sir. I tried to stop her, but she insisted on seeing you right away," said the officer.

Guin stopped in front of Detective O'Loughlin, slightly out of breath.

"And to what do I owe this honor, Ms. Jones?" asked the detective, just the hint of a smile on his face.

"I heard you were about to arrest my ex-husband for a crime he couldn't possibly have committed."

The detective's right eyebrow shot up.

"And where did you hear that, Ms. Jones?" replied the detective.

Guin shot a look over at Art, who refused to meet her eye. In a moment of panic, while the others were being questioned, he had texted her.

"Ah," said the detective.

"Well, I'm sorry to inform you, Ms. Jones, but you've been misinformed."

Guin looked from the detective to back at Art. Art cleared his throat and continued to look down at the floor.

"So, you're not going to arrest Art?"

"Not right now, no," replied the detective.

Art shot a quick look at the detective, then looked down again.

"But I suggest you don't leave the island for the next twenty-four hours, Mr. Jones. I may have some additional questions for you."

"You have my word, detective," said Art solemnly, looking up at the detective.

Guin snorted.

"Is there a problem, Ms. Jones?" asked the detective.

"Yes, but it has nothing to do with you, detective," she said, looking directly at Art.

The detective looked from Guin to Art.

"Come along, Arthur," Guin said, glaring at her ex.

CHAPTER 9

Guin walked briskly down the hall and back into the small reception area, Art trailing behind her. She looked around.

"Where are your buddies?" she asked.

"They left," he said, looking up at her.

"They didn't wait for you?" she asked, bewildered.

"I told them they should go, that I could take a cab back to the hotel."

"Fine. You need the number for a taxi service?"

"Actually," he said, "I was hoping maybe you'd let me take you out to dinner."

"What?!" said Guin, taken aback. "Why?" She looked suspiciously at Art.

"To thank you."

"For what?" she asked, still regarding him.

"For coming to my rescue," he said, smiling at her.

Guin felt herself blushing. When Art smiled like that… No! She said to herself. Do not let him get to you.

"So, would you let me buy you dinner?" he asked her.

"I'm not hungry," said Guin.

Just then her stomach rumbled, quite loudly. Guin looked mortified, but Art just chuckled.

"Come on, let me buy you dinner. No strings attached."

"Don't you have some welcome reception you need to go to?" Guin asked.

"I don't care about the reception."

All I care about is you, he wanted to add, but he knew how corny that would sound.

"Come on, Guin. We both need to eat. Pick a place. My treat."

She was about to protest, but her stomach gurgled again. She glared down at it. Traitor.

"Fine," she said.

She tried to think of a place that wasn't the slightest bit romantic, where they wouldn't have to sit too close together.

"Let's go to Doc Ford's," she said. "We can sit at the bar."

"Whatever you say," said Art.

He followed her out of the police department, down the stairs, and to the purple Mini. Guin unlocked the door. "Get in," she growled, unhappy that she had been trapped into having dinner with him.

He got in and closed the door.

Art and Guin were seated at a booth in a quieter area of the restaurant, despite Guin's desire to sit at the bar, where she would be surrounded by other people. But Art had asked the hostess if she had a quiet table available, flashing her his winning smile, and she said she would check—and came back a minute later saying she had a booth available.

They sat down and ordered some beer. Then Guin turned to Art.

"Now tell me what the hell happened on that boat, Arthur Jones, and don't leave out a single detail."

Their beers, along with a couple of menus, arrived as he had begun to tell her about the trip. He paused in his story a couple of minutes later, when a server came to take their order. Then he resumed.

"So, all they found of Rick was a baseball cap with a little blood on it?"

"And don't forget the knife," added Art.

"Still, we don't even know if it was Rick's blood on the knife or the cap, or if that was even Rick's cap," said Guin.

"I'm pretty sure it was Rick's cap," said Art, staring at his beer.

"Pretty sure but not positive?" asked Guin.

"No," said Art, sighing and looking up at Guin. "I know he was wearing a baseball cap, but I didn't pay attention to what kind. The less I paid attention to Rick, the better."

"So, you and Rick weren't close?"

"Hardly," said Art, making a face. "We were both up for the same job, and Rick was doing whatever he could to suck up to Alan and make me look bad."

"As I recall, Alan was not the type who could be won over with flattery."

"It wasn't that Rick was flattering Alan as much as bad-mouthing me. He was always finding ways to tweak me or make it sound like I was slacking off."

"You, slacking off? I can't believe Alan thought that. Part of the reason we got divorced, as you may recall, is that you were more married to that damn job than you were to me. Didn't you tell me you were going to exceed your quota last year?"

Art gave her a rueful smile. "I did—and I did. But, I can't explain it. Rick just had a way of making me look bad." He took another sip of his beer.

Guin watched Art. Where had the confident man from this morning gone? She sighed.

"So, did anyone else have a grudge against Rick?"

"Sure, lots of guys. Rick was a total brown-noser—and back stabber. A lot of guys didn't like him."

"Any of the guys on your fishing trip?" asked Guin.

Art thought for a minute. Justin lived and worked in Canada, so it was unlikely he had met Rick before the sales conference. It was possible Murph and Rick knew each other, even though they covered different territories. Alan obviously knew Rick, but as far as he could tell, the two of them got along famously.

He relayed this to Guin, who listened attentively.

"So it would seem you were the only one with any motive to get rid of him."

"Get rid of him, yes, but not in that way," Art clarified.

Just then their food arrived. Guin was starving and dug into her crab cakes. Art watched her and smiled.

"What?" said Guin, looking up.

"I love to watch you eat," said Art, still smiling.

They ate in silence for a couple of minutes. Then Guin continued her questioning.

"So you said you were all drinking, a lot, and Justin, Murph, and Alan were busy at the front of the boat while you were in back talking to Rick, yes?"

"That's correct."

"And then you went to the front of the boat, but Rick stayed in the back?"

"Yes. What's your point?"

"So, it would have been pretty easy for Rick to slip over the side or back of the boat without anyone seeing him."

"Have you seen one of these fishing boats, Guin? They're not that big. And Captain Ben said the water in Pine Island Sound, where we were, was pretty shallow in most places. Even if he did get drunk and fall overboard, which I sincerely doubt, it's unlikely he would have drowned—and we would have heard or seen him."

Art drained the last of his beer. He looked morose.

"So, what did you think of tarpon fishing?" asked Guin, trying to change the subject slightly.

"It was okay," said Art.

"Had you ever gone before?" she asked.

Art smiled at her. "No, but I must have watched a hundred hours of tarpon fishing videos."

Guin laughed, and Art joined her. She could just picture him watching and re-watching clip after clip, to make sure he sounded like he knew what he was doing. That was Art's way, at least when trying to close a sale—and what made him such a good salesman. He learned everything he could about a client, and he made sure he had the right solution to address that client's particular need or problem.

The server came over and asked if they wanted dessert or coffee.

"Do you have key lime pie?" Art asked.

"The best!" replied the server. "Bring us a slice of that," commanded Art, "along with two forks."

"Would you like some coffee?" asked the server.

"I'm good," said Guin.

"None for me," said Art.

"I'll be right back with that key lime pie," said the server, who departed, taking their plates with him.

"So, what about the knife?" asked Guin.

"What about it?" replied Art.

"Did you happen to notice if there was blood on the knife when you picked it up?"

Art thought for a few seconds, trying to picture the knife. "I honestly don't recall," he said. "I knew Ben was in a hurry, so I just grabbed it."

"Is it possible someone else had used the knife?"

"I don't know," said Art. "It's possible Rick might have handled it. He was at the back of the boat."

Art could see Guin's wheels turning.

"What?" said Guin, looking at him.

Art smiled. "You were thinking about something."

"I'm always thinking about something," said Guin.

"You make that face whenever you're trying to work something out," said Art, still smiling at her.

The server returned with a large piece of key lime pie and two forks.

"Here you go!"

"Thanks," Art said. "Looks good."

He stuck his fork in and took a big piece.

"Mmm…" he said.

Guin took a bite, closing her eyes as she tasted the sweet-tart lime. She opened her eyes to find Art smiling at her.

"What?" she said, a bit defensively.

"Nothing," said Art. "I had just forgotten what you looked like when you ate something you really liked."

Guin blushed.

"We should get the check. I have a big day tomorrow," she said. It was an exaggeration, but she was starting to feel uncomfortable.

Art signaled for the check, which the server brought over a minute later.

"I got this," said Art, grabbing it.

"Be my guest," said Guin, taking another bite of the key lime pie.

Art took out his wallet and slid a credit card into the folder.

They headed outside a few minutes later.

"Well, goodnight," said Guin.

"Aren't you going to give me a lift back to my hotel?" asked Art.

Guin made a face. "I thought you were going to take a taxi."

"Please?" asked Art. "It's what, less than ten minutes from here?"

He gave her that look that in the past always made her melt.

"Fine," she growled. "Let's go."

Art smiled and followed her to the Mini.

A few minutes later, Guin pulled into the San Ybel Resort & Spa.

"You sure I can't interest you in a nightcap?" asked Art, as Guin stopped in front of the entrance.

"No thanks," said Guin.

Art thought about leaning over and giving Guin a kiss goodnight. But the look on her face changed his mind.

"Well, goodnight," he said, opening the passenger side door. "Thanks for helping me out and driving me back here."

"Just try to stay out of trouble for the next couple of days, okay?"

"Okay," said Art, smiling. "And don't forget about Saturday!" he called from the entrance.

Oh crap. That's right, she recalled. She had promised to go to that stupid dinner with Art on Saturday night. Guin clenched her teeth. This was going to be a long weekend.

CHAPTER 10

Friday morning Guin got up early and drove over to Blind Pass beach to meet her friend Lenny. Lenny, a retired science teacher, was a Shell Ambassador, which meant he had taken the course and passed the shell identification test given by the Bailey-Matthews National Shell Museum. Lenny loved to comb the beaches of Sanibel looking for shells—and looking for people to share his shelling knowledge.

Guin had begged Lenny not to wear his Shell Ambassador t-shirt that morning. She didn't have time to stop and chat with every person they ran into on the beach, she told him, which is what happened every time Lenny wore the shirt. He had just laughed and replied that he didn't chat up *everyone*, to which Guin had rolled her eyes.

So she was a little nervous as she approached the entrance to the beach and saw Lenny a little way away, down by the water. She squinted to see what t-shirt he was wearing. She breathed a sigh of relief when she didn't see the royal blue of his Shell Ambassador tee. But her relief quickly turned to dismay as she saw that he was wearing his Sanibel Shell Seekers t-shirt instead, which was also a magnet for beach combers.

Guin sighed. "Really, Lenny?"

Lenny smiled. "What, you don't like what I'm wearing?" he said in mock dismay.

Guin made a face and crossed her arms.

"You told me not to wear my Shell Ambassador t-shirt, and I didn't," said Lenny.

"Well, it's a good thing the beach is pretty quiet this time of year. Maybe, if we're lucky, we won't run into anyone, or anyone with questions about shells."

"Don't you want your fellow beachgoers to be informed?" asked Lenny.

"Yes, but not today. I have a lot of work to do, and I can't spend two hours hanging around while you answer questions and play mollusk master to hordes of amateur shellers."

"Hordes?" said Lenny, raising an eyebrow.

Guin gave his arm a gentle slap. "You know what I mean. Now, let's get going. I need to be at my desk by nine."

Lenny saluted. "Lead on, *mon capitaine.*"

They proceeded to walk down the beach, toward Silver Key and Bowman's Beach.

"So, what's new?" asked Lenny, bending down to pick up a good-sized lightning whelk.

"Nice one!" said Guin, eyeing the shell. "Other than my ex showing up, telling me he wants me back, then his becoming the chief suspect in a missing person's case? Not much."

Lenny stopped and looked at Guin. "You okay, kiddo?"

"Yeah, I guess," she said. "I just don't know what to think." She spied a lettered olive and bent down to get it, rinsing it off in the water before putting it into her shelling bag. "I thought it was over between me and Art. It *is* over," she clarified. "But he's been so nice. And he's apologized at least a dozen times. I just don't know."

"You still have feelings for him?" asked Lenny. "If you did, nothing wrong with it. You guys were together a long time. You've got history."

"I know, Len, but he hurt me pretty badly," Guin replied. "And I thought I had moved on. Ris is a really great guy."

They walked in silence for the next few minutes, stopping every few feet to pick up shells.

"So, what are you going to do?"

"Nothing," said Guin.

"So what's the problem?" asked Lenny, reaching down to grab a shell. He held it up.

"Ooh, a Florida cone!" said Guin. "I'd love to find one."

"You want it?" asked Lenny, holding it out to her.

"Oh no, you found it. You should keep it."

"I don't mind. I have dozens at home," said Lenny.

"That's very sweet of you, Lenny, but I can't accept it. You know my rule: I have to find the shell myself. Otherwise it doesn't count."

"Suit yourself," said Lenny, putting the pretty orange Florida cone in his bag. "So, you going to see your ex again?"

"Yeah, I agreed to go to this dinner with him tomorrow. It's a company thing, and he thought it would help with his promotion. Besides Ris is out of town."

Lenny regarded Guin.

"What?" asked Guin, stopping.

"Just be careful," said Lenny.

Guin sighed. She knew it was a bad idea to go to the dinner, even if there would be lots of people there. She didn't want to give Art, or anyone else, the idea that they were back together. But she had stupidly agreed, and she felt it wouldn't be right to cancel.

Lenny, sensing Guin's anxiety, remained silent as they continued their stroll down the beach.

By the time Guin had showered and had breakfast, it was almost nine-thirty. Oh well, she thought. Better late than....

She sat down at her desk and started up her computer. As she did so, Fauna, her black cat, jumped into her lap.

"Oh, hello, Fauna," said Guin, petting the cat.

Seconds later Flora jumped up on her desk and started rubbing herself against Guin's monitor. She sighed. "Hello, Flora." Flora sat directly in front of the monitor and batted Guin with her paw. Guin rubbed her ears.

"Listen, guys," she said, addressing the two felines. "I need to do some work. So either you lie down and behave yourselves or I'm evicting you."

Flora continued to paw the air in front of Guin as Fauna curled up in a ball in Guin's lap. Guin sighed.

She had two articles to write this weekend, and she had wasted enough time. So she ignored the cats and got to work, putting her phone on silent and placing it in a drawer, so she wouldn't be disturbed or distracted.

Finally, at one-thirty she decided she needed a lunch break. She got up and stretched, then took her phone out of the drawer and saw that her message light was flashing. She checked her voicemail first. There was a message from Art, thanking her for "rescuing" him last night. She rolled her eyes and deleted the message before it had finished playing. There was also a voicemail from Ris, telling her he missed her and that he hoped they were still on for Sunday. Immediately, Guin felt guilty. She thought about calling him back and telling him she'd decided to accept his offer regarding the key, and of course they were on for Sunday. She was about to hit call back when she changed her mind. Instead, she checked her text messages. There were several texts from Shelly, the last one asking why she hadn't texted her back. Guin groaned. There was also a text from her brother, Lance, asking if it would be too hot and sweaty to come for a visit in late July. "No worse than New York in July," she wrote him back, "and we have much nicer beaches. :-)" She smiled. She had been trying to get her brother to come down to Sanibel with his husband, Owen, for months, but something always prevented him. Maybe this time he'd finally come down.

She quickly checked her email to make sure there wasn't anything urgent. Amazing how many messages you can receive in just a few hours, she thought, scrolling through her inbox. She deleted all the junk and unimportant messages, starring the ones she'd need to get to later.

"And now, food!" she said aloud. As if in response, her stomach gurgled. She got up, put her phone in her back pocket, and headed to the kitchen to make herself a sandwich.

As she sat at her dining table eating a cheese, lettuce, and tomato sandwich, she stared out past the lanai onto the golf course. It was a beautiful day, and this was probably the closest she would get to being outside. She continued to gaze out at the trees and the birds flying by, taking bites of her sandwich.

As she was watching a flock of ibis make their way across the fairway, her phone started buzzing. She grabbed it and saw her message notification light flashing. It was another text message from Shelly.

"You OK?!" read the text. "I haven't heard from you in FOREVER!"

Guin smiled and texted Shelly back. "I've been busy! What's up?"

"When am I going to see you?" replied Shelly.

Guin thought about it, but she didn't have an answer.

"How about you join me and Steve for happy hour at Doc Ford's on Captiva tonight? There's a guitar player Steve likes playing there."

Hmm, thought Guin. Ris was away, and she didn't have plans. "Sure," she replied. "What time should I meet you?"

"How about 5:15?" texted Shelly.

"OK. C u then. Gotta go!" wrote Guin.

Guin finished her sandwich, then rinsed off her plate and placed it into the dishwasher. Back to work, she said to herself, and headed back to her bedroom/office.

CHAPTER 11

Guin arrived at Doc Ford's, located at the South Seas Resort, promptly at 5:15 and immediately spied Shelly and Steve sitting on the deck. They were intently listening to the guitar player, so they didn't see her approach.

"Boo!" said Guin, standing just behind Shelly.

Shelly jumped and whipped her head around. Guin smiled.

"Oh my goodness! Don't ever do that again!" said Shelly, placing a hand on her heart. "I nearly had a heart attack!"

"Hi, Guin," said Steve, turning to face her. He pulled out the chair next to him and Guin sat down, giving each of them a peck on the cheek.

A minute later a server came over. "What can I get for you?" he asked. Guin eyed what Steve and Shelly were drinking. Steve was drinking a beer, as per usual.

"What are you having?" Guin asked Shelly, looking at her drink.

"It's called Babe on the Bay," said Shelly, taking a sip. "And it's yummy."

Guin smiled. "I'll have a margarita, no salt."

Shelly rolled her eyes. "You're so predictable!"

"I like what I like."

"You all want any appetizers?" asked the server.

"How about some fried calamari?" asked Steve, looking at Guin and Shelly.

"Sounds good to me," said Guin.

"Me too," said Shelly.

"One order of fried calamari," said Steve to the server, who repeated the order and left. "So, what've you been up to, Guin? I feel like I haven't seen you in ages."

"Just working," said Guin.

"How's Ris?"

"Good. He wants me to have a key to his place."

"He does?!" said Shelly, leaning over and putting her hand on Guin's arm.

"Down girl," said Guin.

"So, he must be serious," said Shelly.

"I didn't accept," said Guin, wishing the server would hurry up and bring her margarita.

Steve and Shelly exchanged a look.

"What?" asked Guin, looking from one to the other.

"Why don't you want his key? I thought you really liked Ris," said Shelly.

"I do," said Guin. "I'm just not sure I'm ready for that level of commitment."

Steve chuckled.

"What's so funny?" asked Guin.

"You sound like a guy."

Shelly swatted him.

"Ha ha," said Guin. "I know I'm making a bigger deal out of it than I should, but it's barely been a year since the divorce, and I'm not sure I'm ready to live with someone just yet."

"You just take your time then," said Shelly, patting Guin's arm.

"And now Art's here," added Guin, staring at the guitar player.

"What?! Art is *here*?!" said Shelly, looking around. "Where?"

"Not *here* here," said Guin. "His company's sales

conference is being held on Sanibel this year, over at the San Ybel Resort & Spa. I thought I told you that."

"I must have forgotten," said Shelly.

"You're slipping dear," said Steve, smiling. She swatted her husband, gently.

"So have you seen him?" asked Shelly, leaning close.

Just then the server returned with Guin's margarita. She thanked him, and he said he'd be back in a few with their fried calamari. Guin took a healthy sip of her drink.

"I met him for breakfast yesterday."

"AND…?!" said Shelly.

"And it was fine," said Guin, taking another sip of her margarita.

Shelly stared. "FINE?! It was *fine*?! What does *fine* mean?"

Guin sighed and turned to face Shelly. "It means we didn't kill each other. Actually, Art apologized, several times—"

"As he should!" said Shelly, indignantly.

"And he told me he missed me, that leaving me was a huge mistake."

"Duh," said Shelly.

"Are you going to keep interrupting Guin, dear, or are you going to let her finish?" asked Steve, smiling at his wife.

Shelly glared at him.

Guin looked from one to the other and smiled. If only her marriage had been as happy as Shelly and Steve's. They had been together for over 25 years, and clearly still cared about each other.

"So, what else did he have to say? You're not going to get back together with him, are you?" asked Shelly.

"No, we are not getting back together. I'm with Ris now."

"Did you tell Art that?"

"I did," said Guin.

"And how did he take it?" asked Shelly.

"I think he took it as a challenge."

"How exciting!" said Shelly, clapping her hands. "Are you going to see him again?"

"We-ell," said Guin, slowly, not sure how much she should tell them. She took another sip of her margarita and sat back. "So, Art and a bunch of his sales buddies went on this fishing trip after I saw him, yesterday afternoon—"

"Who did they go with?" asked Steve. "Did they hire Captain Al?"

"No, they went with a captain by the name of Big Ben Johnson," said Guin.

Steve made a face.

"What?" asked Guin.

"They should have hired Captain Al," said Steve.

"As in Al Boudreaux?" asked Guin.

"Yes," said Steve. "Captain Al is the best."

"You have something against Captain Ben?"

"I don't know him, personally. But you hear things. Apparently, he's gotten into trouble a few times. Always seems to come out okay, but I don't trust him."

"But you like Al Boudreaux?"

"Oh yeah, Captain Al is great. We tell all our guests to go with Captain Al. He knows a lot about the islands. He's also big on the environment."

"Well, as it happens, I gave Art both Captain Ben's and Captain Al's information," said Guin. "My colleague, Craig, recommended them both. But Art went with Ben. No doubt swayed by the pictures of guys with large fish, drinking beer."

"Did they have a good time?" asked Steve.

"They did, until one of the guys went missing."

"Missing?" asked Shelly.

"Yeah, apparently while two of the guys were trying to

reel in tarpon, one of the other guys, Rick, Art's nemesis, disappeared."

"Nemesis?" asked Steve.

"They're up for the same job, and Art says the guy had it in for him. Anyway, they discovered he was missing after they had reeled in the tarpon. They went looking for him. But all they found was his cap, which had some blood on it. So they called the Coast Guard and the police when they got back to shore, but the Coast Guard didn't find him, and the police had them in for questioning. Art was sure they were going to arrest him, even though he swore he had nothing to do with it."

"And you know all this how?" asked Steve.

"I was at the police department."

"Why?" asked Shelly.

"Art had texted me. He was sure they were going to arrest him, and he asked what he should do."

"So you just drove over there?" asked an astonished Shelly.

"I did," said Guin.

"Very Christian of you, Guin," said Steve, with a slight smirk.

"I think Art was pretty freaked out, though he'd never admit it," said Guin, ignoring Steve's comment.

"Why did he think they'd arrest him? Sounds like an accident."

"Apparently, Art was the last one to see Rick, and there was a knife at the back of the boat with blood on it."

"Oh no!" said Shelly. "Was it covered in Rick's blood?" she asked, gripping Guin's forearm.

"They don't know yet," replied Guin.

"Was Detective O'Loughlin there?" asked Shelly.

"He was. He was the one doing the questioning," replied Guin.

"So, did they arrest Art?" asked Steve.

"No," said Guin.

"Well, that's a relief, right?" asked Shelly. "So that's that then."

"Not quite," said Guin, taking another sip of her drink, which she noticed was almost empty.

Just then the server returned, depositing their order of fried calamari in the middle of the table. Guin reached over with her fork and speared a piece, dipping it into the red sauce. Shelly and Steve followed suit.

"Would you like another drink?" the server asked Guin.

Guin looked down at her glass. She was sorely tempted. But she had to work tomorrow, and she wanted to go to the beach early.

"No, thank you. Just some water, please."

"So...?" asked Shelly. "What happened?"

"After he was finally dismissed by O'Loughlin, we wound up having dinner."

"You had dinner?! Alone?" asked Shelly.

"Well, there were other people at the restaurant," said Guin, grinning.

"What happened to his friends?" asked Shelly.

"They left."

"That wasn't very considerate," said Steve.

"Art had told them to go," replied Guin. "He was counting on me showing up and then driving him back to the resort when he was done being questioned."

"Very presumptuous of him!" said Shelly. "So where did you go for dinner?"

"Doc Ford's on Sanibel," replied Guin, spearing another piece of calamari.

"Did he try any funny business?" asked Shelly.

"No," said Guin, not wanting to discuss their dinner or their drive back to the resort.

"You going to see him again?" Shelly asked, narrowing her eyes.

"Actually…" said Guin, trying to avoid Shelly's gaze, "I told Art I'd go with him to the sales dinner on Saturday."

Steve and Shelly exchanged looks.

"All the other guys are bringing their wives or dates, and Art felt weird about going stag."

"Oh boo hoo hoo," said Shelly. "Poor Art. Why didn't he just bring that chippy of his, the one he threw you over for?"

"They broke up," said Guin, looking into her empty drink, wishing she had ordered another margarita.

"You mean she ditched him," said Shelly.

"Her mom has cancer, and she went to be with her, back in Texas."

"So, Art's come running back to you, with his tail between his legs, begging you to take him back," said Shelly.

Guin took a sip of water. When Shelly put it that way, it didn't make Guin feel good. She thought again about bailing on dinner the next night.

As if reading her mind, Shelly added, "You know, you can cancel on him. No one would blame you."

Guin sighed. "I know, Shell. And I know it's probably stupid of me to have accepted. But I really need closure."

"And you think going to a sales dinner with your ex is the way to get it, Guin?" asked Steve.

"I don't know, maybe," said Guin, suddenly feeling stupid.

"You want another drink?" asked Steve, seeing Guin staring at her empty margarita glass.

"I really shouldn't," said Guin. "What I could use, though, is more food."

"Me, too," said Shelly. She looked around, trying to find their server. She finally spied him by the door to the restaurant and waved her arms. A few seconds later, he came over.

"What can I get you folks?"

"How about some of your chicken wings?" said Shelly, looking around the table. Steve and Guin gave her a thumbs up.

"One order of wings, it is. Anything else?"

They ordered some margarita flatbread, and Steve ordered another beer. Then the waiter left.

"So, what time's this dinner Saturday, and what do you plan on wearing?" asked Shelly.

"It's at seven at the resort. And I'm not sure. I was hoping maybe you could come over and help me pick something out?" said Guin, questioningly, looking over at Shelly, who had her arms crossed over her chest and a look on her face that reminded Guin of her mother, and not in a good way.

Shelly sighed. "Fine. What time should I come over?"

"Five-thirty okay?"

"I'll be there. Let's make Art regret he ever left you."

Guin took another sip of water, then she stood up. "I need to run to the Ladies' room. I'll be back in a couple of minutes."

She walked inside and headed to the restrooms. On the way, she saw a couple in a booth who looked vaguely familiar. She paused and stared, trying to place them, but she was unable to. She shook her head and continued to the Ladies' restroom. When she came out, she glanced again at the booth, sure she had seen the man and the woman somewhere. She waited a few seconds, but the booth was dimly lit, and she felt weird about going over there. Then they got up to leave, and she scurried back to her table on the deck, not looking at the couple.

"You okay?" asked Steve.

"Why?" replied Guin.

"You look a little flushed."

"Oh, I just thought I saw someone I knew."

"Happens to me all the time," said Shelly. "If you're like me, you'll suddenly remember at three a.m."

"At least Guin won't wake me up to tell me," said Steve, grinning at his wife, who poked him in the ribs.

Just then the wings and the flatbread arrived. The three of them dove in, devouring both in just a few minutes, and the topic of Art, and the mystery couple, didn't come up again.

CHAPTER 12

Saturday morning Guin got up early and went for a walk on the beach by herself. She hadn't thought about the couple at the restaurant. She had, however, been thinking about Art, who had texted her just before she had gone to bed, saying how much he was looking forward to tonight.

As she walked along Bowman's Beach, looking for shells, she again questioned why she had agreed to go to the dinner with Art. As she was lost in thought, several brown pelicans dove for fish. She stopped and watched them. Then she continued walking.

The beach was quiet, which was not that unusual for June, especially before eight a.m. However, people weren't the only things missing from the beach that morning. There were very few shells, too. But it was a beautiful morning, and Guin enjoyed her walk nonetheless.

When she got home a little while later, she was greeted at the front door by the cats, whom she had forgotten to feed before she left.

"Sorry!" she said, as they mewed their disapproval and ran ahead of her into the kitchen. She opened the door to the pantry, grabbed the bag of cat food, and poured some into their bowls. They immediately dove in.

"Better now?" she asked Flora and Fauna. As usual, they ignored her. "Fine, be that way," Guin said.

"I'm going to fix myself some coffee and something to eat," she announced. The cats continued to ignore her. She sighed and went about making coffee in her little French press. Then she took out some eggs and whole grain bread from the fridge. She cracked two eggs into a bowl and immediately Fauna trotted over and started meowing.

"I just fed you!" said Guin, looking down at the black cat.

Fauna let out a plaintive meow.

Guin sighed (again). "Fine. You can lick the bowl when I'm done with it."

She put two slices of bread into the toaster and started heating up a pan for the eggs. A minute later, she added the eggs, then placed the bowl on the floor, in front of Fauna.

"Here," she said. Fauna immediately stuck her head in and began licking up the remaining egg. Guin smiled.

When everything was ready, she took her plate and mug of coffee to the table in her living-dining area, where she read the paper on her phone as she ate.

Guin had been cranking on work and had lost track of the time. It often happened when she was writing an article. She was nearly done when the doorbell rang. She looked at the clock on her computer. How did it get to be nearly five-thirty?

The doorbell rang again. "Coming!" Guin called as she ran to the front door. She opened it to find her friend standing there.

"Hey, Shelly, thanks for coming over," Guin said, giving her a hug and then letting her in.

They headed back to the bedroom and into Guin's walk-in closet. By now, Shelly was quite familiar with Guin's wardrobe, having helped Guin pick out outfits for several events. But as she was always reminding Guin, no two occasions were the same, and it was important to dress appropriately if she wanted to make a good impression.

"So, what are we going for here?" asked Shelly, flicking through Guin's hangers. "The aren't-you-sorry-you-dissed-me look? Professional badass? Confident fortysomething woman? I'm too sexy for my ex?"

Guin laughed. "How about all of the above?"

Shelly smiled. "There's always that sexy little gold number you wore to the Shell Show reception…"

"Bad memories," said Guin. (That was the night the Golden Junonia had gone missing, which had started a chain of unfortunate events, including the murder of Gregor Matenopoulos, the former king of Captiva real estate.)

"Okay," said Shelly, continuing to sort through Guin's clothes. "How about this one?" She pulled out a pretty, long blue-green dress with a scoop neck that buttoned down the front. "What did you call this one again?"

"My mermaid dress," said Guin.

Shelly held it up against her. "Yes, I think this will do nicely. It brings out the blue in your eyes and complements your strawberry blonde hair."

"You don't think it's too casual?"

"You're on a tropical island. It's perfect," said Shelly. "Besides, I bet half the guys there will be wearing Hawaiian shirts."

Guin laughed.

"So, do you know any of these people?" asked Shelly, as she waited for Guin to put on the dress.

"A few. I know Art's boss, Alan, and his wife, Emily. We used to have dinner together. And I probably know a few of the salespeople, the ones who've been there awhile."

Guin finished buttoning up the dress and then spun around in front of Shelly.

"Looks good! Now let's pick out some jewelry, then do your hair and makeup."

"You sure you don't want to get a job as a professional stylist, Shell?" asked Guin, following Shelly back into the closet, where they retrieved her jewelry box. "You could make a killing over on Captiva."

"Nah, I just like helping my friends."

They picked out some jewelry, then headed into the bathroom. Shelly ordered Guin to sit on the chair by the vanity, then she opened a drawer and retrieved Guin's makeup bag. "Girl, you need to get some new makeup," she said, looking through Guin's collection of old and used up lipsticks and mascara.

"You know I'm not a big fan of makeup, Shell."

"I know," said Shelly, "but we're not getting any younger, and you need to do something about those freckles of yours."

"I like my freckles," said Guin. "I think they suit me."

"Yeah, yeah, yeah," said Shelly. "Now sit still, so I can do your hair and makeup."

A half hour later, Guin was made up and dressed, her hair down, as Shelly had given up on the up-do. She spun around.

"How do I look?"

"Like Art is going to wonder why he ever left," said Shelly.

Guin leaned over and gave Shelly a kiss on the cheek.

"Thank you. You're a good friend."

"We still on for brunch tomorrow? You know I'm going to want all the details."

"Yes, we are still on for brunch tomorrow," said Guin, escorting Shelly out.

"Okay, now don't stay out too late," called Shelly as she made her way down the stairs. "And don't do anything you'll regret in the morning!"

"Goodbye, Shelly," called Guin.

"Call me if you need anything!" Shelly shouted back.

Guin laughed and closed the door. When she turned around, the cats were directly in front of her.

"Well, how do I look?" she asked them.

Flora tilted her head and stared. Fauna walked over and rubbed herself against Guin's leg. Guin gently scooted her away.

"Not tonight, Fauna. I don't want to be covered in cat hair."

She walked into the kitchen and grabbed the lint roller, removing the black fur Fauna had deposited on her dress.

She looked at the clock. "Okay, time to go," she said aloud. She gave the cats some food, then grabbed her bag and her keys, put on her high-heeled sandals, and headed out the door.

CHAPTER 13

Guin arrived at the San Ybel Resort & Spa in her purple Mini Cooper a few minutes after seven and handed her keys to the valet. She took a deep breath and headed to the reception area, not sure where the banquet was being held. As she was waiting in line, Art's boss, Alan, walked by, absorbed in conversation on his cell phone. Guin saw him and waved. He glanced at her, at first confused, then recognition dawned and he headed over, muttering something into his phone before putting it in his pocket.

"Guin? Is that you?" he said, smiling.

"It is indeed," she replied.

"What are you doing here?" asked Alan, eyeing her appreciatively.

"I'm supposed to meet Art, but I don't know where exactly the dinner is being held, so I thought I'd ask at reception."

"Are you and Art back together then? I always thought he was an idiot for dumping you—" he caught himself and looked abashed. "Sorry, that was rather clumsy of me."

"No worries," she said. "I thought he was an idiot, too."

Guin grinned at him, and he smiled back at her.

"Well, since Art isn't here, may I escort you into the banquet, my lady?" asked Alan, proffering his arm.

"I would be honored, kind sir," said Guin, making a little

curtsy before taking his arm. "So, is Emily not here with you?" asked Guin, looking around.

"She is, but she isn't feeling well. A headache," he added, in what sounded to Guin like a somewhat sarcastic tone.

"I'm sorry to hear that," said Guin. "I hope she feels better soon."

"I'm sure she will," said Alan.

As she took his arm, Guin could hear Alan's phone buzzing.

"Do you need to get that?" she asked.

"If it's important, they'll leave a message."

They walked through the resort, Guin admiring the decor and the view.

"This place is lovely," she said.

"It is," Alan agreed. "Have you been here before?"

"No, it's actually my first time."

They made their way to the private banquet room, which had a view of the Gulf of Mexico, and entered. There were a few dozen people there already, standing near the open bar and the hors d'oeuvres table, mingling. Guin looked around for Art but didn't see him.

"Maybe I should text him," said Guin, suddenly feeling a bit nervous.

"Tired of me already, are you?" said Alan.

"Oh no!" said Guin.

Alan held up his hands. "I was just kidding. Go ahead and text Art. He's probably doing his hair—or closing a deal," he said, smiling. "I'm going to go get a drink."

He headed over to the bar, stopping to say hello to several people along the way.

Guin opened her bag, took out her phone, and texted Art. "I'm here at the banquet. Where are you?"

She waited for a reply but did not receive one. That's odd, she thought. He knew I was going to be here at seven.

She continued to stare at her phone for a minute.

"Excuse me, is everything okay?"

Guin looked up to see a handsome blond man in his thirties, a younger version of Art, wearing a collarless shirt and chinos, looking at her.

"I'm not sure," said Guin, a bit flustered.

"I'm Joe, Joe Walton," said the man, extending a hand. "I'm the rep from the Midwest. And you are?"

"I'm Guin, Guinivere Jones," replied Guin, shaking his hand. "And I'm just a guest."

"Well, Guinivere Jones, may I get you a drink?" said Joe, smiling at her. "I believe guests are entitled to at least one free drink."

Guin looked around the room. Still no sign of Art.

"Sure, why not?" said Guin. "I'll head over to the bar with you."

They walked over to the bar. The bartender smiled and asked what they'd like to drink.

"Guinivere?" asked Joe.

"Please, call me Guin," she said, smiling at Joe. "I'll have a white wine spritzer," she said, turning back to the bartender.

She was tempted to order something stronger, but the last thing she wanted was to become tipsy at Art's sales conference, in front of his boss and coworkers. Though, looking around at all the men, and women, with drinks in their hands, they probably wouldn't notice.

"I'll have a beer," said Joe.

"We have…"

The bartender rattled off a bunch of names, but Guin wasn't paying attention. She was looking around the room, trying to see if Art was lurking somewhere. But there was no sign of him.

"You looking for someone?" asked Joe.

"Oh, yes, sorry," said Guin, giving him a bashful smile. "I was just looking for my, for my… friend."

Friend? Thought Guin. She suddenly realized she didn't know how to refer to Art. Yes, she could have said "my ex-husband," but that sounded odd. And no way was she going to refer to him as her "date."

"What does your friend look like?" asked Joe, scanning the room.

"Well," said Guin, thinking how best to describe Art. (She thought about saying "like an older version of you," but stopped herself.) "He's a little over six feet, with dirty blond hair and brown eyes. Kind of looks like an aging surfer or a former lacrosse player."

"Oh, so your friend is a guy," said Joe, sounding a bit disappointed.

"He is," said Guin, smiling. "You probably know him. Arthur Jones?"

"Oh, Art!" said Joe, smiling again. "He's a rock star! He's been the top sales guy for, like, three years in a row now. So, how do you know him?"

"I used to be married to him," said Guin, taking a sip of her drink and acting as nonchalant as she could.

Joe hit his palm against his forehead. "Right! You said your last name was Jones. I should have connected the dots," he said, eyeing Guin more closely.

Guin glanced down at Joe's left hand.

"Oh, I'm not married," said Joe, following her gaze and smiling.

"I bet you have a girlfriend, though," said Guin, teasingly. (He was very good looking.)

Joe blushed slightly. "Actually, I do, but she's back in Illinois. She's a teacher. I wanted her to come to the conference with me, but she couldn't get time off. End of year and all. Probably just as well."

"What does she teach?" asked Guin.

"High school French," said Joe. "I'm hoping to take her to Paris over Christmas."

How sweet, thought Guin. "I'm sure Paris is magical at Christmastime. The perfect place to pop the question," said Guin, slyly.

"Or go on your honeymoon," said Joe, grinning. "I'm planning to propose to her over July Fourth. But please, don't tell anyone. It's a secret."

Guin smiled. "Scout's honor," she said, holding up three fingers.

Joe smiled, then frowned, spying something toward the back of the room.

"Everything okay?" she asked Joe. She looked where he was looking and saw Art making his way toward them, looking disheveled and distracted.

"Hey, Art!" said Joe, holding up a hand in greeting as Art approached them.

Art stared at Joe, looking slightly confused.

Joe held out his hand. "Joe, Joe Walton. I'm the Midwest rep. We chatted the other day after the seminar."

"Oh right," said Art, his face breaking into his salesman's smile. "Now I remember."

Guin interrupted. "Where have you been?"

She gazed at Art, taking in his untucked shirt and slightly bedraggled appearance. Normally, Art was very fastidious about his appearance, always making sure he dressed to impress. He was always telling Guin, "You only get one chance to make a first impression."

"Something came up," he said, cryptically. He tucked his shirt into his slacks, ran a hand through his hair, and then leaned over to give Guin a kiss on the cheek.

"Have you been on the beach?" asked Guin, noticing a bit of sand on Art's pants.

"Uh, no, why?" replied Art.

Just then Murph came up to them and slapped Art on the shoulder.

"And who might this lovely lady be?" he asked, eyeing Guin.

"This is my wife, Guin."

"*Ex*-wife," interrupted Guin.

Murph smiled. "A pleasure to meet you, Guin," he said, extending his hand. Guin shook it but didn't say anything. "Did your husband here—"

"*Ex*-husband," repeated Guin.

"Excuse me, *ex*-husband, tell you I caught a huge tarpon the other day on our little fishing expedition? Though I was unable to reel it all the way in. But you should have seen it!"

"As a matter of fact, he did mention it," said Guin, smiling at Murph.

Murph turned to Joe, putting a hand on his shoulder.

"So, Joseph, me boy," he said in a fake Irish brogue. "How you be enjoying the conference?"

Judging by Murph's happy-go-lucky attitude and his breath, Guin guessed he had already had a couple of drinks.

"It's great," said Joe, smiling at Murph. "I'm learning a lot."

"Young Joe here is relatively new to the company," explained Murph to Guin, his arm around Joe's shoulders. "I'm showing him the ropes, so he can be a big shot like Art here."

Murph grinned while Joe tried not to look uncomfortable.

"Well, if you both will excuse us, I need to have a chat with my wife," said Art, putting his hand on Guin's back.

"*Ex*-wife," hissed Guin. She turned to Murph and Joe. "Nice meeting you both," she said, trying to ignore Art's hand.

Art maneuvered her outside.

"What is up with you?" she asked, slightly annoyed.

He looked down at Guin.

"Have I told you that you look beautiful tonight?" he asked, a smile spreading across his face, a genuine one.

"No, you haven't," she said, flustered. "But don't change the subject. What's up?"

He held up his hands. "Nothing, I swear! I was just attending to some last-minute business and lost track of the time."

"Business on a Saturday?"

"You know I'm always working, babe."

Guin winced. She hated when Art called her "babe."

"Let's get some food and go grab a seat," said Art.

Guin looked over at the hors d'oeuvres table. The food did look good.

"Is there going to be a sit-down dinner, or is this it?"

"Worried you won't get fed?" he asked, still smiling.

Guin made a face.

"Yes, there will be dinner—and karaoke," said Art, his smile broadening.

"Oh no!" said Guin. "I did *not* sign on for that!"

Art laughed. "Okay, okay. No karaoke. But there will be dancing," he said. He continued to smile at Guin, remembering what it felt like to hold her in his arms.

"Hello? Anybody home?" asked Guin, waving a hand in front of Art's face. He had been staring at her.

Art continued to smile at her.

"Okay, let's get some food and go have a seat," he replied. "And Guin?"

"Yes?" she replied, a bit warily.

"You really do look wonderful. I mean that."

Guin smiled. "Thank you."

They headed over to the hors d'oeuvres table and grabbed plates. Guin was starving and quickly picked out a variety of things. Then they found a couple of seats at a table near the patio.

They sat down to dinner a little while later, and Guin half-listened as the men discussed golf, fishing, and various company-related things. At their table were Alan, Murph and Murph's wife, Maura, and Justin Campbell and his spouse, Felicity. Emily, despite Alan's assertion that she would appear, was a no-show.

The dessert plates were just being cleared away, and the DJ was getting ready to start playing, when there was a commotion at the back of the room. Guin turned around to see Detective O'Loughlin, accompanied by two uniformed officers, heading toward the mic stand.

"Ladies and gentlemen," said the detective, speaking into the microphone.

There were lots of confused looks and buzzing in the room.

"Who's he then?" asked Justin.

"He would be Detective William O'Loughlin of the Sanibel Police Department," answered Guin.

"What's he doing here?" asked Murph.

"I have a feeling we are about to find out," said Alan.

The detective continued. "Ladies and gentlemen, I'm sorry to break up your little gathering, but we're investigating an incident here at the hotel, and we need to question everyone."

There was loud groaning heard around the room.

"That'll take all night!" someone at a nearby table groused.

Guin looked around the room, then back at the table, and noticed Art gripping the back of his chair.

"If I could have your attention, please," said the

detective, tapping the microphone. The two officers both took a step forward and the room immediately quieted down. "We will try to get through this as quickly as possible and ask for your patience."

There was continued grumbling amongst the crowd.

"We'll call each table up, one at a time, beginning over there," he said, pointing to a table in the far-right corner. "In the meantime, feel free to go about your business. Just please do not leave the room until we've finished questioning you."

The detective nodded at the DJ, who began playing some music, and then indicated to one of the officers to escort the first table out of the banquet room.

"Any idea what this is about?" asked Justin, looking at Alan.

Alan shrugged.

Murph's wife, Maura, who seemed the good-natured type, like her husband, piped up. "Well, I can think of worse places to be stuck. May as well have another drink!"

Murph smiled at her. "That's my girl."

Guin watched as the first table of people left the room, escorted by one of the officers as the other officer stationed himself by the door. Not long after, most of the people from the first table had returned and the first officer escorted the next table of people out of the room. Things proceeded apace for the next couple of hours, until it was just her table left.

In the interim, Guin had allowed herself to have another drink, and some dessert, and had even danced, taking turns dancing with Art and Joe, who reminded her more and more of a young Art.

Finally, it was time for their table to be questioned.

"If you all would come with me," said the officer.

"Happy to, officer," said Justin, getting up.

The rest of the table followed suit.

"This way, please," said the officer, gesturing toward the door.

They followed him out the door of the banquet room down the hall.

"I say, he's rather cute," Maura whispered to Guin.

Guin smiled at her.

They arrived at one of the meeting rooms.

"Ladies first," said the officer, holding the door open.

"Do you want all three of us to go in?" asked Justin's wife, Felicity.

"Yes, ma'am," said the officer.

Maura looked at the other two women, shrugged, and stepped into the room. Guin and Felicity followed her.

Sitting at a table at the far end of the room was Detective O'Loughlin. Guin marched up to him and stopped, folding her arms over her chest.

"What's this all about, Detective?"

The detective looked up at her.

"Ah, Ms. Jones, so nice to see you. Won't you have a seat?"

CHAPTER 14

The detective had asked the women what they had been doing earlier that evening. All three of them had replied that they had been getting ready for the banquet and had been in their rooms (or at home, in Guin's case) most of the afternoon. He then asked them if they were acquainted with Richard Tomlinson.

Immediately upon hearing Rick's name, Guin's eyebrows shot up. She did not have a good feeling. She glanced at the detective, who was impassively scanning the three women's faces.

"I didn't *know* him, if that's what you're getting after," stated Maura, who had clearly had a fair amount to drink.

"I don't think I've actually met the man," answered Felicity.

The detective looked over at Guin.

"I knew *of* him," she replied. "But I can't say I really knew him."

The detective wrote something in his notebook.

"Thank you, ladies," he said. "You're free to go."

The three women got up and were escorted out of the room by the officer.

Alan, Art, Justin, and Murph were standing there, waiting.

"Everything okay?" Murph asked his wife.

Maura glanced over at the officer, then turned back to her husband and nodded.

The officer came over to the group.

"Gentlemen," he said, gesturing toward the door. He opened it and waited for the men to enter.

Guin laid a hand on Art's arm as he passed her. He stopped.

"What?"

Guin was going to say something, but she just shook her head. Art smiled down at her.

"Worried about me?"

Guin opened her mouth, then quickly closed it.

"Sir?" said the officer, who was holding the door.

"I'm sure everything's fine, Guin. Be out in a few."

He went through the door, into the meeting room, the officer closing the door behind them.

Maura and Felicity had announced that they were going up to their rooms, but Guin had decided to wait for the men. It was quite late, but she didn't care. She had a bad feeling and wanted to find out what was going on, not having had a chance to ask the detective when she had been in the room.

A few minutes later, the door opened and Alan, Justin, Murph, and Art, accompanied by the detective, came out. Guin glanced at Art, but he wouldn't look at her.

"Art?" she asked.

She looked over at the detective.

"We're taking Mr. Jones here over to the Police Department for some additional questioning," he said. "You should go home."

"What?" said Guin, looking from the detective to Art. "Why?"

But the detective didn't reply.

"I'll be fine, Guin," Art said, though he didn't look it. "Go home. I'll call you in the morning."

Guin watched as the detective escorted Art down the hall.

"Don't worry, Guin," said Alan. "I'm sure everything will be fine."

Guin hated that word, *fine*. Things were clearly not fine.

"What's this all about anyway?" she asked him.

Alan sighed.

"Rick was found dead earlier this evening."

"What?!" said Guin. "Where?"

"In one of the cabanas the company had rented for the conference," Alan replied.

"How did he die?"

"The detective didn't say," said Alan.

"He thinks Art did it, doesn't he?" Guin asked, looking from Alan to Murph.

The men looked a bit uncomfortable.

"I'm sure it's nothing," said Murph. "Just procedure."

"Nothing?" said Guin, clearly upset. "Did the detective ask any of you to go to the police station?" she said, glancing from Murph to Justin to Alan.

"No, but..." began Murph.

Guin glared at him.

"But he did tell us not to leave the island," said Murph.

Alan put a hand on Guin's arm. "We all know that Art had a killer instinct," he said, smiling at his play on words. "But I doubt that he killed Rick, much as he may have wanted to at times."

Guin tried to picture Art killing Rick, but she couldn't. Did Art have a bit of a temper? Sure. Did he occasionally get so frustrated he would slam his hand against the wall? Indeed. But in all their years together, Guin had never seen Art hurt anyone or even threaten violence, at least not seriously, as far as she knew. Then again, she had never thought Art was capable of cheating on her.

"You going to be okay?" asked Murph. "You need a ride?"

"I'm good," said Guin.

"Well, let me know if you need anything," said Alan. "You can call me anytime. We'll be here at the resort for a few more days."

He leaned over and gave Guin a kiss on the cheek.

"Goodnight, Guin. Don't worry too much about Art. He'll be fine."

But Guin was a worrier by nature, and she knew the detective would only have brought Art back to the station if he had a good reason.

"Goodnight, Alan, and thank you," she said. "If you gentlemen will excuse me?"

She hurried off to the lobby, pulling her phone out of her bag on the way. It was nearly eleven-thirty, but she had a bad feeling regarding Art, and her feelings were rarely wrong.

"Forgive me, Ginny," she said, in a whisper as she pressed speed dial.

Ginny's mobile rang several times, and just as Guin was sure the call would go into Ginny's voicemail, she picked up.

"Hey, Guin, what's up? Is everything okay?"

"The Sanibel police just brought my husband—I mean my ex-husband—Art in for questioning. They think he killed someone, and I need to find him a lawyer, pronto," Guin blurted.

Ginny whistled.

"Can you help me out?"

"At eleven-thirty on a Saturday night?" said Ginny. She paused, and Guin held her breath. "Give me a few minutes. I'll call you back."

"Thanks, Ginny. Appreciate it. And sorry for calling you so late."

"As long as we get the exclusive," said Ginny and hung up.

Guin let out a bark of laughter. That was Ginny, always out to get a good story.

Guin paced around the lobby for several minutes, waiting for Ginny to call back. She thought about going to her car and driving home—Ginny may not even call her back until the morning—when her phone started buzzing.

It was a text message from Ginny.

"Reach out to Tricia Parker," she wrote. "She's the best. Tell her I recommended you call her."

Ginny had included a phone number.

"OK to call her now?" Guin typed.

"Yes," replied Ginny.

"Thanks Ginny," Guin wrote. She immediately called the number Ginny gave her, despite her nervousness at calling so late.

"Tricia Parker."

"Hi, Ms. Parker? Sorry for phoning so late. My name is Guinivere Jones. My boss, Ginny Prescott, told me to call you. My husband—ex-husband—was just taken in for questioning by the Sanibel police regarding a murder case, and he needs a good lawyer."

"I see," said Ms. Parker. "As it happens, I'm at a party over on Captiva, and I was just about to leave," she replied. "Give me a few minutes. I'll meet you over there."

"Thank you," said Guin.

She ended the call, shoved her phone back in her bag, and strode quickly to the valet stand, where she gently tapped the valet, who looked like he had nodded off. She smiled and handed him her ticket. A few minutes later, she was in her purple Mini, on her way to the Sanibel Police Department.

CHAPTER 15

Guin was pacing around the small foyer at the Sanibel Police Department. She had announced herself at the front desk and had asked to speak with Detective O'Loughlin, but she had been told he was in with someone.

"Yes, my ex-husband!" she practically shouted at the young officer on duty.

"Sorry, ma'am," said the officer. "But I can't let you back there."

"Could you just please tell the detective that Ms. Jones is here?"

But the officer had refused, explaining that the detective had told him he was not to be disturbed.

Guin made a face and sat down, bouncing one leg atop the other while she waited.

A few minutes later, a tall, striking woman with long brown hair walked through the door. She was dressed in a sarong and wore a shell necklace and must have been at least half a foot taller than Guin, more with her heels. Guin tried not to stare, but it was hard not to. The woman commanded your attention.

"Ms. Jones?" asked the woman, looking down at Guin.

Guin collected herself and stood up, extending her hand. "Yes, I'm Ms. Jones—Guinivere, Guin," she said. "You must be Ms. Parker."

The woman smiled and shook Guin's hand. "Guilty as charged."

Guin smiled politely at the joke.

"Sorry, lawyer humor," said Ms. Parker.

Guin looked up at the attorney. She felt like a midget compared to her. (Guin was five-foot-four, five-six in her heels, and Tricia Parker was easily over six feet with her heels.)

"Thank you for coming on such short notice."

"No problem. Any friend of Ginny's...." she trailed off, looking around, then returning her gaze to Guin. "So, is he in back?"

"Yes, speaking with Detective O'Loughlin. But they won't let me see him."

"Well, we'll fix that," said the lawyer.

She went over to the desk. "Good evening, I'm Tricia Parker, Mr. Jones's attorney. Can you please tell Detective O'Loughlin I'm here to see my client?"

The officer at the desk hesitated. The detective had told him he was not to be disturbed.

Ms. Parker leaned over and smiled down at him. It was not a friendly smile, rather one that warned people that Tricia Parker was not a woman to be messed with. "Please tell him I'm here. I'll wait."

The officer excused himself and said he'd be right back.

Guin chuckled to herself. If only she could have that effect on people.

A couple of minutes later, the detective appeared in the doorway. He did not look happy. He looked over at the attorney.

"Ms. Parker," he said. "And what brings you to our little precinct so late on a Saturday night?"

"Good evening, William. Nice to see you, too."

Guin looked from one to the other.

"I believe you are holding a client of mine," said Ms. Parker.

"And who might that be?" asked the detective.

"A Mr. Arthur Jones."

Just then the detective spied Guin, who had been standing silently in the corner, hidden in shadow.

"Ah," he said. "I should have known." The detective ran a hand through his closely cropped auburn and gray hair.

"Fine, come on back. But just you," he said, addressing the attorney. "Ms. Jones, you stay right where you are."

"But—" said Guin.

"No buts," said the detective. "Just the lawyer."

Guin registered her displeasure but didn't say anything. The detective opened the door and gestured for Ms. Parker to go through.

"Don't worry, Ms. Jones," said the attorney, standing in the doorframe. "We'll have this sorted out in no time. If you like, you can go home."

"I'll wait here for a bit, if you don't mind," said Guin.

"Suit yourself," said the lawyer.

Guin watched as the door closed behind them. Then she leaned against the wall as there was no place in the vestibule to sit. She reached into her bag and pulled out her phone. She sent Shelly a text, letting her know she was at the police station, waiting for Art, even though it was long past Shelly's bedtime and her phone was probably turned off.

But a few seconds later, Guin's phone began to buzz. It was a text from Shelly.

"WHAT?!" she had written.

Guess she's still up, said Guin to herself, smiling.

"What are you doing up?" replied Guin.

"Forgot to turn off my phone," wrote Shelly. "What's going on? Why are you at the police department?"

"I'll fill you in at brunch tomorrow," Guin wrote back.

"Oh no," wrote Shelly. "Tell me NOW! Call me!"

"Hold on a sec," Guin texted her.

She went outside and called Shelly on her mobile.

"What the heck is going on?" asked Shelly as soon as she picked up.

"And that's everything I know," said Guin, a few minutes later, after recounting the events of the evening.

Shelly whistled. "That husband of yours…"

"*Ex*-husband," corrected Guin.

"Whatever. He's nothing but trouble."

It was Guin's turn to sigh now. She knew Shelly was right.

"Remind me again why you're helping him?" asked Shelly.

Guin could hear Shelly's disapproval.

"Because even though he was a total jerk to me, I don't think he deserves to be sent to prison for a crime he didn't commit. Art may be a lot of things, but a killer? I don't think so."

"How can you be so sure?" asked Shelly. "You didn't think he was a cheater either."

Guin paused. Shelly had a point. If you had asked her several years ago if Art was the type to cheat, she would have immediately said no. But she had been wrong. Could she also be wrong about this? She sat down on a bench.

"Hello? Anybody there?"

"Oh, sorry, Shell. I was just thinking."

"About?"

"About what you said."

"Well, just be careful," said Shelly.

"I will, Shelly, promise."

Shelly let out a yawn. Guin did the same. They both laughed.

"I should go back to bed," said Shelly. "You sure you're going to be okay?"

"I'll be fine," said Guin, letting out another yawn. "You go to sleep. I'll see you tomorrow at Over Easy at ten."

"Okay," said Shelly. "Goodnight."

Guin ended the call and got up. She paced on the walkway in front of the police department, waiting for the attorney to come out. A few minutes later, she finally did.

"Ms. Jones?" she called, stepping outside.

Guin quickly walked over. "Yes?"

"Would you come with me, please?" said the attorney.

Guin nodded her head and silently followed her back inside, through the door to the back, to Detective O'Loughlin's office. She entered and saw the detective seated behind his desk, a sour look on his face. Her ex-husband sat across from him. She ignored Art and looked right at the detective.

"Did you arrest him?" she asked.

"Not yet," said the detective.

"So, he's free to go?" asked Guin, looking from the detective to the attorney.

"Not exactly," said Ms. Parker.

Guin was confused.

"The detective has enough evidence to hold your husband," explained the attorney.

"*Ex*-husband," said Guin.

"*Ex*-husband," said Ms. Parker, smiling and looking at Guin. "However, out of the goodness of his heart—"

The detective glared at Ms. Parker.

"He has decided to release your ex-husband into your custody," she explained.

"WHAT?!" said Guin, jerking her head from the attorney to the detective to Art. "Who decided that? He can't stay with me!"

"Why not?" asked Ms. Parker, calmly. "I understand you live alone and have an extra bedroom that is currently unoccupied."

Guin glared at the detective.

"He can't stay with me!" Guin repeated, resisting the urge to stamp her foot.

"Would you rather see him in jail?" asked Ms. Parker.

Guin was tempted to say "Yes!" But she looked down at Art, whose brown eyes were practically pleading with her, and she felt herself soften.

"Why can't he just stay at the hotel?"

"Because right now he is the prime suspect in a murder investigation, but the police don't have enough evidence to formally charge him," explained the attorney. "And we thought placing him in your custody for at least the next twenty-four hours would ensure that he didn't leave Sanibel."

"I can't believe you agreed to this," said Guin, looking at the detective.

The detective said nothing.

Guin turned back to the attorney, "Fine, I agree. What happens now?"

"I suggest you take Mr. Jones home with you and get a good night's rest," said Ms. Parker. "Then tomorrow morning the two of you should go to the hotel and gather his things."

A good night's rest, with Art sleeping under her roof? Ha!

"So, is he under house arrest?" asked Guin.

"In a manner of speaking," said Ms. Parker. "He doesn't have to wear a tracking device, but we suggest you keep a close eye on him. I'm sure the detective will want to speak with him again, soon," said the attorney, smiling at the detective.

"But I have plans for tomorrow," said Guin, trying not to sound too whiny.

"You are not joined at the hip," said Ms. Parker. "Just keep an eye on him."

The attorney looked down at Art. "I trust you can behave yourself, Mr. Jones?"

Art made a face.

"Well, now that that is all settled," said Ms. Parker, "I must be off. You have my number, Ms. Jones, if you need to reach me." She turned to the detective. "William."

The detective remained stony faced as the attorney left the room.

"So he's free to go?" said Guin, addressing the detective.

"For now," replied O'Loughlin.

"You heard the man," said Guin, looking down at Art. "Get up."

Art glanced at the detective then stood up. "Thank you," he whispered quietly to Guin.

"Don't thank me yet," said Guin, clenching her teeth. "Let's go."

"Goodnight, detective," said Guin, turning back to face him. "I'm sure we'll be seeing each other again very soon."

"Goodnight, Ms. Jones," said the detective. "I look forward to it."

As Guin looked back at the detective, she could have sworn that was a little smile on his face.

CHAPTER 16

They drove back to Guin's condo in silence. When they got there, Guin escorted Art to the guest room and gave him one of the spare toothbrushes she kept for guests.

"Do you need something to sleep in?" Guin asked. "I probably have an old concert tee that would fit you."

"You know I don't need anything, Guin," said Art, a mischievous look on his face.

Guin blushed. She had momentarily forgotten that Art liked to sleep in the buff.

"Well, goodnight then," she said, eager to be out of the guest room. "I'll see you in the morning."

Despite not going to bed until very late, Guin got up at her usual time the next morning and knocked on the guest room door.

"Rise and shine, jailbird. I have a brunch date, so we need to head down to your hotel now."

The door opened and Guin looked away.

"Relax," said Art. "I'm dressed."

Guin hesitated.

"Don't you trust me?" he asked.

"No," replied Guin.

"Well, I'm telling you the truth. Turn around."

Guin turned around to see Art in the clothes he was wearing the night before.

"You ready to go over to the hotel and get your things?"

"Could I have some coffee first?" he asked.

"I was about to make some," said Guin.

She went into the kitchen and put some coffee and water in the coffee maker. As she was doing so, the cats trotted in, stopping to look up at Art.

"Hello Flora. Hello Fauna," said Art, looking down at the felines.

The cats looked from Art to Guin and back again.

"I think they're confused," said Guin.

She gave them some food and fresh water.

"Coffee's almost ready," said Guin.

Guin eyed Art, in his rumpled clothes, his hair mussed, and hated that she still found him attractive.

"So, what's on tap for today?" he asked her.

"Like I said, I have a brunch date with my friend, Shelly. So I need to get you back to the hotel, so you can pick up your things."

"Anything else?" asked Art.

"Why?" said Guin.

"I thought maybe we could do something together this afternoon."

"I have to work," said Guin, which was the truth.

Art eyed Guin. "Is this the way it's going to be?"

"What do you mean?" asked Guin.

"I mean, are you going to be snapping at me the whole time I'm here? I've already told you how sorry I am, Guin. I'd apologize to you a million times, if I thought it would help. I don't know what else I can do."

Guin looked at Art.

"Tell me what the hell happened back at the hotel. Why are you the prime suspect in Rick's death?"

"You don't beat around the bush, do you?" said Art, smiling at her.

"I'm serious, Art. Tell me what happened. What did you say to the detective?"

Art sighed and leaned against the counter. "You know that Rick disappeared from the boat the other day?"

"I do," said Guin.

"Well, yesterday, shortly before the dinner, I received a message from Rick."

"Did he text you?"

"No, it was a note left for me at the front desk."

"Go on," said Guin.

"Like I said, the front desk called the room to say I had a message. So I went downstairs to retrieve it. It was a note from Rick. It said to meet him at six-thirty in Cabana 5. That's one of the private cabanas we rented for the conference."

"Well, I guess he didn't drown."

"Apparently not," said Art, taking a sip of his coffee. "I thought about blowing him off. After all, I was meeting you at seven, and I didn't want to be late. But I wanted to give the guy a piece of my mind for that stunt he pulled on the boat."

"Go on," said Guin.

"I arrived at the cabana at six-thirty. The lights weren't on, which I thought a bit odd, and it was very quiet. I called Rick's name, but he didn't answer. I felt around for a light switch and flipped on the lights. I saw Rick, seated in a chair at the table, with his back to me. I stood in the doorway and said, 'turn around, Rick.' But he didn't respond. So I walked over to him. Like I said, his back was to the door, so I leaned over and tapped him on the shoulder. Nothing. I said his name again, and probably a few other things, but he didn't respond.

"Now I was starting to get a bad feeling. I said, 'Come on, Rick!' and gave his shoulder a little shake, and he slumped over onto the table. There were bottles of beer on the table, along with a couple of glasses. I figured Rick been drinking and had passed out. I knew he liked to drink, but I thought he could hold his booze. Anyway, I said, 'Fine, when you sober up, you know where to find me.' And I left."

"You didn't check to see if he was okay?"

"Like I said, I thought he had just had too much to drink and passed out."

"You didn't check to see if he was breathing, or if he had a pulse?" asked Guin, staring at him.

Art ran a hand through his ash blond hair. "To be honest, I was more worried about being late for you than about Rick," he said. "I know how you hate it when people are late."

Part of Guin was touched, but a bigger part couldn't believe how stupid Art had been.

"So then what?"

"So then I headed to the banquet room to meet up with you."

Guin eyed him warily.

"You were late."

"I was stopped on the way by this new rep who had a bunch of questions. She talked my ear off."

"Is that why your shirt was untucked and your hair was mussed?" asked Guin.

"Was it?" Art replied innocently, giving her a boyish smile. "It must have come out while I was hurrying to meet you."

"Uh-huh," said Guin, not believing him.

"I swear, I'm telling you the truth, Guin."

They stood there for a minute looking at each other. Then Art put down his coffee and moved toward Guin, his hand outstretched. "Guin—"

Guin held up a hand. "Stop. We need to go if I'm going to make my brunch date. You can grab a to-go mug if you want to take your coffee," she said, pointing at a cabinet.

A few minutes later, they were in Guin's Mini, heading to the San Ybel Resort & Spa to pick up his things.

"Guin, I'm sorry," said Art, looking over at her from the passenger seat of the Mini, where he had crammed his over six-foot frame.

Guin gripped the steering wheel and said nothing.

"Is there anything I can do to make it up to you?"

Guin turned her head slightly, to glance at Art, still keeping one eye on the road in front of her.

"Just tell me you didn't do it."

"Of course I didn't do it!" Art replied. "How could you even think such a thing?"

Guin turned back to face the road, keeping her eyes out for the entrance to the resort.

"Well, the detective wouldn't have brought you in without a good reason."

"I know it looks bad," said Art.

"Ya think?" said Guin, turning into the resort's driveway.

They pulled up to the entrance.

"I'll just be a couple of minutes," said Art, getting out of the car.

"I'm going with you," said Guin, getting out of the car. "Wait up."

"Suit yourself," said Art.

The valet came over to Guin.

"The keys are in the car. We'll just be a few minutes," she told him.

She then followed Art into the hotel. They avoided the elevator, taking the stairs instead. Art's room was on the third floor. They entered, and Art flipped on the lights.

"Nice room," said Guin, looking around.

"It's all right," he said.

Art had grabbed his suitcase and was throwing his clothes into it, not paying attention to Guin.

"All right?" said Guin, walking over to the large windows. "It's got a view of the Gulf—and I think it's bigger than my first apartment in Manhattan!"

"When you travel as much as I do," said Art, not looking up from his packing, "all hotel rooms look the same."

"Well then I hope I never have to travel as much as you," said Guin, plopping down on one of the queen-sized beds.

Art looked up at her and smiled. Suddenly Guin got that funny feeling she always used to get whenever Art looked at her a certain way.

"You almost done packing?" she asked.

Art continued to smile at her. "Just need to grab my toiletries and make sure I have everything. Then I'm all set."

Guin followed him into the bathroom.

"Very nice," she said, eyeing the big shower head. "Don't forget your toothbrush," she added, spying it by the sink.

"Thanks, Mom," he replied, picking it up.

Guin made a face.

A few minutes later, Art was all packed, and they were back in the Mini, heading down Sanibel-Captiva Road to Guin's condo.

"Back again," said Guin, opening the door to the condo and turning on the light.

As soon as they heard the door, the cats ran over—and Flora immediately started rubbing herself against Art's legs. He bent down and scratched her head and back.

"Traitor," Guin said, looking down at Flora.

Art smiled as he continued to scratch the cat.

"Happy to see me, Flora? Did you miss me?"

Guin folded her arms across her chest and made a face as Flora continued to rub herself against Art's legs and purred loudly. Fauna looked up at Guin and meowed. Guin sighed and bent down to scratch the black cat.

"So, you want to show me around?" Art asked.

She led him down the short hallway.

"This is the kitchen," she said. "As you no doubt figured out. If you need a glass of water, help yourself. Glasses are in the cabinet above the dishwasher."

"Thanks," said Art.

"You're already familiar with the guest room," said Guin, walking him back over there. "Hope you don't mind the twin beds."

"I'll be fine," said Art.

"You know where the bathroom is."

"Yes, I figured it out all by myself."

Guin made a face, then headed back down the hall.

"No doubt your keen powers of observation have told you that this is the living room, and dining room," said Guin. "And over there is the lanai."

"And what's that room, over there?" asked Art, pointing to a closed door.

"That's my bedroom and office," said Guin.

"Aren't you going to show me?" asked Art.

"No," said Guin. "That room is off limits to you."

"You're not even going to show it to me? I thought I paid for the whole house tour."

Guin stood in front of the door, glaring at Art.

"You may think this is funny, but it's not a joke, Art. You could be arrested for murder. And for some ungodly reason, I have been tasked with keeping you out of trouble, which means keeping you out of my bedroom."

"Okay, okay," said Art, holding up his hands. "It's not like I was going to pick you up and throw you on the bed and ravish you."

Guin felt her face turning pink.

"Okay then. I have to go meet my friend, Shelly, for brunch in town. Do you need anything before I go?"

"Do I need a password to get on your wifi?"

"I'll go write it down for you," said Guin.

She walked into the kitchen and grabbed a piece of paper and a pen.

"Here you go," she said, handing him the paper.

Art smiled at the password.

"No comment, please," said Guin.

Art held up his hands, still smiling.

"Now, if there's nothing else..."

Guin paused in the doorway.

"I'm good. See you later."

"Text me if you need me to pick up anything for you in town," said Guin, as she headed back out the door.

CHAPTER 17

As Guin drove back toward town, an image of Art picking her up, throwing her on the bed, and ravishing her kept popping into her head.

"Stop it!" she said aloud.

She gripped the steering wheel tightly and gritted her teeth.

She arrived at the Over Easy Café a little before ten and pulled out her phone. She then entered the detective's mobile number and sent him a text.

"URGENT," she wrote, in all caps. "Call me as soon as you get this." She hit send and then paced around the parking lot. A minute later, her phone rang. It was the detective. She immediately picked up.

"You okay?" asked the detective.

"No, I am most certainly *not* okay," replied Guin, stopping by the little pond.

"Did something happen? Did he hurt you?" asked the detective. Was that a note of concern in the detective's voice?

"What? Art? No," replied Guin.

"Then what is so urgent at nine-fifty on a Sunday?" asked the detective.

"I can't have him there, with me, at the condo. You have to take him back."

The detective snorted.

"What's so funny?" asked Guin, irritated.

"You sound like one of those people who adopts a puppy only to realize they're a lot more work than expected."

"For your information, detective, Art is no puppy. He's more like of a fully-grown Saint Bernard. And I did not ask to take Art home with me. You and that lawyer were the ones who came up with the brilliant idea of putting him under house arrest at my house, and I want him gone. Now. Or by this evening."

The detective snorted again.

"What?!" said Guin, glaring at her phone. "It's not funny!"

"I'm sorry, Ms. Jones," said the detective, composing himself. "It's likely only for another day. I'm sure you can handle him."

"You don't know Art!" she replied, testily.

"No, I do not," replied the detective. "Do you believe he is a threat to you?"

Guin, who had resumed her pacing, stopped. Was Art a threat? To her sanity, maybe. But would he actually hurt her, physically? Even during their most tempestuous arguments, and they'd had some beauts, Art had never hit her.

Guin sighed. "No, I don't think Art would ever harm me."

"Then he stays, at least for now."

"Fine," said Guin, resignedly. "But I'm not happy about it. What if he does something?"

"I have every confidence that you will get him to behave, Saint Bernard or no," said the detective, who Guin just knew was smiling that smug little smile of his.

"Fine," said Guin, again. "Just let me know if you plan on formally charging him."

"You'll be the first to know," he replied.

Guin downed another piece of French toast and waited for Shelly to say something. She had just finished telling Shelly about her house guest, and she could tell from Shelly's expression she was about to burst.

"You have got to be kidding me! What were that lawyer and the detective thinking?"

"Beats me," said Guin, taking a bite of her bacon (extra crispy, as requested).

"Have you told Ris?" Shelly asked.

Guin took a sip of her coffee. "No, not yet."

"Aren't you two supposed to have dinner tonight?"

"We are."

"And?" asked Shelly. "You going to cancel?"

Guin took another sip of her coffee and thought. Would she cancel? Should she cancel? And what would she tell Ris, 'Hey, can't do dinner tonight because my ex is shacking up with me'? 'He's the prime suspect in a murder investigation, and his lawyer and Detective O'Loughlin thought it best if he stayed with me, under house arrest, until they find enough evidence to formally arrest him.' Yeah, that would go over real well.

"Hello? Anybody home?" said Shelly, waving a hand in front of Guin's face.

Guin refocused.

"Sorry. Do *you* think I should cancel?"

"You can always use the Marcia Brady excuse," suggested Shelly.

Guin looked momentarily confused.

"You know, 'something suddenly came up.'"

Guin smiled. "As I recall, that didn't end well."

"Well, you know what I mean," said Shelly, tucking into her pancakes.

"I think I should be straight with Ris, tell him what's

going on."

"He's not going to like it," said Shelly.

"I know, but it's better than lying to him."

Shelly sighed. "Girl, you have a lot to learn about relationships."

Guin laughed. "Clearly."

They continued to eat and catch each other up.

"So, do you think he did it?" asked Shelly, downing the last bite of pancake.

"No, I don't," said Guin.

"How can you be so sure?" said Shelly.

"Call it intuition," said Guin.

"Well, call it whatever you like, but unless you find evidence to the contrary, sounds like they're going to arrest your ex."

Guin sat back, nursing her coffee. Shelly had a point.

"I can see those wheels turning," said Shelly, leaning forward.

Guin put down her coffee. "Is it that obvious?"

"So, Nancy Drew, you going to investigate?" said Shelly.

Guin smiled. "Maybe."

"I'll take that as a 'yes,'" said Shelly, grinning. "Can I help?"

"We'll see. First, I need to find out what the detective has on Art. Maybe I can get Ginny to officially assign me to the story. You okay if I send her a quick text?"

"Text away," said Shelly. "I'll just check my messages."

Shelly made beautiful shell jewelry that she sold on Etsy and was very active on social media, with thousands of followers, many of whom had become friends over the years. And she was always checking her Instagram and Facebook feeds.

"Okay, sent!" said Guin, putting down her phone. "You mind if we get the check? I should be getting home."

"Uh-huh," said Shelly, who was busily typing something into her phone.

Guin smiled and signaled to the server for the check.

A few minutes later, they said their goodbyes.

"Keep me posted!" called Shelly, walking to her car. "And let me know if we can go shelling later this week!"

"Will do," Guin called back. She unlocked the Mini and climbed in, checking her phone for a text message from Ginny. But there was nothing. She then texted Art, asking him if he wanted her to pick him up something for lunch.

"Would love a turkey sandwich, on whole wheat, with lettuce and tomato," replied Art.

"OK," typed Guin. "Will pick one up at Bailey's."

"And some chips," added Art.

"OK," replied Guin.

She then put away her phone, started the engine, and headed across the way to Bailey's General Store to pick up a sandwich and chips for her prisoner.

CHAPTER 18

As she was leaving Bailey's with Art's lunch, Guin's phone rang. She stopped at one of the outdoor tables, putting down her bag, and answered it.

"Guin Jones." (She hadn't had time to see who was calling, so gave her generic greeting.)

"Guin!"

"Ris! I was just about to call you," lied Guin. "What's up?"

"Bad news. My flight's been delayed, and I'm not going to be able to make dinner tonight."

Guin let out a silent sigh of relief.

"Sorry to hear that. How's Costa Rica?"

"Great! Amazing. I'll tell you all about it when I see you."

"And when will that be?" asked Guin.

"I have meetings all day tomorrow, assuming I make it home tonight. You free Tuesday night? I'm going to be at the museum that afternoon and we could go to Doc Ford's for dinner afterward."

"Sounds like a plan," said Guin. "Though I'm sorry I won't get to see you later," she added, somewhat disingenuously.

While she had been looking forward to seeing him, with her ex now staying at her place, she was relieved that the subject of Art could be put off for a couple of days. Maybe by then he'd be gone.

"Same," said Ris. "Hey, I've gotta go. But I'll text you when I've landed."

"Okay," said Guin. "Safe travels. I'll confirm with you on Tuesday."

She hung up and breathed out, not realizing she had been holding her breath. Thank God. She sent up a silent prayer, then picked up her bag of groceries and walked to her car.

She arrived back at her condo to find a freshly showered, shaved, and dressed Art pacing around the lanai, talking to someone on the phone. No doubt a customer, even though it was Sunday. She caught his eye and waved the bag from Bailey's. He smiled and held up his index finger, indicating he'd be with her in a minute.

She walked into the kitchen and placed the still-wrapped turkey sandwich and the chips on the counter, along with a plate. Having just eaten brunch, she wasn't hungry.

A couple of minutes later Art walked into the kitchen. Immediately, Guin smelled his aftershave, the one that she always found a bit erotic.

"So, who were you talking with?" she asked, trying not to breathe in Art's scent.

"Alan. This whole Rick thing is a mess. He and a couple of the other guys have been asked to stay on the island until everything's been sorted out."

"I can think of worse places to be stuck," retorted Guin.

"Yeah, but they're not happy. They've got work to do."

"Can't they do it from here?" asked Guin.

"They can, but…" Art ran a hand through his hair.

"Any word from your attorney?"

"Yeah, she phoned me earlier."

"And?" asked Guin.

Art eyed the wrapped sandwich and chips. "Hey, are those for me?"

"As requested," said Guin.

She watched as Art unwrapped the sandwich and placed it on the plate, along with the chips.

"Mind if I eat? I'm starving."

"Be my guest," she said. "So, you were saying, about Ms. Parker?"

"Nothing much to say. She was just checking in to see if I was comfortable."

"How nice of her," said Guin, her voice laced with sarcasm.

Guin leaned against the counter, watching as Art ate his sandwich and chips.

"You want some water?"

"Thanks," said Art.

Guin reached into the cabinet and retrieved a glass, then filled it with water from the fridge.

"Here," she said, handing it to him.

He took the glass and drank.

"So tell me more about Rick," said Guin. "Why would someone want to kill him?"

"Oh, I can think of a dozen reasons," said Art, continuing to eat his sandwich.

"Care to elaborate?"

"Let's just say Rick was not beloved, at least not by a lot of the guys we worked with. He was a total brown-noser: good at managing up but not so nice to the people under him or on the same level, though Rick thought no one was on his level."

"Not even you?" asked Guin.

"Especially not me," said Art, taking a handful of chips. "Rick thought everyone was a slacker. There was nothing he wouldn't do to close a deal. And a lot of guys thought some of his tactics weren't kosher."

"Not kosher?" asked Guin, amused by Art's use of the expression.

"You know, not right or proper. You know how sales guys are assigned a specific territory?"

"Yes," said Guin.

"Well, Rick was known to occasionally blur the lines."

"Meaning?"

"Meaning he had boundary issues."

Guin gave him a questioning look.

"Rumor had it he was pursuing deals outside his territory."

"I thought that wasn't allowed. Wasn't he reprimanded?"

"I heard some of the guys complained, but who's going to punish a guy for bringing in millions of dollars of business?"

"So, Alan didn't say anything?"

Art shrugged.

"Is there anyone you know of who had a big deal poached by Rick?"

"Not off the top of my head, but I can do a little research."

"What about women?"

"What about them?" asked Art.

"Was Rick married?"

"Divorced."

"Did he have a girlfriend?"

"Rumor has it he was seeing someone."

"Was she at the conference?"

"I don't think so. As you know, Rick and I weren't exactly bosom pals."

"And yet you invited him on your little fishing trip."

"Believe me, I didn't want to, but I had to. It would have looked petty if I didn't."

"So who besides you would want to kill Rick?"

"Hey, who says I wanted the guy dead?" asked Art.

"You were both up for the same promotion, and it was

common knowledge you didn't like each other. Did he steal any deals from you?"

"No," said Art. "He wouldn't be that stupid. And yeah, we were up for the same promotion, but I wouldn't have killed for it. Come on, Guin. You know me better than that."

Guin eyed Art. She had thought she knew him. Then he went and cheated on her with their hairdresser.

"Look, I'm sorry about that," said Art, reading her mind.

"About what?" asked Guin, startled.

"About the whole Debbie mess. I was an idiot. Mid-life crisis. Mea culpa. I love you, Guin," he said, taking a step toward her.

Guin immediately took a step back. Art held up his hands.

"Sorry. I just want you to know I appreciate what you're doing for me, and I really do regret everything."

"Do me a favor and make a list of all the people who had it in for Rick, or didn't like him, who are at the conference," said Guin. "Don't leave anyone out, and include as much information as you can."

Art smiled and saluted.

"And what will you be doing?"

"Work."

She made to leave the kitchen but stopped.

"And put your plate in the dishwasher or wash it when you're done."

Art stood at attention and saluted her again. Guin made a face and then headed to her office.

CHAPTER 19

Guin shut the door and called Detective O'Loughlin.

"This better be good," said the detective.

"I don't think he did it."

"Wonderful," said the detective, sarcastically. "Thanks for saving me the trouble of investigating."

"I'm serious, detective. I spoke with Art, and I don't think he killed Rick. It's just not like him. And besides, there are plenty of people who had just as much, if not more, motive to kill the guy."

"Ms. Jones, while I greatly appreciate your assistance, I don't think you are in a position to be objective."

"I am being perfectly objective," retorted Guin. "And I have access to insider information."

The detective sighed.

"Also, as you may recall," Guin continued, "if it wasn't for me, the wrong man would have been tried for the murder of Gregor Matenopoulos," she reminded him.

"And need I remind *you*, Ms. Jones, that your efforts nearly got you raped?"

"Anthony Mandelli would not have raped me," Guin huffed.

"I wouldn't be so sure of that," said the detective.

He had been at the Sanctuary Club during Guin's attempt to ferret out information about the murder of Gregor

Matenopoulos from his partner and noted womanizer Anthony Mandelli. And he had seen first-hand how Mandelli had looked at Guin, and how angry he was when Guin dodged his advances—and how scared Guin, who had drunk too much, had been when Mandelli had grabbed her and insisted she leave with him. He had seen too many scenes just like that back up in South Boston, where he had worked for many years before transferring to Sanibel, which is why he had insisted on escorting Guin home himself. But he also knew that no matter what he said, Guin would stick her nose in this case.

The detective sighed again. "Fine. Come see me at the police department at eight a.m. tomorrow."

Guin was going to protest that she had planned on going shelling tomorrow morning, but she stopped herself.

"Fine. I'll be there."

"I look forward to it," said the detective.

The call ended, and Guin could envision the detective leaning back in his chair, that smug grin of his on his face.

Next, she called her colleague, Craig.

"Hi Craig, it's Guin," she said when he picked up. "I hope I'm not interrupting anything."

"Nah, Betty is out with one of her friends, and I was doing some reading. What's up? I heard they took your hubby in for questioning regarding that guy they found over at the San Ybel."

"*Ex*-hubby," said Guin. "How'd you know?"

"Word travels fast."

"Ginny told you, didn't she?"

"Yup."

"Did she assign you to cover the story for the paper?"

"She did," said Craig.

"How would you feel about us working together again?" asked Guin.

Craig had enjoyed working with Guin on the Matenopoulos murder, but he wondered if Guin could be objective in this case and told her so.

"Why does everyone keep asking if I can be objective?" Guin complained. "I just want to find out the truth, Craig. And if Art really did do it, I want to know."

Craig hesitated. Even though Guin claimed she had no feelings for Art, that it was over between the two of them, he doubted that she was impartial. But he admired her research skills and knew this case and story meant a lot to her.

"Okay, Guin, but we need to go over some ground rules. No going rogue. There's a killer out there, and it could be your ex-husband."

"If the detective really thought Art was a killer, would he have agreed to let him stay with me?"

"He's staying with you?" asked Craig. Guin could hear the surprise in his voice.

"Guess Ginny didn't mention that little tidbit."

"No, she did not. How the heck did that happen?"

"I'll fill you in later," said Guin. "So, where do we start?"

"Well, I reached out to my buddy, Al Boudreaux, the charter boat captain."

"The one you told me about."

"Yeah, him. I want to know what happened to Rick from the moment he disappeared on that boat trip to the moment the police found him."

"I'm down with that," said Guin.

"So I asked Al if he would take me out to the spot where Rick supposedly disappeared in Pine Island Sound, by Wulfert Keys, over by Ding Darling."

"Can I come?"

"I don't see why not."

"When are you two going?"

"Tomorrow, late afternoon."

"Count me in!" said Guin. "Where's his boat?"

"I'll text you the information," said Craig. "It's a little hard to find."

"Great. See you tomorrow. And thanks, Craig."

"No problem."

Guin ended the call, feeling rather pleased with herself, until she realized she had several stories she was supposed to be working on the coming week. She immediately texted Ginny, asking her to give her a call. Her other stories could wait, but a murder was high priority. Surely Ginny wouldn't object to her working with Craig again, especially on such a big story?

A few minutes later Guin's phone rang. It was Ginny.

"What's up?" she asked.

Guin relayed her conversation with Craig and asked Ginny if it would be okay to delay or even reassign her stories, at least for the next week.

"Please?" said Guin.

Ginny was slow to reply.

"You sure you can be impartial?" she asked.

"Of course I can be impartial!" said Guin. "I'm a journalist."

Ginny made a face. She knew how involved Guin got in her stories, how passionate she could be about some of her subjects.

She sighed. "Fine, but Craig is the lead on this. And if I hear about you doing something reckless again, I'm pulling you off, you got it?"

"Got it," said Guin.

"As for your articles, get me the piece on things to do on Sanibel in the summer by Tuesday. I can reassign the others. But I want to run this one in this week's print edition."

"Absolutely, I'm almost done with it," said Guin. "I'll get

it to you by midday Tuesday at the latest, promise."

"Okay then. Now don't get yourself killed."

"Will do," said Guin, smiling.

She had neglected to tell Ginny that Art was staying with her, but she figured Ginny would find out soon enough—and would harangue her then. In the meantime, Guin had work to do if she was going to hand in that piece by Tuesday. And there was the matter of a murder to solve.

CHAPTER 20

Guin was so busy, she had lost track of time. Wow, six o'clock already? She got up, stretched, and went to see what Art was up to.

She found him hunched over his laptop at the dining table, Fauna curled up in his lap, asleep, Flora napping in the chair next to him. Guin smiled.

She waited for Art to notice her there, but he was too absorbed in whatever it was he was working on. She cleared her throat.

"Whatcha working on?"

"Research," said Art, not looking up.

Guin waited for Art to elaborate.

"So, what do you want to do about dinner?" she asked. "I was thinking we could order in."

"Whatever you want to do," said Art, his focus entirely on his computer screen.

"That must be some research project," said Guin, taking a couple of steps closer to him, trying to see what he was working on.

"It is," he replied.

She leaned over, brushing against his back.

Art stopped typing and turned to look up at her.

"Sorry," he said, shutting the laptop.

Guin took a step back. "No biggie. I know how you get."

"I'm just trying to figure out what Rick was working on before he died. Word is he was working on a couple of big deals. Even told Jake, the rep from Southern California, that he was sure he was going to be top salesman this year."

Guin raised an eyebrow.

"Rick was always bragging."

"Could he have been telling the truth?"

"That's what I was trying to determine," said Art. "You remember how I was telling you earlier that Rick sometimes went after deals outside his territory?"

"Yes…" said Guin, slowly. She looked down at him. "You think maybe one of the deals Rick was bragging about was in some other guy's territory?"

"I do," said Art. "I was in the CRM system trying to see if there was any information, but Rick's account is password protected and I don't have the password, though I took a couple of guesses. No dice."

"You have a buddy in the IT department who can help you out?"

"No. I'm not exactly on a first-name basis with IT," said Art.

"What about Alan? Could he find out?"

"Probably," said Art. "He was Rick's boss."

"But you don't want to ask him. Is there some other way of finding out if Rick was about to close a deal outside his territory?"

"I could ask some of the guys. There's a chance he shot his mouth off to someone about it."

"And you think maybe one of the guys he was undercutting found out about it and then killed him?"

"I don't know," said Art. "How would you feel if you had been working on some big story and then got scooped by someone you knew?"

Guin didn't have to imagine. She knew the feeling first

hand. She had been repeatedly scooped by Suzy Seashell, the nom de plume of the woman who ran the popular blog Shellapalooza.com. Suzy knew everything that happened on the island, and if it had anything to do with shells or shelling, such as the world's largest junonia being stolen and the alleged thief being murdered shortly thereafter, Suzy wrote about it. Fortunately, for Guin, Suzy and her husband were cruising around Europe. So she didn't have to worry about being scooped, at least by Suzy.

"I'd be pretty pissed off," said Guin. "But I wouldn't go and murder the guy—or gal," she quickly added.

"You clearly don't know sales guys," said Art, a grim look on his face. "A really big deal can make a guy, or break him if he loses it."

"Would you have killed a guy if he had stolen a multimillion-dollar deal from you?" asked Guin.

Art looked up at Guin. "No! Come on, Guin! I thought we had gone over that."

He was clearly irritated.

"Fine. How about we discuss dinner instead?" suggested Guin.

"You were saying something about ordering in?"

"I was."

"How about we go out instead? I've been cooped up inside all day."

Guin thought for a minute. She really didn't want to run into anyone she knew and then have to explain Art's presence. But she couldn't blame the guy for wanting to get out.

"Fine. Let's go to the Sunset Grill. It's just down the road. The food is very good, and you can see the sunset from outside."

"Sounds like a plan," said Art, getting up. "My treat."

"You don't have to pay," said Guin.

"I insist," said Art. "It's the least I can do. Just give me a minute to change."

"You don't have to change," said Guin, looking at him. Art was in a short-sleeved shirt and board shorts.

"I should at least put on a pair of pants."

"Do whatever you want," said Guin. "Sanibel is pretty casual."

"I'm putting on pants," said Art. "So do we need a reservation?"

"I'll call over there and find out," said Guin.

Art went into the guest room to change, and Guin decided she would put on a sundress. She then called over to the restaurant. No need to make a reservation, the host informed her. Just come on over.

When she re-entered the living room Art was in a fresh shirt and slacks and was busy typing on his laptop again.

"We're all set," said Guin. "We can head over there whenever."

"Great," said Art. He glanced up at her. "You look nice!"

"Thanks," said Guin, smiling.

"I'm just finishing up that list you had me make, of all the suspects."

"Email it to me when you're done. I'm meeting with the detective at eight tomorrow."

"Isn't that rather early?" asked Art.

"Not for Sanibel," Guin replied. "Anyway, you can finish up that list later. I'm hungry."

"Okay," said Art. "I don't want you to starve."

He smiled up at her and closed his laptop.

Guin walked into the kitchen, gave the cats some food and fresh water, then she grabbed her keys.

"Let's go," she said.

CHAPTER 21

The next morning, Guin arrived at the Sanibel Police Department promptly at eight and asked for Detective O'Loughlin.

"Is he expecting you?" asked the officer manning the desk.

"He is. Tell him Guinivere Jones is here to see him."

The officer, a young woman Guin didn't know, picked up the phone and dialed the detective's extension. "A Ms. Jones is here to see you, sir." She paused and looked over at Guin. "Yes, sir. I'll tell her."

"He'll be out in a couple of minutes," said the officer.

"Thanks," said Guin, smiling at the young woman. "I'll go wait outside."

She stepped outside the entrance to the police department, onto the walkway that ran along the building, leaning over the railing to gaze out at the trees. It was a beautiful morning, still not too hot, and Guin breathed in the fresh air. As she waited for the detective to appear, her mind wandered back to dinner the night before.

She and Art had gone to the Sunset Grill. And it had felt, for a moment or two, like they were still married. Guin shuddered at the thought. Despite how charming and considerate Art had been the last few days, she had not forgotten how poorly he had treated her the last year of their marriage. So while she had smiled at him and had even laughed at his jokes over dinner, she never forgot that Art had betrayed her—and that she was with someone else now.

"Ms. Jones?"

Guin jumped. She was so lost in thought that she hadn't heard the detective approach. She turned around.

"Detective! You startled me."

The detective smiled. At least Guin thought it was a smile. With O'Loughlin it was often hard to tell.

"Would you like to come in, or would you rather continue to commune with nature?" he asked.

"We could both commune with nature," replied Guin. "Why don't we go for a walk? It's a beautiful morning."

The detective stood still for several seconds, not saying anything, his face not revealing what he was thinking.

"Fine. Let me just go in and tell Officer Bianchi I'm stepping away for a few minutes," he finally replied.

"I'll be waiting," said Guin, with a smile.

The detective went back inside and came out a minute later.

"Let's go, but I need to be back before nine."

"No problem," said Guin.

"Any place in particular you had in mind, Ms. Jones?"

"Let's head over toward the library," she suggested.

The detective gestured for her to proceed.

"So, do you know how Rick—Richard Tomlinson— died?" asked Guin as they walked.

"Not yet," said the detective. "We're waiting for the toxicology report. The preliminary finding was heart failure."

"Do you think Rick was poisoned?"

"That's what we're trying to determine."

"So, theoretically, it could have been natural causes, like a heart attack. Though Art said Rick wasn't even forty. Did he have any pre-existing conditions?"

The detective stopped and Guin did, too.

"Ms. Jones," said the detective.

"Yes?" said Guin, looking into his eyes, which were a kind of tawny brown.

"It is barely after eight o'clock on Monday morning. I have only had one cup of coffee so far, and the work day hasn't even officially begun. If you could exercise a little patience…"

Guin's cheeks turned pink.

"As I was saying, it appears Mr. Tomlinson died of heart failure, but, as you noted, Mr. Tomlinson was not even forty and appeared to be in good health. Of course, that doesn't mean he didn't have some kind of heart condition. As I said, we are looking into it. However, due to the laws around patient privacy, it can take a while. And Mr. Tomlinson had no spouse or children who could give us access to his medical records."

"What about parents?"

"We have been trying to locate them."

They spent the next few minutes in silence as Guin mulled over what the detective had told her.

"Art said Rick had been drinking, quite a bit by the look of it," said Guin, stopping on the trail. "Maybe Rick met with someone earlier that evening, and that person slipped something into his drink?"

The detective stopped again and looked at Guin.

"Has it occurred to you that the person Mr. Tomlinson was sharing a drink with was your husband, Ms. Jones?"

"*Ex*-husband," said Guin. "And if you really thought Art was the killer, shouldn't he be in jail instead of staying with me?"

The detective rubbed his face and wished he was back in his office, drinking a nice, strong cup of coffee.

"Did you find any fingerprints?" asked Guin.

"Just the deceased's," replied the detective.

"On both glasses?" Guin asked.

"No," replied the detective.

Guin waited for the detective to provide more information.

"One of the glasses appeared to have been wiped clean," he added, a few seconds later.

"But you're checking both glasses for traces of poison, yes?"

The detective stopped again and looked at Guin.

"Would *you* like to conduct the investigation, Ms. Jones? Maybe I should put you in charge."

Guin blushed.

"Sorry. Will you let me know if they find anything?"

The detective eyed Guin, not saying anything, then he continued to walk. Guin hurried to catch up.

"Was there any sign of a struggle?" she asked.

"No," said the detective, still walking. "Though there were some cuts and bruises on his body."

"He could have gotten those when he went over the side of the boat," said Guin. "Speaking of which," she said, turning to the detective, "any idea what happened to him after he disappeared? Art said no one had seen Rick since the boat ride, or at least that's what the people he spoke with said."

They had reached the library and the detective had stopped.

"I need to get back to the office," he said, not answering Guin's question.

They turned around and headed back toward the police department.

"Did the medical examiner say what time Rick died?"

"He believes it was shortly before your husband found him. In fact, it's possible Mr. Tomlinson was still alive when Mr. Jones found him."

Guin stopped.

"Are you okay, Ms. Jones?"

Guin had gone pale, though it was hard to tell with her fair skin. Breathe, she told herself. Art wouldn't have let Rick die. Though he had told her he thought Rick had just passed out and hadn't bothered to check if he was breathing or had a pulse.

"I'm fine," she replied, pulling herself together.

They continued walking.

"Any more questions?"

"Any suspects?"

"Other than your ex-husband?"

Guin made a face. "Yes."

"We are conducting a thorough investigation," he replied.

Guin waited for the detective to say more, but in typical fashion he did not.

"Speaking of my ex, Art made a list of all the people who had a motive or reason to kill Rick, or would at least want him incapacitated."

The detective glanced at Guin, his eyebrows raised.

Guin fished in her pocket. "Art created a spreadsheet. It's on this flash drive."

She handed him the flash drive, which was decorated with a picture of a junonia.

The detective eyed the drive, then placed it in his pocket.

"You're welcome," said Guin.

They walked the remaining way in silence.

"Well, it's been lovely, Ms. Jones, but now I must get to work," said the detective at the foot of the steps leading up to the police department.

"Will you let me know if you find out anything?" said Guin, placing a hand on the detective's arm as he climbed the first step.

The detective looked down at Guin's hand, and she removed it.

"I'm covering the story for the paper, with Craig," she hastily added.

The detective looked at her, then turned around and proceeded up the stairs.

"Detective!" called Guin as the detective was about to enter the building.

He turned around. "Yes, Ms. Jones?"

Guin had wanted to ask him a couple more questions, but from the look on his face, she decided it would not be wise. She sighed.

"Have a good day!" she called instead.

"The same to you, Ms. Jones," said the detective, opening the door.

Guin watched as he disappeared back inside the building. One day, she thought. She stood staring up at the police department for a few more seconds. Then she turned around and headed to her car.

CHAPTER 22

"You don't need to come with me, Art. I—"

"But I want to go," Art interrupted. "I can show you where I last saw Rick."

Guin was leaving to meet Craig and Captain Al Boudreaux when Art had stopped her and asked if he could go with her. Art had a point, but she really didn't want him tagging along.

"Craig says Captain Al knows the area Big Ben took you fishing quite well. We'll be fine, Art."

"Please?" said Art, making the face that back in the day Guin couldn't say no to. "It's my neck on the line. Just let me come with you. Captain Al doesn't know the exact spot, but I do, or close to it."

Guin sighed. "Fine. Let's go."

The dock where Captain Al kept his boat was a less-than-10-minute drive from the condo, down a dirt road.

"Where's the dock?" asked Art, looking around.

Guin, too, looked confused.

"I plugged the address into the GPS," she said. "It should be right around here."

A few seconds later, Craig pulled in a short distance away.

"There's Craig," said Guin. "So this must be the right place."

She got out of the car, as did Art, and waved at Craig.

"Hey, Craig," she said, walking over to him. "So, where's the dock?"

Craig smiled.

Just then Art came over, extending his hand, his salesman's smile on his face.

"Art Jones, a pleasure to meet you, Craig."

Craig looked down at Art's hand and scowled, begrudgingly shaking Art's hand. "Craig Jeffers. Guin's told me all about you," he said, eyeing the tall blond man.

"You can't believe everything you hear," Art said, still smiling.

Craig continued to scowl, then turned his attention to Guin.

"I didn't know your ex was coming along."

"Neither did I, until a few minutes ago," said Guin. "He insisted."

"I can show you where Rick went over, or where I last saw him," Art chimed in.

Craig eyed Art again, then he turned and headed toward some bushes. "Al's boat is over here," he said, pointing toward the bushes.

Guin and Art followed Craig. As they got close to the bushes, they could see a narrow path. They continued to follow Craig and soon saw a white fishing boat tied up to a small wooden dock. Seated at the helm, reading a book, was a man in a baseball cap.

"Al!" called Craig.

The man, Al, looked up and smiled at Craig. "Craig!" He put the book down and came over to the side of the boat. "I see you brought your friends."

"Al Boudreaux, this is my colleague, Guinivere Jones," he said, smiling over at Guin.

"Thank you so much for agreeing to take us out," said Guin, smiling at Captain Al.

"Thank your friend Craig here," said Captain Al, nodding to Craig as he helped Guin onto the boat.

Craig followed Guin down onto the boat, followed by Art.

"And who's this?" asked Captain Al, looking up at Art, who stood several inches taller than him.

"That's her ex," said Craig, making a face.

"Art Jones," said Art, extending his hand.

Captain Al didn't take it.

"So, you ready?" asked Captain Al, looking at his passengers.

"Nice boat you have here," said Art, looking the boat over.

"She's all right," said Captain Al, casting off. "So, you said they lost this guy over in Wulfert Keys, by Ding Darling. That right?" he asked, addressing Craig.

"That's right," replied Art. "I remember Big Ben—Captain Johnson—saying we were right by the Wulfert Keys Trail."

"Mmph," said Captain Al, steering them along the waterway.

Craig and Captain Al chatted while Captain Al navigated the ship into Pine Island Sound.

"Over there's a manatee," said Captain Al, pointing off the port side.

"Where?" said Guin, looking down into the water. "Oh, I see it!" she said, excitedly, locating the sea cow. "My first manatee sighting!"

They continued to motor along, Captain Al relaying different facts about the area.

Just as Guin spied the familiar pole marking the end of Wulfert Keys Trail, Art shouted "Here!"

Captain Al cut the motor. "You sure?"

"Yes," said Art, looking around. "Rick was there," he said, pointing to a spot on the starboard, or right, side. "He grabbed me and tried to pick a fight, but I just shook myself loose and told him to back off. That was the last time I saw him."

"It's pretty shallow around here," said Captain Al. "If the tide was low enough, he could have practically walked to one of those islands or that area over there," he said, pointing towards Ding Darling.

"I'll check the tide charts for that day," said Craig. "You remember what time it was?"

"I think it was around six," said Art.

"Even if the tide was high, he could have easily swum over to the shore," said Captain Al.

"Or back to the boat," said Craig.

"Unless he was trying to disappear," said Art.

Craig and Captain Al looked at Art.

"Now why would he want to do that?" asked Captain Al.

"To cause trouble," said Art.

"He's certainly done that," said Guin.

"Well, unless he was unconscious, he could have easily gotten back to the boat or gone ashore someplace," said Captain Al.

"Was he drinking?" asked Craig.

"Yes, we all were," said Art.

"Could he have passed out and fallen overboard?" asked Guin.

"It's possible," said Art, "but knowing Rick, unlikely. No, Rick was up to something. I'd bet my commission on it."

"You and this Rick not on good terms?" asked Captain Al.

"Not exactly," said Art. "We were competing for the same

job," he explained. "Though Rick thought he had already won. That's why he pulled me aside on the boat, to gloat."

"But why pull a stunt like that and disappear?" asked Craig. "How would that make you look bad? And if he was so hot to get that promotion, he'd have to show up at some point."

"You don't know Rick," said Art. "He'd do whatever it took to close a deal or get what he wanted—and make me look bad in front of Alan, our boss."

"I know you and Rick didn't get along, but do you really think he's that devious?" asked Guin. "Isn't it possible he drank a little too much and fell overboard? Maybe he was attacked by a shark or something."

"The sharks round here are pretty small and don't usually attack people," said Captain Al, smiling at Guin.

Guin colored slightly.

"My guess? Rick had this whole thing planned, to make me look like a jerk, or worse," said Art, looking around the water. "He probably picked that fight with me on purpose, hoping I'd slug him or throw him overboard."

"That sounds pretty far-fetched," said Craig.

"Like I said, you don't know Rick," replied Art.

"Okay, let's assume that Rick was as devious as you say and deliberately picked a fight with you," said Guin. "Why disappear? Why not just pop out of the water and accuse you of throwing him overboard?"

"Guin's got a point there," said Craig.

As they were talking Captain Al was staring at something off in the distance.

"What you looking at, Al?" said Craig, following Captain Al's gaze.

"You see over there," said Captain Al, pointing to the big utility poll near the end of the Wulfert Keys Trail.

Craig, Guin, and Art looked where Al was pointing.

"About halfway up the poll, there's a video camera," said Captain Al.

Guin squinted.

"That thing on all the time?" asked Craig.

"Pretty sure," said Captain Al.

"So maybe there's some footage showing Rick jumping off the boat and swimming to shore," said Guin.

"It's possible," said Captain Al. "You said the last time you saw him was around six on Thursday? It's still pretty light then. There's a chance the camera may have captured something."

"Who do we contact to find out?" asked Guin.

"The U.S. Fish and Wildlife Service," said Captain Al. "They're in charge of the refuge."

"You know anyone?" asked Guin, looking from Captain Al to Craig.

"I bet Hank could help us out," said Captain Al, looking at Craig.

Craig smiled.

Guin looked from Captain Al to Craig. "Who's Hank?"

"Hank Rawlins," said Craig. "He's a volunteer over at Ding. Practically runs the place."

"You want to know about that camera up there, you ask Hank. He doesn't know, he'll know who does," said Captain Al.

"Great!" said Art. "Let's go talk to Hank."

"Hold your horses," said Captain Al. "Let me and Craig go talk to Hank. He can be a bit prickly."

Art made a face. "Fine. Just keep me posted. It's my ass on the line."

Craig shot Art a look.

"And I'll follow up with the detective," said Guin. "He probably knows about the camera and may have already requested the footage."

Captain Al turned the boat around and headed back toward the dock. On the way back, Art and Guin stared out at the water while Craig and Al made plans to go fishing the following week.

CHAPTER 23

When they got back to shore, Art and Guin thanked Craig and Captain Al, then headed back to Guin's Mini.

"You want to get something to eat?" asked Guin.

"I'm not really hungry," Art replied.

"How about we go get some fried chicken? I know how you love fried chicken," said Guin, trying to cheer him up—an old habit.

He turned to look at her and his expression changed.

"Sorry," he said. "I'm just frustrated."

"I know," said Guin, who was tempted to put a hand on Art's arm, but quickly nixed the idea. "But I bet some food will make you feel better."

"You say this place has really good fried chicken?" asked Art, a small smile creeping over his face.

"The best," said Guin, smiling. "And really good biscuits and coleslaw, too."

"Then what are we waiting for?" said Art, smiling once again. "Start the engine and let's go!"

They were eating their fried chicken—with biscuits, coleslaw, and collard greens—at Guin's dining table, the cats lurking just underneath, hoping to get a treat, when Guin's phone started buzzing. She grabbed it and took a look. It was a text from her brother Lance.

"Hey, Sis! Long time no text. What's up? You free to chat?"

Guin made a face.

"Everything okay?" asked Art.

"Everything's fine," said Guin. "It's just Lance, asking why he hasn't heard from me."

"Give him my best," said Art, continuing to work his way through the chicken and sides.

Guin regarded him. "You really think that's a good idea? You know, Lance was never crazy about you to begin with."

"That's just because he was jealous," Art replied with a grin. "He totally wanted to date me."

Guin rolled her eyes. "Seriously?"

"He totally had the hots for me," said Art. "But he's not my type," he added, grinning at her.

Guin's brother Lancelot (their mother had a thing for Arthurian legends) lived in Brooklyn and ran a boutique ad agency. He had been with his partner, now husband, Owen, who ran a gallery in Chelsea, for years. And if Lance had "had the hots" for Art at one time, it was news to Guin.

Lance and Owen had yet to visit Guin on Sanibel, though she had invited them down several times. But they were always too busy. Instead, she spoke with Lance once a week, and they texted each other regularly. However, she had been so busy with Art the last few days that she had completely forgotten about Lance.

"You going to reply to him?" said Art.

"Can't talk right now," Guin typed into her phone. "Can I call you later?"

"Sure thing," replied Lance. "Owen and I are staying in tonight."

"Great. Call you in a bit," replied Guin.

She put the phone down and stared at her plate.

"What's up?" asked Art, taking another bite of chicken and surreptitiously passing a bite to Fauna, who immediately gobbled it up. "By the way, you were right, this chicken is great. Next time, we should get more," he said, dropping another piece onto the floor.

Guin looked over at Art. She was not smiling. "There is not going to be a next time," she informed him. "As soon as this matter has been cleared up, you're going back to Connecticut."

Art put down the chicken and held up his hands. "Hey, no need to get nasty."

Guin glared at him. "I'm not being nasty, Art. I'm being real. I just realized I haven't communicated with my brother, or my mother, who's probably wondering what happened to me and is this close to calling the police to find out why I haven't called her in days, because I've been so busy running around with you or on your behalf. In fact, I've pretty much blown everything off since you've come to town, and for what?"

Art reached out to touch Guin's arm, looking very serious.

"Don't touch me," Guin said, pulling her arm away. "I mean it, Art. As soon as we figure out who really killed Rick, it's over. For good this time."

Art was about to say something, but he took one look at his wife—ex-wife—and thought better of it. "Whatever you say, Guin." he said.

"Good," said Guin, getting up. "I trust you can clean up? You should be familiar with the place by now."

"No problem," said Art. "But where are you going?"

"I need some air," said Guin. She walked over to where she kept her keys, grabbed a set, and headed to the door. "I'll be back in a little while."

Art looked down at Flora and Fauna, who were waiting

to be fed more chicken. There was still a little left of Guin's plate. Art reached over, ripped some meat from the bone, and dropped it onto the floor.

"Don't tell Guin," he said, smiling down at the cats, who gobbled up the chicken.

Guin stormed down the stairs, barely able to contain her anger, and immediately regretted not putting on bug spray. She frantically swatted at her arms. "Argh!" she grunted. She started walking toward the end of the cul-de-sac, but it was too dark to see, so she quickly turned around. However, she was not ready to go back into the apartment. Instead, she walked over to the garage, opened the garage door, and got into the Mini. She pounded on the top of the dashboard. Suddenly her phone started buzzing. She took it out. It was a call from Ris. She debated whether to answer it, finally tapping "answer."

"Hey!" said Guin, trying to sound cheerful.

"Hey yourself," replied Ris. "Sorry I haven't called sooner. I've been crazy busy."

"No worries," said Guin. "I've been pretty busy, too."

"Working on a big story?" asked Ris.

"Yeah, I guess you could say so," replied Guin.

"So, we getting together tomorrow night? You want me to come over to your place?"

"No!" Guin practically shouted.

"Haven't tidied up again?" asked Ris, laughing. When they had first started dating, Guin was always nervous about having Ris over to her place, claiming it wasn't as nice, or as neat, as his place, which had been designed by a former girlfriend of Ris's who did killer decor.

"Something like that," said Guin, who had yet to tell Ris about Art, though she knew at some point soon she would have to.

"Fine, you want to meet someplace?"

"That would be great," said Guin. "You going to be on Sanibel, at the Shell Museum, tomorrow, or are you working over at FGCU?"

"At the museum, which is why I suggested your place. Hey, I know: Why don't you come to the museum around five, just before it closes. Then we can go to happy hour or out to dinner someplace on the island."

Guin glanced up toward the condo. And what would she do about Art? Screw him.

"Five o'clock at the Shell Museum it is," replied Guin. "See you tomorrow."

"Excellent. See you then. And Guin?"

"What?" asked Guin, somewhat distracted.

"I've missed you."

Guin smiled down at the phone. "I've missed you too. See you soon."

She hung up and got out of her car. It was too hot to stay in the garage, even with the garage door open, and she didn't want to waste gas or electricity by turning on the car's A/C. She closed the garage door and headed up the stairs.

She walked in to find the dining table cleared of food. She peeked into the kitchen. It, too, was clean.

"Art?" she called from the hallway just outside the kitchen.

Instead of Art, Flora and Fauna came running.

"You guys know where Art is?"

Flora headed back down the hall, toward the lanai. Guin followed her. Art was out there, talking on his phone, pacing.

Guin walked over to the glass sliders and gently knocked on them, to get Art's attention. He saw her, smiled, and held up a finger, indicating to give him a minute.

"I'll be in my office," Guin mouthed and pointed.

Art nodded, though he didn't seem to be paying too much attention to her. Guin waited a second. Then she turned around and went into the bedroom, the cats following her.

She looked at her clock. It was just past eight-thirty. She should really call Lance back. She was also itching to speak with the detective, to tell him about their little boat trip, and ask him if he knew about or had seen the footage from the camera over at the end of the Wulfert Keys Trail.

As she decided who to call first, she went to the bathroom to brush her teeth. She walked back and forth, moving the toothbrush around her mouth, once again going over Rick's disappearance from the boat. Something just wasn't adding up.

She rinsed her mouth and spit into the sink—and heard a loud knock coming from the bedroom door.

"Guin? You in there?"

It was Art.

Guin wiped her mouth and made her way to the bedroom door. She opened it and looked out. "What do you want?"

"You told me to come look for you when I was off the phone. You going to let me in?" asked Art.

"Most definitely not," said Guin, opening the door wider and stepping into the hallway. "Who were you talking to on the phone?"

"Alan," Art replied. Apparently he and a few other guys have been asked to extend their stay on Sanibel another few days."

"Ah," said Guin. "And I take it they're not happy about it."

"No, they are not," said Art. "But it probably means I'm not the only suspect."

"So, who's been asked to stay, other than Alan?"

"Just Murph and this other sales guy, Joe Walton."

"The nice young man I met at the dinner?"

Art looked momentarily confused. Then he remembered.

"Yeah, him."

"How come?" asked Guin.

"Alan was able to access Rick's CRM account. Apparently, he had a couple of big deals about to close."

"And?"

"And remember how I was telling you there was a rumor going around, about Rick doing deals in other guys' territories?"

"Yes," said Guin, hoping Art would cut to the chase.

"Well, apparently, he was working on a deal down here, which, as you know, is Murph's territory."

"Interesting," said Guin. "Go on."

"And he had a big deal in the Midwest, too. That's Joe Walton's territory."

"Ah," said Guin.

"Alan was a bit vague, but knowing Rick, the deals were probably worth a lot of money, otherwise why risk it?"

"So, you think maybe Murph or Joe found out about Rick doing deals in their territories?" asked Guin.

"I think it's a distinct possibility."

"Still, you don't kill someone over a deal," said Guin.

"We're talking potentially millions of dollars, Guin. I know guys who would kill for less," said Art. "Well, maybe not literally kill a guy. But, you know. It's the principal of the thing, Guin. You don't go steal another guy's deal."

"Money is a pretty powerful motive," said Guin.

"Definitely," said Art.

"Did you notice any tension between Murph and Rick on the boat?" asked Guin.

"No, but…"

Art thought back to the boat trip.

"It's possible Murph didn't know then," he said.

"So when did he find out?"

"I don't know, but Alan may have said something to him after Rick disappeared. I know he'd hate to lose a really big deal."

Guin mulled it over.

"And what about Joe?"

"Same thing," said Art.

"Though…" Guin frowned. "Wouldn't you know if some guy was working on the same deal you were?"

Art regarded Guin. "You have a point," he said. "Though if I heard about some guy trying to horn in on one of my big deals, I'd…"

"Kill him?" Guin asked, regarding Art.

Art looked momentarily flustered.

"So did Alan tell you anything else?" Guin asked. "Any way you could find out what Rick was working on, get into his CRM account? There may be some information there that would help."

"I asked Alan about it, but he said he'd need to check with the detective."

"A shame you don't have a buddy in IT," said Guin.

"I'll put it on my to-do list," said Art.

"How's Emily doing?" asked Guin, changing the subject. "Is she feeling better? I know I should have called her…"

"We didn't discuss Emily," replied Art.

"I assume she's staying down here with Alan," Guin said.

"I don't know. I guess so," said Art.

"I should give her a call," said Guin.

"I'm sure she'd appreciate that," said Art. "Though I don't know if she's still here."

"Only one way to find out," said Guin. "I should have reached out to her sooner. I'll call over to the hotel in the morning."

"That's very good of you, Guin."

"Speaking of calls, I need to call my brother back. So if you will excuse me…"

Guin turned around and opened the door to the bedroom. As she was about to step in, Art gently placed a hand on Guin's arm. Guin turned and looked at Art's hand on her arm. It felt warm. She looked up at Art and recognized the look on his face.

"Goodnight, Art," she said. "I'll see you in the morning."

She shook off his hand and walked quickly into the bedroom, shutting the door behind her. She took a deep breath, then exhaled. The sooner she solved this case and got rid of Art, the better.

Instead of calling her brother right away, Guin went into the bathroom and slapped some cold water on her face. She looked in the mirror. Pull yourself together, Guin. She wiped her hands and face on the hand towel, then walked into her closet and changed into a big tee. She took another deep breath and exhaled. Then she sat on her bed and picked up her phone.

"I hear you have information to share," she texted the detective. "I have some, too. When can we meet to discuss?"

She stared at her phone, hoping for an immediate response, even though it was long after business hours. The detective did not respond.

Oh well, thought Guin. What was I expecting? She sighed and then pressed her brother's number. He picked up right away.

"Sis!"

"Hey, Lance," Guin replied.

"Long time no speak."

"Yeah, sorry about that," said Guin.

"Everything okay?" asked Lance, sensing something in Guin's voice.

"Yes—no," said Guin, sighing.

"Tell big brother all about it," said Lance.

"It's Art," said Guin.

"What about Art?" asked Lance. "I thought you were done with him. And good riddance, I say. I never did like the guy."

"I know. He's staying with me."

"WHAT?!" said Lance, practically screaming into the phone. "Have you gone insane? More importantly, how did he get an invite to Sanibel before I did?"

"I've invited you and Owen down here a zillion times, Lance. You've just been too busy, or so you've said."

"Well, we're coming down in July. I just need to finalize things."

"Uh-huh," said Guin, knowing there was a good chance that, once again, they wouldn't make it.

"You don't believe me?"

"No," said Guin. "But eventually I'll get you down here."

"So," said Lance, having calmed down, slightly, "what is the ex doing staying with you?"

"It's a long story," said Guin.

"I deal in stories," replied Lance. "Shoot."

Guin then told him everything, or nearly everything.

Lance whistled. "I've heard of taking your work home with you, but sister, this takes the cake."

Guin laughed.

"Well, at least you can laugh about it," said Lance.

"Beats the alternative," Guin replied.

"True. So have you told mom?"

"God no!" said Guin.

"You know she's going to find out," said Lance.

"The only way she'd find out is if you told her," said Guin, squinting at the phone.

"My lips are sealed."

"Uh-huh," said Guin.

Lance sighed. "Well, you should call mom and just tell her yourself."

"I will, eventually."

"Call her, Guin. You know she'll wheedle it out of me."

He had a point. "Fine, but not tonight."

"Whatever you say."

They spoke for several more minutes, with Lance telling her about work and what fabulous new restaurants he and Owen had tried. Guin smiled. Lance was a good story teller. Must run in the family, she thought. Guin suddenly let out a yawn.

"Past your bedtime?" said Lance. "I know you Floridians like to go to bed early."

It actually was getting close to Guin's bedtime.

"You know me too well," replied Guin, yawning again.

"Well goodnight, Sis. Thanks for the call. Don't be a stranger!"

"Goodnight, Lance," said Guin.

"And make sure you keep the door to your bedroom locked!"

"Goodbye, Lance," said Guin, making a face.

She ended the call and checked her messages, or for one specific message, from Detective O'Loughlin. But there was still no reply to her text. She yawned again and looked down at the bed. The cats were on it, asleep. If she kept her door closed, they wouldn't be able to get out and would probably wake her up in the middle of the night to let them out. But if she kicked them out now and closed the door, they would no doubt start yowling and scratching at the door to get back in later.

She weighed the risk of Art trying to sneak into her bedroom against the cats waking her up in the middle of the night and decided to leave the door open a crack. Then she walked back over to her bed, turned down the comforter, and climbed in, gently kicking Fauna, so she would move over.

It had been a long day, and, despite all the thoughts going through her brain, she quickly fell asleep.

CHAPTER 24

Guin got up early the next morning, determined to get in a beach walk. She quickly got dressed, scribbled a note to Art that she would be back before nine, gave the cats some food and fresh water, grabbed her keys and her shelling bag, and was out the door.

She ran down the steps and opened the garage. A few minutes later, she was parking the Mini across from Blind Pass beach. In her haste, Guin hadn't turned on her phone. Now, feeling it in her pocket, she debated whether she should. She pulled it out and stared at it for several seconds. Finally, she decided to turn it on, just in case there was an emergency, but she set it on vibrate. Smiling at her good sense, she locked the car and headed across the road to the beach.

It was a beautiful morning, with just a few wispy clouds in the sky. The sun had barely risen, and there was hardly anyone on the beach, though there were lots of gulls, terns, and brown pelicans. Guin headed east, her eyes cast down, hoping to find some good shells. But she knew that shelling on Sanibel could be unpredictable. One day you could find a bucket full of nice shells—and maybe a great big horse conch—the next you would be lucky to find a single Florida fighting conch or a lightning whelk.

She paused a little way down the beach and looked out

at the Gulf. As she gazed out at the sea, she sent out a silent prayer: O Mighty Neptune, send me a junonia! She looked down, transfixed by the lapping of the waves against the shore, hoping this time Neptune would hear her, and a junonia, or an alphabet cone, would magically appear. But as she watched the waves come and go, she became discouraged. Oh well, she thought. The day was still young, it was a beautiful morning, and she could still find some good shells farther down.

Guin continued to walk. She spied a pile of shells and made a beeline for it. Using her foot, she moved the shells around, hoping to discover a scotch bonnet or an apple murex or a king's crown conch or a cone underneath. But she was having no luck. She sighed and continued walking, ignoring the giant cockles and pen shells she came across. She was about to turn around and head back toward her car when she caught sight of two dolphins frolicking in the waves. She watched as they made their way toward Captiva and smiled.

She continued walking and then, about halfway back, while lost in thought, she tripped. She looked down and beheld a giant horse conch, half buried in the sand. Guin bent down and immediately started digging. As luck would have it, it was whole, or nearly, with a beautiful black patina and an orange interior. She took the horse conch down to the water and rinsed it out. Well, the morning's not a total loss, she said to herself. Thank you, Neptune.

She then continued the rest of the way, a smile on her face, proudly carrying her prize.

Guin arrived back at the condo a little after eight-thirty. As the shelling hadn't been great, except for finding the horse conch, she hadn't tarried on the beach. She walked into the kitchen and was greeted by the smell of freshly brewed coffee.

She looked around, but there was no sign of Art, just a carafe full of coffee in the coffee maker. Then she spied a mug Art had left out for her, with a note underneath it. "Gone running," it said. "Took the spare keys. Be back in a bit. Help yourself to coffee." It was dated "8—" in the upper right-hand corner. Guin wondered how long he would be out. In their younger days, they would often go running together, sometimes as much as five or six miles.

Don't mind if I do, thought Guin, pouring herself a mug of coffee. She took a sip, closing her eyes. Damn, that was good. She wasn't that hungry, but she knew she should eat something, so she grabbed a peanut butter protein bar from the fridge and took her coffee and the protein bar to her desk in the bedroom.

She took another sip of coffee and booted up her computer. Immediately, Flora jumped onto the desk in front of her, looking for attention. Guin obliged, scratching Flora's head and rubbing her ears. Then Flora flopped down on Guin's notes, rolling around on top of them.

Guin sighed. "How am I supposed to do any work with you rolling around on top of my notes, cat?" she said to the feline. But Flora ignored her and continued to roll from side to side, purring.

Guin shooed Flora away from her monitor and opened the document containing her notes regarding Rick. She reviewed what she had written. Then she took out her phone to see if the detective had gotten back to her. He had not. As it was now nine o'clock, she decided to give him a call over at the police department.

"Sanibel Police Department," said the masculine voice at the other end of the line.

"Detective O'Loughlin, please," said Guin, using her professional voice.

"Who's calling?"

"Tell him Guinivere Jones. He's expecting my call," or should be, thought Guin.

"Oh, hi, Ms. Jones," said the voice. "It's Officer Pettit."

"And hello to you, Officer Pettit. So, is he in?"

"I'll go check," said Officer Pettit.

Guin had come to know Officer Pettit while she was investigating the disappearance of the Golden Junonia and the murder of Gregor Matenopoulos. He was a good-looking young man—*young* being the operative word. Guin couldn't believe he was in his twenties. He looked like he had just graduated from high school. But he was a very competent police officer, and he was always very polite to her.

A minute later he was back on the line. "The detective asked if he could call you back. He's kind of busy right now."

Guin made a face. She had the distinct impression that the detective was avoiding her.

"Fine. But tell him if he hasn't called me back by eleven, I'm going to call him back, and text him."

"Will do, Ms. Jones. I'll pass along the message."

Guin thanked him and hung up.

I should probably give Emily a call, thought Guin. She dialed the number for the San Ybel Resort & Spa and asked for Emily Fielding's room. A few seconds later, she was connected.

"Hello?" said a wary voice.

"Emily?" said Guin.

"Yes, who's calling?"

"Emily, it's Guin, Guinivere Jones."

"Oh Guin! Alan said he saw you the other night. I meant to phone you the next day, to apologize for not attending the dinner, but I had this horrible headache."

"You feeling better?" asked Guin.

"Much."

"In that case, how about getting together tomorrow?"

"I would love that," said Emily. "The resort life may be nice for some, but it's not for me."

"How about I pick you up around nine tomorrow morning, show you the island?"

"Wonderful!" said Emily.

Guin suddenly had a thought. "Emily, do you like shells?"

"Shells? I used to collect them as a kid. Why?" She paused. "Oh, that's right. Sanibel is known for its shells."

"It is," said Guin, "and if you are interested, I could pick you up a bit earlier and we could go shelling over on Lighthouse Beach."

"Sounds like a plan. Let's do it!" She paused. "Uh, how early are we talking about?"

Guin laughed. "Not too early. How about I pick you up at the hotel at eight? We can go have a late breakfast after. Sound good?"

"It's a date! So what should I bring?"

"Just a bag for collecting shells. I'll bring one of my extras, just in case. And put on plenty of sunblock and bug spray. And bring your camera! I'll take you over to Ding Darling, that's the wildlife refuge, after breakfast and to the Shell Museum, too. Have you been up to Captiva yet?"

There was a pause on the other end of the line.

"You still there?" asked Guin.

"Sorry," said Emily. "What were you saying?"

"I wanted to know if you'd been up to Captiva."

Again there was a slight pause. "No."

"Well, I'll take you up there, too."

"You don't have to, Guin, really. Don't you have work to do?"

"I do," Guin replied, thinking she should really call Craig.

"But I can take a few hours off to show an old friend around."

"Okay then. See you tomorrow at eight. Let me give you my mobile, in case you're running late or something comes up."

She rattled off her mobile number, which Guin wrote down.

"I'll send you a quick text, so you'll have mine. See you tomorrow!"

"Thanks, Guin," said Emily. "See you tomorrow."

They hung up and Guin was about to call Craig when she heard the front door. Art, no doubt back from his run. She got up and headed toward the kitchen. She walked in to find a very sweaty Art downing a banana.

"Potassium," he said, holding up the banana.

"You want a towel?" asked Guin, watching the sweat roll off him.

"Nah, I'm okay."

Guin made a face and went to get Art a hand towel. When she returned, he had consumed the banana and was gulping down a glass of water.

"How many miles did you run?" asked Guin.

"I don't know, five, maybe six? I wasn't keeping track."

"Feeling better?" asked Guin.

"Not right this minute, but I will after I've taken a shower."

"Well, don't let me stop you," said Guin, as she watched rivulets of sweat make their way down Art's sculpted torso, his white running shirt now see-through.

"Care to join me?" said Art, a grin spreading across his face.

"Oh no!" said Guin, holding up a hand. "I shower alone these days."

"So no showers with the new beau?" said Art. "What a shame."

Guin glared at him. "Go take a shower."

"Sure you don't want to join me?" he said, taking a step toward her. "I remember, back in the day..."

"GO!" said Guin, flinging the hand towel at him.

"Thanks," he said, grabbing it and wiping his forehead. He then turned and headed toward the guest room, whistling a jaunty tune.

"ARGH!" grounded out Guin, after he had left. She could feel her face burning. She wasn't sure what she was more annoyed with, Art's behavior or her reaction to it.

She stood another minute in the kitchen, fuming. Then she headed back to her office, slamming the door behind her. When she sat back down at her desk, she saw there was a voicemail message. She quickly played it. Of course, O'Loughlin. The message was very brief. She deleted it and called him back on his mobile. Why were all the men in her life so infuriating?

Of course, when she called him back the call went straight to voicemail, but half an hour later, he called her back.

"You rang," said the detective, at the sound of Guin's voice.

"I did. I have news, and I want to know what you've found out. Can we meet later? I can come over to the police department."

"You have lunch plans?" asked the detective.

Guin flashed on Art. She made a face.

"Nope."

"Meet me over at Doc Ford's at one then."

"Fine," said Guin. "I'll see you then."

She ended the call. Then she sent an email to Craig, letting him know what Art had found out about Rick, and asking if he had been able to get in touch with Hank. She ended the email by saying she would be having lunch with the detective and would let Craig know if she found out anything. Then she hit 'send.'

As she had some time until she had to leave to meet the detective, she decided to give her article one last pass before sending it to Ginny. She opened the document and re-read it, making a couple of minor tweaks. Satisfied, she closed it and sent it off to the *San-Cap Sun-Times* with a brief cover note. She leaned back in her chair and looked out at the golf course. There was a foursome playing just outside her window. She watched as a man in a pink polo shirt, Bermuda shorts, and a baseball cap hit his ball down the fairway. Something about him rang a bell in her head. She got up and went into the living area, to look for Art.

He was sitting at the dining table, working on his computer.

"How's it going?" asked Guin.

"Slowly," said Art.

"Still doing your research on Rick?"

"I am. I'll say this for the guy, he was no slacker. Alan sent me over the report, which listed the various deals Rick had been working on. He must have had a dozen different deals brewing. He traveled more than I did," said Art, shaking his head.

"About Rick," said Guin. "Do you happen to have any recent pictures of him?"

"I think I have a few from our fishing trip. Why?"

"Can I see them?" asked Guin.

"Sure," said Art, picking up his phone and scrolling through the photos.

"Here's one of the four of us. Rick's on the end there, wearing a baseball cap and sunglasses. You can't really see his face."

Guin held out her hand for the phone, which Art handed

to her. She enlarged the photo to try to get a better view of Rick. "You're right, you really can't see his face that clearly, what with the hat and the glasses, but I have a feeling this is the guy I saw at Doc Ford's over on Captiva Friday night."

"You saw Rick at Doc Ford's on Captiva Friday and you didn't say anything?" said Art.

"I didn't realize it was Rick until just a few minutes ago," Guin retorted. "I knew the guy looked familiar, but I couldn't place him. It was kind of dark inside where he was sitting, and he was wearing a baseball cap, so I didn't get a good look at his face. But I'm pretty sure it was him, and he was with a woman who also looked familiar. But I haven't been able to place her."

"You tell that to your friend, the detective?" asked Art.

"I only put it together a minute ago, but I'll tell him when I see him for lunch."

"Lunch, eh?" said Art, giving Guin a funny look.

"What? You have a problem?"

"That my wife is cozy with the guy who could put me away? Yes, I have a problem with that," said Art.

"*Ex*-wife," said Guin. "You jealous? As you recall, we're no longer married."

"How does your boyfriend feel about you having lunch with the detective?"

Guin fumed. As it happened, Ris wasn't crazy about the detective either, but as Guin explained, her job required her to be on good terms with the Sanibel police force, especially the detective. And if that meant the two of them having lunch every so often, so be it. Was that such a big deal?

"He's totally fine with it," Guin lied.

"Well, bully for him," said Art, turning back to his computer.

"Let me know if I can pick you up something," said Guin.

Art turned to look back up at her.

"As a matter of fact, I'm also going out for lunch."

"Oh?" said Guin. "How are you planning on getting there?"

"Alan and the guys are going to pick me up. We're going to have lunch over at the Sunset Grill and discuss a few things."

"Fine. Have fun. Just remember to take the spare keys—and keep them someplace safe." (During their marriage, Art was always losing or misplacing his keys.)

Art made a face. "Yes, Mom."

Guin resisted the urge to say something snarky. Instead she only asked what time they were picking him up.

"Twelve-thirty," he replied, looking at his computer again.

"I'll be heading out right after you."

Art did not reply.

Guin stood there for a few more seconds then went back into her room.

CHAPTER 25

Guin sat in a booth with the detective.

"So, how's the investigation coming along?" she asked.

"You said you had some information for me," replied the detective.

Guin sighed. "I went out on a boat with Craig and his buddy, Al Boudreaux, the other day. He's a charter boat captain."

"I know him," said the detective. "Good guy."

"We checked out the place where Art said he last saw Rick, over by Wulfert Keys, and apparently there's a video camera on the pole over there, down at the end of the Wulfert Keys Trail."

Guin watched the detective's face, looking for a reaction, but as usual it registered nothing. She continued.

"And we wondered if the police department had seen the footage from the camera, from the afternoon Rick disappeared."

Guin waited for a reply.

"Anything else?" said the detective.

Guin made a face.

"I assume you've been checking out Rick's colleagues. So you probably know that he had been poaching."

"Poaching, Ms. Jones?"

"You know, going into another guy's territory and taking a deal away without telling him."

The detective smiled, or it could have been a smirk.

"We are currently looking into Mr. Tomlinson's business dealings. He was a very busy man, from what we've uncovered."

"There are two deals in particular that concerned me," said Guin, wanting to leave Art's name out of it.

The detective raised an eyebrow and waited for Guin to continue.

"Apparently, Rick was about to close a big deal down here, which is Murph's territory—Bob Murphy, that is. All the guys call him Murph. He's in charge of Florida and Georgia," said Guin, clarifying. "Though you probably knew that," she quickly added. "He was also about to close a big deal in the Midwest. That would be Joe Walton's territory. I'd question both of them."

"Thank you for telling me how to do my job, Ms. Jones," said the detective.

That was definitely sarcasm.

"I'm actually speaking with the two of them later today, along with Mr. Tomlinson's boss, Alan Fielding."

"Well, let me know what you find out," said Guin. "You know they're all having lunch together?"

The detective eyed Guin.

A minute later their lunch arrived. Guin had ordered the fish tacos, the detective the grouper sandwich. They ate in silence for a few minutes, then Guin continued to query the detective.

"So you didn't tell me whether you obtained the footage from the video camera," said Guin.

The detective was about to take another bite of his sandwich but stopped.

"No, I didn't."

"Does that mean you haven't obtained it—or that you have and you just don't want to share?"

The detective sighed and put the sandwich back on the plate.

"We are in the process of obtaining the footage, Ms. Jones."

"Well, when you get it, can Craig and I have a look at it?" Though Guin was secretly hoping Craig and Al's buddy, Hank, would be able to get them their own copy.

"Maybe," said the detective.

Guin took another bite of her remaining fish taco, followed by a sip of her Arnold Palmer, while the detective finished off his grouper sandwich.

"There's something else," said Guin.

The detective regarded her and waited.

"I'm pretty sure I saw Rick the other night, over at Doc Ford's on Captiva."

"And you didn't tell me? Frankly, I am shocked, Ms. Jones."

Was that a twinkle in the detective's eye? Guin wasn't sure.

"At the time, I didn't know it was him."

"And now you're sure?"

"Well, pretty sure," said Guin. "It was kind of dark where he was sitting, and he was wearing a baseball cap. I just thought the guy looked familiar. He was sitting with a woman who also looked familiar, but I couldn't place her."

The detective looked thoughtful. Guin continued.

"I thought about going over there, to get a better look, but…" She trailed off. "Anyway, it finally came to me this morning that the guy was Rick, or looked a lot like him. I'm still trying to figure out who the woman could be, why she looked familiar. Rick isn't married, and, according to Art, he didn't bring a girlfriend with him to the conference. Though I guess it's possible he knew someone down here…"

The detective caught their server's eye and signaled for the check.

"I need to get back to work."

"So do I," said Guin. She reached for her wallet, but the detective stopped her.

"Are you ever going to let me pay for lunch?" she asked.

"Maybe," said the detective, giving Guin a rare smile.

"Well, it's been lovely," said Guin. "Thank you. You know what else would be nice?"

"What?" asked the detective.

"If you would share your information with me. I have a story to write—and an ex-husband who wants to remove that 'ex.' The sooner we solve this case, the sooner Art goes back to Connecticut."

"We?" said the detective.

"You know what I mean," said Guin.

"All right, Nancy Drew," said the detective, his lips curling into a smile, or what passed for a smile on the detective. "I'll keep you posted. And if your ex gives you trouble, let me know. Just try to stay out of trouble."

Guin did her best not to roll her eyes.

The server returned with the check. The detective took a quick look, then placed some bills inside the folder.

"You sure I can't contribute?" asked Guin.

"You've already contributed," said the detective. "You ready?"

"Do you need change?" asked Guin.

"No, I'm good," said the detective. "Let's go."

They headed to the front of the restaurant and out the front door, into the parking lot.

"Well, goodbye, detective. Let me know about the camera footage and if you find out anything from Art's colleagues."

"Good day, Ms. Jones," replied the detective.

"So, how was your lunch?" asked Guin when Art returned. She had beaten him back to the condo.

"Good," he replied.

"That's it? Just 'good'?"

"What would you like me to say? You want me to tell you what everyone ordered? I had the—"

Guin hit him.

"Ow, what was that for?" said Art, though, from his expression, Guin knew he knew exactly what the slap was for.

"Did they tell you they had an appointment over at the police department this afternoon, to speak with the detective?"

"Yeah," said Art.

"And?"

"What do you want me to tell you, Guin?"

"Did you talk about Rick?"

"What do you think?"

Guin sighed.

"How was lunch with the detective?" asked Art.

"Fine," said Guin.

Two could play at this game.

They stayed there staring at each other for several seconds.

"So, you have any idea who Rick could have been having dinner with Friday night?" asked Guin. Was he seeing someone down here?"

"No idea," said Art. "Like I said, I tried to stay as far away from Rick as possible."

"Well, could you ask Alan and some of the other guys? This mystery woman may know where Rick was hiding out... or could even be the killer."

Art looked thoughtful. "I'll ask, but..."

"Thank you," said Guin.

She paused.

"You think Joe or Murph could have offed Rick?" asked Guin.

"It's possible," said Art.

"By the way, the detective should have the toxicology report back any day."

"Does he think Rick was poisoned?" Art asked.

"It does seem the most likely cause of death," Guin replied.

"Well, let me know what your good friend, the detective, finds out."

Guin made a face.

"I'm going to my office to do some work," she announced.

"Fine," Art replied. "I have work to do, too."

Guin walked to her bedroom, slamming the door shut behind her.

Guin spent the rest of the afternoon in her office/bedroom, speaking with Craig and Ginny. Craig had spoken with his buddy, Hank, who was working on getting them a copy of the videotape. Craig had also suggested that Guin go back to Doc Ford's on Captiva and see if anyone could remember the couple Guin saw.

"Good idea," Guin had said, wishing she had thought of that sooner. I know, she thought. I'll take Emily there for lunch tomorrow, then ask. She smiled at the thought.

After she hung up with Craig she phoned Ginny, who was in a chatty mood. Guin caught Ginny up on the case, and Ginny caught Guin up on the local gossip.

"And here I thought Suzy Seashell was the queen of Sanibel gossip," said Guin, chuckling over one particularly juicy story.

"Who do you think taught her everything she knows?" replied Ginny. "She used to work for me before she started Shellapalooza."

Guin smiled.

"So, how are things going with your ex?" Ginny asked.

Guin frowned.

"Okay, but I can't wait to wrap up this case, so he can go back to Connecticut."

"So, not feeling the love?" asked Ginny.

"No way," said Guin. "That ship has sailed."

"And here I thought it was still docked in your harbor," said Ginny.

"Ha ha," said Guin. "I am not getting back together with Art, Ginny."

"Fine," said Ginny. "So, do I get to meet him?"

"Why on earth do you want to meet him?" asked Guin.

"Professional curiosity," said Ginny.

"Uh-huh," said Guin.

"Oh, come on, Guin. Let me meet him."

Guin sighed. "Fine."

"Excellent. How about we meet for drinks over at Timbers tomorrow, say six o'clock?"

"I'll ask him."

They ended the call and Guin looked at the clock on her monitor. It was just past four-thirty, and she was supposed to meet Ris at the Shell Museum at five. She texted him to let him know she was going to be a few minutes late.

"Text me if the door is locked," he wrote back. "I'll come get you."

"Thanks," typed Guin. "C u soon."

Guin went into her closet and changed into a pair of skinny jeans and a loose-fitting top. Then she went into the bathroom to fix her hair. It was frizzy, as usual. She ran a comb through it, but quickly stopped, realizing there was no point. She sighed and put on some lip gloss, then headed into the living room.

Art was still sitting at the dining table, working on his

computer. (Or he could have been looking at porn. She had no desire to check.)

"I'm heading out."

"Have fun," said Art, not looking at her.

"If you need food, you can order in something. There are some menus on the counter."

"Thanks, but I had a pretty big lunch, so I should be good," he said, continuing to look at his computer screen.

"Well, if you need anything, text me," said Guin.

She waited for a response, but when none came she turned and walked down the hall. She stopped at the front door and called out, "And if the cats start bugging you, just give them some food!"

Again, no response from Art. Guin sighed, put on her high-heeled sandals, then headed out the door.

CHAPTER 26

Guin arrived at the Bailey-Matthews National Shell Museum a few minutes after five to find the door still open. She entered and went over to the front desk, where Bonnie, the treasurer of the Shell Club, who volunteered at the museum, was seated.

"Hi Guin!" said Bonnie. "You here to see Dr. Hartwick?"

Guin smiled. "How'd you know?"

Bonnie smiled back.

"Can you let him know I'm here?"

"Sure thing," she said. She picked up the phone and dialed Ris's extension. "A Ms. Jones here to see you, Dr. Hartwick," she said, winking at Guin.

Bonnie nodded, then hung up. "He said to go on up."

"Thank you," said Guin.

Guin headed up the stairs to the second floor and down the hall to Ris's office. The door was closed, so she knocked.

"Come in," called a male voice.

Guin opened the door to find Ris seated at the desk, surrounded by piles of papers, books, and shells. "Did a hurricane blow through here?" she said, looking around.

Ris gave her a sheepish grin. "No, I'm just trying to organize things."

Guin gave him a skeptical look.

"I thought I would help Luis out by going through the backlog while it's slow, but I got a little carried away, and now I feel like I'll never finish."

"Anything I can do?" asked Guin, looking at the piles dotting the office.

"Thank you, but that's okay," said Ris. "I've enlisted one of the summer interns to help me. So you should be able to see the floor by next week," he added with a grin.

Guin looked for a place to sit, but both chairs were already occupied.

Ris followed Guin's gaze and quickly got up and started removing things from the chair closest to him.

"Here, have a seat," he said, gesturing to the now empty chair.

"Thank you," said Guin, smiling up at him.

She remained standing, continuing to look at him.

"Is everything okay?" he asked, looking confused.

"Aren't you going to give me a kiss hello?"

Ris quickly moved toward Guin, took her face in his hands, and kissed her.

When he finally broke off, several minutes later, Guin nearly fell back into the chair.

"Is that better?" he asked, a sly smile on his face.

Guin blushed and sat down.

"So, um, what are you working on?" she asked, trying to collect herself.

"Stuff. Things," said Ris, returning to the seat behind his desk.

"Well, if you need a little time to finish up, I can read the paper on my phone."

"Thanks," said Ris. "But I just need a few minutes. Then we can go over to Doc Ford's."

"Actually, can we go someplace else?" asked Guin. "I just had lunch there."

"Oh?" said Ris. "With whom?"

Guin debated whether she should tell Ris about her lunch with the detective. Then she chided herself for being silly. She had nothing to hide. Well, except for her ex staying with her.

"Detective O'Loughlin," she replied.

Ris raised an eyebrow.

"I'm working on a big story and needed to speak with him."

"This wouldn't have to do with the missing guy who turned up dead, the one who was a rival of your ex?"

Guin stared at Ris, her mouth open. Did everyone know about Rick and her ex? Clearly, she needed to pay more attention to the local scuttlebutt.

"How do you know about that?" asked Guin.

"I have my sources," said Ris. "So, you didn't answer me. Does your big story have to do with the murder?"

Guin bit her lip.

"Yes, but Art didn't do it," she said, a bit too quickly.

Ris gave her a look.

"I know what you're thinking, but Art swears he's innocent. And I believe him."

Ris continued to regard Guin, a skeptical look on his face.

"Don't you think you may be a bit biased?" asked Ris.

"Maybe," Guin admitted. "But I also know Art. He may be a lot of things, but he's not a killer."

"If you say so," said Ris.

Guin could tell Ris did not believe her, but she forged ahead.

"There's something else you should know," she said, taking a deep breath and holding it.

"I have a feeling from your expression that I'm not going to like it," Ris replied.

Guin willed herself not to look or feel guilty.

"Art's been staying with me."

Ris opened his mouth to stay something, but Guin put up a hand to stop him.

"It was not my idea. It was Art's attorney's idea, and the detective agreed to it. They figured I could keep an eye on him."

"Well, isn't that nice of them," said Ris. "And you went along with it?"

"I didn't have a choice!" said Guin, trying not to raise her voice (too much).

"Of course you had a choice!" Ris retorted. "The guy should be in jail."

Guin felt exasperated. Clearly, nothing she could say would make Ris trust her on this score.

They stared at each other for several seconds. Then Ris sighed.

"Sorry. I just don't like the idea of you being alone with the guy."

Guin leaned over and put a hand on Ris's arm.

"I don't like it either, believe me. That's why I'm working with the detective to help solve this case. The sooner we figure out who killed Rick—that's the name of the guy who disappeared and got killed—the sooner Art will be gone."

"Well, in that case," said Ris, a slight grin returning to his face, "how can I help?"

Guin laughed. "I wish you could. Believe me, the sooner Art is gone, the happier I'll be."

"You can always stay at my place," said Ris, taking Guin's hand. "The offer of a key is still out there."

"And I'm very tempted to take it," said Guin, squeezing his hand. "But the whole point of Art staying at my place is so that I can keep tabs on him."

"So, you're his warden?"

"I hadn't thought of it like that, but I guess so," said Guin, somewhat amused by the thought. "Can we please stop talking about my ex now? I'm here to see you, and I want to know all about your trip to Costa Rica."

Ris smiled. "Okay. I'll stop. Just give me a few minutes to sort through some stuff. Then we'll go for an early dinner wherever you'd like."

"Deal," said Guin.

It was nearly six o'clock by the time Ris had finished up at the museum, but Guin hadn't minded. She spent the time catching up on current events—and sent messages to Craig and the detective, asking if they had any news. She had been tempted to text Art too, to see if he was okay, but she restrained herself.

"So where do you want to go for dinner?" asked Ris.

"How about we go to that new pizza place, Dante's, over at the Sanibel Inn?" asked Guin. "That is, if your diet regimen allows for pizza."

Ris, a runner who was also into yoga, was a bit of a health nut and lived by the Mediterranean Diet, though he had a sweet tooth and enjoyed beer.

"I think I can squeeze in a little pizza," he said, patting his stomach (which did not show an ounce of flab—unlike mine, thought Guin).

Guin smiled. "Then it's settled. Let's go."

"They do serve salads there, though, yes?" asked Ris.

Guin rolled her eyes.

"I'm sure they do. Do you want me to double check? I can call them if you're concerned."

"No, that's okay," he said.

They left the museum and stopped at the foot of the stairs.

"Why don't I drive?" suggested Ris.

Guin was about to suggest they take two cars, but she had had enough battles for one evening, so she quickly agreed. A couple of minutes later, they were heading to Dante's in Ris's vintage red Alfa Romeo convertible.

"I do love this car," said Guin, enjoying the breeze.

Ris glanced over at her and smiled. "She's a beauty."

A few minutes later they arrived at Dante's. Ris parked the car and they headed in.

"A table for two, please," he asked the hostess, giving her a big smile, the one that revealed his dimples.

The woman beamed. Ris had that effect on women.

"Would you like a booth?" she asked.

"Please," he said, still smiling at her.

"Follow me," she said.

Guin gave Ris a look, to which he shrugged.

"Here you go!" said the hostess, placing two menus on the table. "Your server will be right over."

She stood there an extra second, smiling at Ris, who continued to smile at her. Guin cleared her throat and looked from Ris to the hostess. The hostess blushed slightly, then left.

"Must you do that?" asked Guin.

"Do what?" asked Ris.

"Be so charming—flirt with every woman you meet."

"I do not flirt with every woman I meet," said Ris.

"Uh-huh," said Guin. She knew first-hand his effect on women, and thought he secretly enjoyed it, despite what he said.

Fortunately, before they could continue that discussion (or argument), the server came over. "Good evening," he said. "My name's Mike. I'll be your server tonight. Can I get the two of you some drinks while you're deciding?"

They ordered two glasses of High Five IPA.

"Very good," said Mike. "I'll be right back."

Guin picked up the menu. "As you can see, they have salads."

"And coal-fired wings," said Ris.

"Those do look good," said Guin. "How about we share some wings and a pizza?"

"Sounds good to me," said Ris. "And a salad."

"Fine, you pick."

A few minutes later, Mike came back with their beers and took their order. The food arrived not long after, and the rest of the evening passed quite pleasantly, with Ris telling Guin all about his trip to Costa Rica.

"It sounds amazing," said Guin, as they finished off their pizza and wings.

"It was," said Ris. "Next time, you should come with me."

"I'd like to," said Guin, "but you know I don't scuba dive."

"I could teach you," said Ris, taking Guin's hand.

Guin looked down at their hands. She loved the feel of his touch, but she did not like the idea of scuba diving. She had been afraid of diving since she was a kid and nearly drowned after hitting her head diving into a pool.

"We'll see," she said, giving him a smile.

They continued to hold hands across the table and smile at each other.

"You two done?" asked Mike, looking down at their near empty plates.

"Yes," said Guin, removing her hand from Ris's.

"I'll just clear these then," said Mike, picking up the plates. "Can I interest you in some dessert?"

Guin glanced at Ris.

"You have a dessert menu?" asked Ris.

"We do," replied Mike. "I'll bring it right over. Any coffee, or maybe a cappuccino?"

"I'll have a decaf cappuccino. How about you, Guin?"

"Same."

"Two decaf cappuccinos and a dessert menu, coming right up!"

Mike returned a few minutes later with the cappuccinos and the dessert menu. "Enjoy!" he said.

"These look good," said Guin, eyeing the foam.

They had a sip. "Mmm… not bad," said Ris.

Guin eyed the dessert menu, then handed it to Ris.

"You see something you want?"

Ris looked up and over at Guin. "Yes."

Guin blushed.

"Let's get out of here and go back to my place," he suggested.

"I'd love to, but I can't," said Guin. "Gotta go watch the prisoner."

Ris made a face. "I hope that guy appreciates that you're keeping him out of jail."

"Probably not," said Guin, "but he'll be out of my hair soon enough."

"I hope so."

Mike returned. "Can I interest you in some dessert?"

They exchanged looks. "I'm good," said Guin.

"Just the check," said Ris.

They finished their cappuccinos in silence. Then Ris paid the bill and they left.

"You sure you can't come to my place, just for a little while," said Ris, pulling Guin close to him in the parking lot.

Guin looked up at his face. It was a nice face, a beautiful face, and Guin would have liked nothing more than to spend the next several hours looking at it. But she felt guilty about being out.

"You know I want to, but…" she trailed off.

Ris let go of her and sighed. "I know."

They got back in the Alfa Romeo and drove back to the museum. The parking lot was empty, except for Guin's purple Mini Cooper. Ris parked next to it. They sat in the Alfa Romeo for a minute, looking at each other. Then Ris leaned over and gave Guin a long, slow kiss. When they finally stopped, Guin wished she didn't have to go back to the condo, and Art.

"Well, goodnight," said Ris, placing a hand on the side of her face.

"Goodnight," said Guin, not moving.

They sat there for a few more minutes, until Guin sighed and finally got out of the car.

"Thanks for dinner."

"My pleasure," said Ris.

"Will I see you this weekend?"

"You tell me," said Ris.

In the darkness, Guin could not read his expression.

"Yes," said Guin.

"Even if…?"

"Yes," repeated Guin, more firmly this time.

Even though it was dark, Guin could tell Ris was smiling. She smiled back, then got in her car and drove home.

CHAPTER 27

It was still relatively early when Guin got back to the condo. The cats ran to the door to greet her. She bent down and petted both of them.

"Did Art give you guys some food?" she asked.

"Meow!" said Fauna, rubbing herself against Guin's leg.

"I'm not sure if that's a yes or a no, as I don't speak cat," said Guin. "Shall we go see?"

Guin walked into the kitchen and eyed their food bowls. She was pleasantly surprised to find some food in them. So Art did feed them.

She walked into the living room, but did not see Art. She walked down the hall to the guest room and knocked on the door. No answer. She knocked again.

"Art, are you in there?"

Again, there was no answer.

"I'm coming in," she called out, as she turned the knob. She entered the room and turned on the light. No sign of Art. The bathroom door was open, so clearly he was not in there either. Where could he be?

Guin checked her phone. No message from Art, though there were a couple of messages from Craig. She would read them in a minute. Right now she was concerned about her missing ex-husband.

"Where are you?" she texted him.

A few seconds later, he replied. "Out with my fellow prisoners."

Guin made a face. Sanibel was hardly a prison.

"Where?"

"At the Bubble Room."

Guin had been meaning to get to the Bubble Room over on Captiva but hadn't yet.

"When will you be home?"

"Miss me?" texted Art.

Guin could feel steam coming out of her ears.

"No. Just wondering where you were," she wrote back.

Art texted back a sad emoji. Guin sighed.

"When you going to be home?" she typed again.

"Soon," Art wrote. "Just finishing up."

"Fine," wrote Guin. "See you soon."

She walked into her bedroom and over to her desk. She sat down in her chair and restarted her computer. As soon as it had rebooted, she opened her email and saw a message from Craig. Apparently he had seen or got wind of the toxicology report. Rick had died from heart failure, which she knew. The cause, however, was something Guin had never heard of, or didn't recall reading about. Per the medical examiner, death was the result of an adverse reaction to ibuprofen, the ingredient in Advil. Apparently, Rick was allergic to ibuprofen and, per his parents, he always wore one of those allergy bracelets, alerting people to the fact. However, he was not wearing the bracelet when his body was brought in, Craig noted.

Interesting, thought Guin.

There was also a substantial amount of alcohol in Rick's blood, Craig wrote, which most likely contributed to his death.

So, did someone deliberately get Rick drunk and then give him ibuprofen? She couldn't imagine Rick ingesting ibuprofen if he was sober. And even drunk, she couldn't imagine someone forcing a pill down his throat. (She immediately pictured herself trying to pill the cats and shuddered.)

She turned back to Craig's message and continued to read. Oh good, she thought, scanning the rest of the email. Craig's friend Hank said they could see the video footage from the camera at the end of Wulfert Keys Trail tomorrow afternoon. They just needed to keep it on the QT. Guin smiled. Craig had certainly been busy.

She replied to Craig's email, thanking him for the information about Rick and asking him what time to meet him over at Ding Darling the next day. Guin had made plans to spend the morning with Emily, but she would probably drop Emily back off at the hotel right after lunch and could meet up with Craig and Hank afterward, on her way back.

As she was pressing 'send,' she heard the front door.

"Helloooo! Anybody home?" called out Art.

Oh God, was he drunk? thought Guin. That's just what she needed.

She sighed and got up to go see him.

He was standing in the hall, just outside her door, about to knock on it when she opened it. He had a goofy expression on his face, which Guin knew too well.

"May I come in?" he said, grinning down at her.

Guin folded her hands over her chest. "No."

"Please," said Art, wiggling his eyebrows suggestively.

"How much did you drink, Art?" asked Guin, eyeing him.

Art started to count on his fingers. "I don't know, maybe three?"

"Three what, Art?" said Guin, losing patience.

"Captiva Coolers," said Art, smiling. "You should try one," he said, poking her in the chest. "It would loosen you up."

"I'm loose enough, thank you," said Guin.

Art leaned down and whispered in her ear. "I could loosen you up."

"You're drunk, Art," said Guin, gently pushing him away.

"Am not," said Art, straightening up, then wobbling a bit.

Guin sighed. "Go to your room, Art. I'll talk with you in the morning."

"Will you come give me a kiss goodnight?" he said, smiling at her.

Despite herself, Guin laughed. When he was tipsy like this, he looked like a naughty little boy.

"Maybe," said Guin. "But only if you are a good boy and go straight to bed."

Art stood tall and saluted her. "Yes, ma'am!" Then he turned around and marched back to the guest room.

Guin watched him, shaking her head. She had planned on asking him about Rick's allergy and the bracelet, and if he had asked Joe and Murph and Alan about those suspicious deals. But it would have to wait until tomorrow. She just hoped Art would be up early as she had to leave a little after seven-thirty to pick up Emily.

A few minutes later, she heard Art calling for her.

"I'm in bed! Come tuck me in!"

Guin debated whether she should go down the hall, but she caved and made her way to the guest room. The door was ajar. She opened it and walked in, to find Art in the twin bed, looking way too big for it, the comforter pulled up to his chin.

"You going to give me a kiss goodnight?" said Art, looking like a little boy.

Guin stood in the doorway, her arms crossed over her chest.

"Please?"

Guin sighed. "Fine."

She went over to the bed and leaned down to give Art a quick kiss on the forehead. But as she did, his hands shot out from under the comforter and he pulled her down to him, his lips finding hers. Guin was too stunned at first to pull away, then she felt herself giving in. Part of the reason she had fallen for Art was that he was a good kisser. And that apparently hadn't changed. It took every ounce of willpower to pull away, but she did, eventually, glaring down at Art as she stepped away from the bed.

"Admit it, you enjoyed that," said Art, resting his hands behind his head and giving her a mischievous grin.

"Goodnight Art," Guin replied, moving toward the door.

"There's more where that came from!" he called as Guin was about to leave. "My door is always open!"

Guin ignored him and immediately closed the door, with a loud slam. She then marched back to her room, threw out the cats, and locked her door.

CHAPTER 28

The next morning Guin got up at six-thirty. She had had a fitful night's sleep, worried that Art would be banging on her door in the middle of the night. But he hadn't. She turned on her phone, then went into the bathroom. When she was done, she went into her closet to get dressed.

She emerged from the bedroom a few minutes later, expecting to find the cats outside her door, but they were not there. Odd, thought Guin. She walked into the living room. No sign of Art or the cats. She walked into the kitchen. Again, no sign of Art or the cats. Guin quietly walked to the guest room. The door was ajar. She peeked in and had to cover her mouth, for fear of laughing out loud. There, curled up on one of the twin beds, was Art, with Flora and Fauna curled up next to him. Guin smiled and quietly walked back into the kitchen. A moment later, both cats came trotting in.

"You two have a good night?" she asked them.

Neither replied, just looked up at her.

Guin went into the pantry and grabbed the bag of cat food. She poured some into each of the cat bowls and then rinsed out and refilled their water bowl.

As the cats nibbled on their dry food, Guin made a big pot of coffee. Art would need it. She then went back into the bedroom to grab her phone while the coffee maker did its thing. She had a few new messages since the night before, but nothing she needed to respond to right away. She checked Facebook and Instagram, liking various posts. Finally, the coffee was ready. She grabbed a mug, poured some coffee into it, and took a sip, closing her eyes. She loved the smell of freshly brewed coffee. She opened them to find Flora looking up at her.

"What?" said Guin, looking down at the cat.

Flora pawed her leg.

"You need some loving, Flora?" Guin asked, bending down.

Flora again tapped Guin's leg with her paw.

Guin stroked the pretty, multicolored cat, scratching her head and back, which elicited a loud purr. Then Flora flopped down on the floor.

"Silly old thing," said Guin, smiling and scratching Flora some more.

Just then Guin's phone started buzzing. It was a text from Shelly.

"You shelling this morning?"

"I'm taking my friend Emily to Lighthouse Beach," Guin replied.

"Okay if I meet you there?" Shelly typed back.

Guin thought about it for a few seconds. "Sure, why not?" she replied. "I'm picking up Emily at the San Ybel Resort & Spa at 8. Should be at Lighthouse by 8:15."

"I'll look for you on the beach," wrote Shelly.

"OK," replied Guin. "C u there."

Guin hoped it would be okay with Emily that Shelly tagged along. She had a few more minutes before she had to head out, so she opened the *New York Times* on her browser and quickly scanned the day's headlines as she drank her coffee. Before she knew it, it was seven-thirty. She put down her phone and went to brush her teeth.

As she went to grab her keys and her bag a few minutes later, she thought about waking Art before she left. But she decided it was probably best not to disturb him. Instead, she left him a note by the coffee maker, letting him know that she was spending the morning with Emily but would check in with him later. She then told the cats to be good and left.

Emily was standing in front of the hotel when Guin pulled up in her Mini. Guin waved to her and got out.

"Nice wheels!" said Emily.

Guin smiled. "Thanks."

She regarded Emily, who was wearing a maxi sundress.

Emily saw her looking at her outfit and looked down.

"I know it's not the most practical thing for going to the beach, but I have barely any clothes left, and I didn't pack shorts and t-shirts since Alan didn't want me to look like, and I quote, 'a beach bum.'"

She held up two fingers, making air quotes as she said it, and both she and Guin laughed.

"Do you maybe have a ponytail holder or rubber band you could use to hold the dress above your knees while we're on the beach?" asked Guin. "I'd hate for it to get wet or sandy."

"I'm sure I do, somewhere," said Emily, rooting around in her bag. "If not, I'll just knot it, no big deal."

"Let's go then," said Guin.

They got into the Mini and drove off.

"So, how are you feeling? Alan said you had a really bad headache."

Emily looked out the window. "Yeah."

Guin waited for her to elaborate. Finally, Emily spoke again.

"I'm not a big fan of these sales conferences."

"But at least it's in a nice place. And I hear the San Ybel Resort & Spa is lovely."

"Sanibel's okay," said Emily. "No disrespect," she quickly added, looking at Guin.

"None taken," said Guin, smiling over at her.

Emily turned back to the window.

"I'm just tired of these sales conferences and the constant sales talk," she said a few seconds later. "Alan has been so on edge lately. All he talks about is work. I thought maybe coming down here, he'd relax a little, but things have just gotten worse. I've barely seen him, and when I have, he's been angry about something or distracted. I finally had it the other night, so I told him I had a headache."

"So you didn't have a headache?"

"Well, sort of. All these guys discussing deals hurts my head. And I dreaded the thought of having to smile and make nice to all those sales guys and their significant others for three hours."

Guin smiled at her. "I know exactly what you mean. I still can't believe I let Art convince me to go."

"So, you two getting back together?" asked Emily, looking over at Guin.

"Hell no!" said Guin.

Emily laughed.

"Speaking of the sales conference," said Guin, casting a quick glance at Emily (and trying to divert the discussion away from her and Art), "has Alan said anything about Rick?"

Guin waited for Emily to reply, but she did not.

"Emily?" asked Guin. She again quickly looked over at Emily, who was looking out the window.

"Sorry," said Emily, a minute later. "I just…"

"Are you okay?" asked Guin.

"To be honest, Guin? No. This whole Rick business…"
She trailed off.

"Did you know Rick well?"

"I knew him… of course," said Emily. "Alan had him over for dinner a few times. But I didn't know him personally," she made a point of adding.

Guin wanted to ask her again if Alan had mentioned anything about Rick, but they had arrived at Lighthouse Beach. Guin parked the car.

"You ready to do some shelling?" Guin asked.

"As ready as I'll ever be," said Emily.

"Oh, by the way, I hope it's okay—my friend, Shelly, may be joining us," Guin said as she grabbed her shelling gear out of the back seat. "You'll like her. She's very friendly and makes gorgeous shell jewelry and things."

"I look forward to meeting her," said Emily. "As long as she doesn't want to discuss sales quotas, I'm good."

Guin laughed. "Come on, let's hit the beach."

"Yoohoo! Over here!" called Shelly, spying Guin and Emily making their way onto the beach.

Guin waved back. "That would be Shelly," she said to Emily.

"So I gathered," said Emily, smiling. (Everyone who met Shelly couldn't help but smile.)

Guin made the introductions and the three of them spent the next two hours looking for shells along the beach. Emily was unsure about what was considered a "good" shell, but Shelly was more than happy to explain, identifying every shell they found.

"You sure know a lot about shells, Shelly," said Emily, clearly impressed (and a bit overwhelmed—Shelly had that effect on people).

"She does indeed," said Guin. "And you should see her shell jewelry."

"I'd love to," said Emily.

"I keep some in my car," said Shelly. "I can show you when we're done."

"Great," said Emily, though Guin wasn't sure if Emily was really interested or just being polite.

"Well, we should get going," said Guin. "But let's show Emily the lighthouse and the fishing pier before we go."

"Sounds like a plan," said Shelly.

The three of them made their way over to the Sanibel lighthouse, which Shelly explained dated back to 1884.

"It was one of the first lighthouses on the gulf coast of Florida," she announced, "and is listed in the National Register of Historic Places."

"Very impressive," said Emily, though Guin, having seen many New England lighthouses, as well as some in the Carolinas, didn't think the Sanibel Island Light, as it was officially called, was that impressive. But she didn't say anything.

The three of them then walked over to the fishing pier and stood at the end, admiring the view of Fort Myers Beach and the Causeway.

"I could stand here all day," said Shelly.

"Oh look, dolphins!" said Guin, pointing.

Shelly and Emily immediately looked where Guin was pointing.

"I love dolphins," said Emily, watching the pod go by.

"Me too," said Guin.

They stayed on the pier a few more minutes, then headed back to the parking lot.

"My car's over here," said Shelly, pointing to a spot across the lot.

Guin and Emily exchanged looks, then followed Shelly to her car.

"Let me just pop the trunk and—voila!"

Inside her trunk was a traveling jewelry case, which she opened to reveal several pieces of jewelry. Guin and Emily moved in take a closer look.

"Ooh, I love this," said Emily, holding up an orange scallop shell necklace.

"It would look great on you, especially with your coloring," said Shelly, beaming.

Emily had olive skin and glossy brown hair, and the bright orange did look good on her.

"How much is it?" she asked.

"For you? Only twenty-five dollars," said Shelly.

"Are you sure?" asked Emily.

"Positive," said Shelly.

"Great! I'll take it. No need to wrap it," she said, smiling. "I'll just wear it."

She put on the necklace.

"What do you think, ladies?"

"Like it was made for you!" said Shelly.

"It's lovely," said Guin.

Emily handed Shelly twenty-five dollars.

"Thanks," said Shelly, pocketing the money. "And what about you, Guin?"

Guin looked through the small pile of jewelry Shelly had on display. Many of the pieces were quite nice, but she wasn't in the mood to go jewelry shopping.

"Not today, Shelly."

"Hold on a sec," said Shelly.

She went around to the passenger side of the car and reached into the glove compartment. Then she walked back to the back of the car.

"Ta da!" she said, unfurling a heart pendant made from a junonia shell, with some pretty beads strung on either side.

"It's lovely!" said Guin.

"I thought you would like it," said Shelly.

Shelly handed it to Guin, who put it on.

"What do you think?" she said, turning to Emily.

"Perfect!" said Shelly.

Emily smiled. "It looks good on you, Guin."

"How much?" asked Guin.

"Twenty-five," said Shelly, "but only because you're one of my very best friends," she added, smiling.

"Sold," said Guin. She reached into her bag and pulled out her wallet, handing Shelly twenty-five dollars. "Now, if you will excuse us, I want to show Emily the rest of the island."

"Run along," said Shelly. "My work here is done."

"Nice to meet you," said Emily, extending her hand.

Shelly gave it a vigorous shake. "Nice to meet you, too. Don't let Guin bore you to tears," she said, winking at Guin.

Guin made a face.

"Bye, Shell. I'll catch up with you later."

She gave Shelly a quick peck on the cheek, then she and Emily headed across the parking lot to Guin's car.

Guin spent the rest of the morning driving Emily around Sanibel, showing her the library, the historic village, and the J.N. "Ding" Darling National Wildlife Refuge. Then they headed toward Captiva.

"I thought we could go and have lunch up on Captiva," said Guin. "There's the Bubble Room, Doc Ford's, the Mucky Duck…"

"Not Doc Ford's," said Emily.

"Alan drag you there already?" said Guin. "I know it's very popular with the guys."

She glanced over at Emily, who looked distracted again.

"I'd just rather not go there, if that's all right with you," said Emily, looking out the window.

"Sure," said Guin. "No problem. Let's go to the Mucky Duck. I haven't been there in ages, and it's right on the beach."

"Sounds great," said Emily, still looking out the window. "Let's go."

CHAPTER 29

Guin drove up to the Mucky Duck, near the end of Captiva. As it was off season, she and Emily were able to get a table near the window, inside. During peak season, there would be a long wait to get a table, Guin explained. They looked at their menus and ordered a few minutes later.

"So, has Alan said anything about Rick?" Guin asked Emily again, casually, as they were sipping their Arnold Palmers. She hoped that this time Emily would answer the question.

A range of emotions crossed Emily's face.

"No," said Emily, not looking at Guin, a faraway look in her eyes.

"Really?" said Guin, keeping her eyes on Emily. "It's all Art can talk about."

Emily turned to face Guin.

"Art hated Rick."

Guin was surprised by the vehemence in Emily's tone.

"I don't know if he hated him," said Guin, carefully. "They were competing for the same promotion, so there was some rivalry. But that's pretty typical, especially for sales guys. And I understand a lot of the guys weren't too fond of Rick."

"That's because they didn't understand him," said Emily.

Guin raised an eyebrow. Was Emily defending Rick?

True, Guin barely knew the guy, and had only heard one side of the argument against Rick, Art's side. But for someone who supposedly barely knew Rick, Emily seemed rather passionate about defending him.

"Oh?" said Guin, sipping her drink.

"Rick grew up really poor. He had to work hard for everything he had. He was a really good salesman, and he hated how cavalier some of the other sales guys were. I think Rick's work ethic just rubbed some people the wrong way."

I'll say, thought Guin. Again, for someone who barely knew the guy, Emily seemed to know a fair amount about Rick.

"Did you know that Rick was doing deals in other guys' territories?" Guin asked.

"I told you, I tuned out sales talk," said Emily.

Guin persevered.

"Word has it Rick was about to close a big deal here in Southwest Florida and another one in Illinois."

"So?" said Emily.

"Well, as you probably know, salespeople have set territories, and you're not supposed to be doing deals, or trying to do deals, on another guy's turf," explained Guin. "I'm surprised Alan didn't mention it."

"He may have," said Emily, looking out the window again. "Like I said, I don't really pay attention when he starts discussing sales stuff."

Guin regarded Emily, who seemed preoccupied.

"So, Alan never said anything about Rick's extracurricular activities?" Guin asked.

Emily's head whipped around. She opened her mouth to say something but closed it as the server arrived with their food.

"Here you go, ladies," he said. "Enjoy!"

Guin thanked him, then dug in. Emily didn't touch her food.

Guin took a few bites, then put down her veggie burger. "Hey, Em, didn't mean to pry. It's just…"

She wasn't sure what to say.

Emily turned to her and gave her a wan smile.

"You haven't really," she said. "I know you're just trying to help out Art, which is very noble of you, considering. I'm not sure I'd do the same for Alan."

She took a look at her food and sighed.

"Things have been kind of tense lately, and this whole thing with Rick has Alan very on edge. Frankly, I've been trying to avoid the subject."

"I understand," said Guin. "But if you remember something, anything, Alan may have said that you think might be useful, would you let me know?"

"Sure," said Emily, dipping a fork into her salad.

Though there was something about her body language that made Guin doubt she would.

They ate the rest of their food in near silence. When they were done, the server came to clear their plates and asked if they wanted anything else. Guin looked at Emily, who shook her head.

"Just the check, please," said Guin.

The server produced the check from his apron.

"Here you go, ladies."

Guin made to grab for it, but Emily put her hand over it first.

"My treat—or, rather, the company's," she said with a smile.

"Well, in that case…" said Guin, also smiling.

Emily took out her credit card and handed it to the server when he returned. A few minutes later, they were heading back to the San Ybel Resort & Spa in Guin's Mini.

Guin said goodbye to Emily at the resort and told her to text anytime. Then she pulled the car over and sent a quick text to Art.

"Headed home. You need me to pick up anything?" she wrote.

"Nope. All good," he texted back a few seconds later.

"OK. C u soon then," she typed.

She put the Mini into drive and headed back to the condo.

When she got there, she found Art sitting at the dining table in front of his computer, Fauna in his lap. Guin smiled.

"Working on something important?"

"Always," said Art, looking up at her and smiling. "Hey, I'm sorry about last night. I guess I had too much to drink."

"You guess?" said Guin, giving him a skeptical look.

"Okay, I was drunk and acted stupid. Forgive me?" he said, doing his best altar boy impression.

Guin snorted. "So did you know that Rick was allergic to ibuprofen?"

"No, or else I forgot. Why?"

"Apparently, that's what killed him, or contributed to his death. He supposedly wore one of those allergy alert bracelets, but he didn't have it on when they found his body."

Art looked thoughtful. "I vaguely remember him wearing a bracelet, but I didn't pay much attention. And I honestly don't recall him mentioning an ibuprofen allergy."

"Well, the killer must have known, or it's a very strange coincidence," said Guin. "You don't happen to recall if Rick was wearing his bracelet when you found him in the cabana?"

"Like I said, it was dark, and I only had the lights on for a few minutes. And I was so annoyed when he slumped over, I just left. I don't even recall what color shirt he was wearing."

Guin regarded Art's face, to see if he was lying. Usually, she could tell, or she used to be able to, until the affair. But if she had to bet on whether Art was telling the truth right now, she'd say he was.

"Do you think other people knew about Rick's allergy?"

"Probably," said Art. "I tried to avoid Rick as much as possible, and I didn't actually see him a whole lot. But anyone who spent time with him or knew him well probably did."

"What about Murph and Joe?"

"What about them?" asked Art.

"Do you think they knew?"

Art thought for a few seconds.

"It's possible. Why?"

"Well, Rick was on the verge of closing a big deal in Joe's territory and one in Murph's. Maybe one of them found out about it and decided to slip him some ibuprofen before the deal closed, to get him out of the way."

"Awfully macabre of you, Guin. Been watching reruns of *Murder, She Wrote* again?" Art said.

"Ha ha," she replied. "And what is wrong with watching *Murder, She Wrote*?"

Art held his hands up. "Nothing."

"Well, *someone* slipped Rick some ibuprofen, enough to kill him, and I'd like to speak with Joe and Murph to find out what they know."

"Fine. But they'll probably just laugh. Should I invite them over here for a drink, or should we do it on neutral territory?"

"Why don't you suggest we meet up for a drink? We can meet them over at the resort or else at the Sanibel Grill or Doc Ford's.

"Okay, I'll ask them. So how was your morning with Emily?"

"Interesting," said Guin.

"Oh?" said Art, looking intrigued.

"She was very defensive when I brought up Rick," said Guin.

Art gave her a questioning look.

"She went on about how Rick was misunderstood, that the guys didn't appreciate his work ethic."

Art raised an eyebrow.

"I know," said Guin. "Like I said, it was odd. When I asked her if Alan had said anything about Rick she clammed up, said she didn't pay attention when he talked about sales stuff."

"Though she wouldn't be the only wife to tune out her husband when he talked about work," he said, looking directly at Guin.

Guin made a face. "I listened to you talk about work plenty," she retorted.

Art looked skeptical.

"Whatever," said Guin.

Just then her phone started buzzing. She took out it out and saw she had a reminder to meet Craig over at the Education Center at Ding Darling.

"I have to go meet up with Craig," she announced.

"Have fun!" said Art, turning back to his laptop.

"I'll be back before dinner," said Guin.

Art held up a hand, in a sort of wave goodbye.

"And remember to ping Joe and Murph and ask them about getting together for drinks!" she called as she walked to the front door.

Art did not respond.

Guin sighed and left. She would follow up with him later.

CHAPTER 30

Guin parked at the Ding Darling Education Center and went to look for Craig. She found him standing at the front desk, chatting with a man in his early seventies who looked like he was about to go on safari. Craig spied Guin and smiled.

"Guin, this is my friend Hank."

"A pleasure to meet you, Hank," said Guin, extending her hand. "Thank you for helping us out."

"Always happy to help Craig here," said Hank, smiling and shaking her hand.

"You been working here long?" asked Guin, looking around.

"Just since dinosaurs roamed the earth," joked Hank.

"The place couldn't run without him," said Craig.

"Well, I don't know about that," said Hank, scratching his head.

"I love the refuge," said Guin. "I drive through it all the time. Though, I confess, I don't often visit the Education Center," she said, looking around.

"Well, come back another time, and I'll give you a personal tour," said Hank.

"Watch out, I'll take you up on it," said Guin, smiling.

"So Hank here has something to show us," said Craig, discreetly.

The two men eyed each other.

"Come with me," said Hank.

He led them out of the Education Center and down the stairs to an area underneath the Education Center that contained offices, and into a room that contained video equipment and computers.

"Have a seat," he said, indicating a couple of chairs placed in front of a computer. "I made a little video of the period Craig here requested, or, technically, one of the gals who work here did. I think you'll find it interesting."

Guin and Craig exchanged looks.

"Here, let me cue it up for you," said Hank, reaching over and waking up the computer.

He typed in a password and then opened a file he had on the desktop.

"Just hit play when you're ready," he said, taking a step back.

Guin and Craig looked at each other.

"You want to do the honors?" asked Craig.

Guin hit play, and they sat back and watched.

The quality wasn't great, but they could make out Big Ben's boat coming into view, with six men aboard. They watched as the boat anchored and then a few seconds later (with editing), Alan and Murph trying to reel in their tarpon.

"Here's the interesting part," said Hank, leaning over and pointing at the screen.

Craig and Guin watched as one of the men on the right or starboard side of the boat, who was standing apart from most of the other men, grabbed the man closest to him. It looked like they were arguing. Then a few seconds later (with editing), the man who had been grabbed jerked himself free and moved to the left, or port, side of the boat, where two of the other men were trying to reel in something. Then, as everyone else was watching the jumping fish, the man who had grabbed the other man picked up something (a knife?)

and seemed to cut himself. Then he put the object back and, when no one was looking, slipped over the side of the boat and swam toward the shore.

"Huh," said Guin, still staring at the monitor.

Craig made a face.

"You can't see anyone's face or what they're wearing," he said, crossing his arms on his chest.

"Let's take another look," said Guin.

She pressed the replay button. While the footage was grainy, you could see a man go over the side of the boat and make his way toward the shore, where there was a wooded area.

Guin sat back, while Craig stared at the monitor.

"That what you were looking for?" asked Hank.

"Is there any way we could get that footage blown up, to make sure that was Rick?" asked Guin.

"I can ask Peta. She's our resident video expert," said Hank.

"That would be great," said Guin.

"You okay if we watch one more time, Hank?" asked Craig.

"Be my guest," said Hank.

Guin hit replay again, and they watched the video one more time.

"Could that be a knife that the man, let's assume it was Rick, picked up and deliberately cut himself with before going overboard?"

"It could be," said Craig. He turned to Hank. "Let me know when you or Peta can get me a blow-up of that footage."

"Will do," said Hank.

"Have the cops seen this?"

"I sent them a copy this morning," said Hank.

"Time for me to have another chat with the detective,"

said Guin, pushing her chair away from the computer.

"Just don't get on his bad side," said Craig.

"Does he have a good one?" asked Guin, a grin on her face.

"Now, now," said Craig. "Give the man a break. He's just doing his job."

"Yeah, yeah, yeah," said Guin. "And I'm just doing mine."

Guin got up and went over to Hank.

"Hank, thank you," she said, extending her hand, which Hank clasped.

"Always happy to help a pretty lady," said Hank, smiling at her.

Guin smiled back at him.

"Craig, I'll catch up with you later?"

"Sure thing," said Craig.

Guin then said her goodbyes and headed back to her car.

Guin drove back along Wildlife Drive, though she was too preoccupied to pay much attention to the birds. She just needed the time (the speed limit was 15 mph) to organize her thoughts. Why did Rick go over the side of the boat, she wondered. And where did he go? And did he intentionally cut himself? That would explain the blood on the knife.

She continued to mull over the video, and what she knew via Art as she made her way back to the condo.

"Art?" she called as she walked in the door.

"In here," Art called from the dining room.

"Did you get up at all?" asked Guin, looking down at him, Fauna again (or still) in his lap.

"Hmm?" mumbled Art, staring at his monitor.

"Can you take a minute and look at me?" asked Guin, folding her arms across her chest.

Art's inattention, or rather laser focus on work and inattention to her, was one of the main things that had led to the divorce.

Art turned and looked at Guin. Fauna did, too.

"Yes?"

"I just saw the footage from the camera down at the end of Wulfert Keys Trail, from when Rick went missing."

"And?"

"And," said Guin, "it's pretty grainy, but it clearly shows someone going over the side of the boat and heading to shore."

Art ran a hand through his hair. "Rick?"

"Unless someone else had a boat anchored over there the same time you did. Like I said, the footage was pretty grainy. Though we asked Hank, that's Craig's contact, if they could blow up some of the images."

"And it looked as though Rick may have cut himself before he went overboard."

"That would explain the blood on the knife," said Art.

"That's what I thought, too," said Guin. "But why do it? Why cut himself and then go overboard and disappear?"

"To pin it on me, and make me look like a deranged lunatic."

Guin looked at Art, wondering if maybe he was being paranoid.

"Rick would do anything to make me look bad in front of Alan. I bet he deliberately picked a fight with me, then made it look as though I was pissed and stuck him with a knife and threw him overboard."

"Doesn't that strike you as a bit extreme?" asked Guin. "And then why disappear? Why not pop out of the water and blame you in front of all the guys?"

Art thought about that for a few seconds.

"Well, the guys were pretty preoccupied with the tarpon,

so they may not have even noticed. And maybe he had some reason to disappear for a day or two."

"Such as?" asked Guin.

"I don't know," said Art, with a sigh.

Suddenly a thought occurred to her.

"What?" said Art. "I know that look, Guinivere Jones. You've thought of something. What is it?"

Guin had thought of something, but she wasn't yet ready to share it with Art. First, she wanted to speak with someone, and the detective.

"Nothing," Guin lied. "So did you speak with Joe and Murph? We going to meet up for drinks and a little chat?"

Art grinned up at her. "I didn't forget. We're to meet them over at the Sanibel Grill at six."

"Tonight?" asked Guin. She grabbed her phone and looked at it. "That's in just over an hour!"

"There a problem?" asked Art, still smiling. "You said ASAP."

Guin made a face. "No problem. It just would have been nice to have had some notice. You could have texted me."

"I was busy," said Art. "And I'm telling you now."

"Thanks," said Guin. "In that case, let me go freshen up," she said.

"You look fine to me," said Art, who had turned his attention back to his computer.

Uh-huh, thought Guin. She stood there for a few seconds, looking at Art, then sighed and went into the bedroom. Flora was asleep on the bed. She looked down at the cat, napping peacefully, and smiled.

"Ah, to be a cat," she said.

She went into the bathroom to freshen up. Then she slipped on a pair of form fitting jeans and a white lacy top. She examined herself in the mirror. Not bad, she thought. She picked up her phone and sent a text to the detective, asking if he could spare her a few minutes the next morning. Then she walked back into the living room.

The bar at the Sanibel Grill was crowded, but they were able to find a table. Guin and Art were the first ones there, but Joe and Murph arrived soon after.

"Thanks for meeting me," Guin said to the two men.

"No problem," said Joe, sitting down.

"Yeah, he's happy to get away from that hotel," added Murph, putting an arm around Joe.

"I thought the San Ybel looked very nice," said Guin.

"Oh, it is," said Joe. "I would just rather be back home."

"I'm sure you would," said Guin.

"So, Art said you had some questions?" said Murph.

"I do," said Guin.

"How about we get a round of beers first?" suggested Art.

"Sounds good to me!" said Murph.

"Fine," said Guin.

Art went over to the bar to order beers for the table. A few minutes later he returned with four mugs. They all took a couple of sips.

"So, what did you want to ask us?" asked Joe, putting down his beer.

May as well cut to the chase, thought Guin.

"Did you know that Rick was working on big deals in your territories?" said Guin, looking from Joe to Murph.

Murph made a face. "Yeah. I suspected something was up when one of my hot leads went cold a few months ago, but I didn't know the reason was Rick until a few days ago, when Alan took me aside and asked me to step in."

"How did Rick even find out about it?" asked Guin.

"I told him," said Murph, staring down at his beer, "like an idiot."

"When?" asked Guin.

"Four, maybe five months ago. He messaged me that he was down here and asked if we could get together. I said 'sure, why not?'"

"And you told him about it then?"

"Yeah, over beer. I didn't think anything of it. You know how guys get," said Murph, looking over at Joe and Art, who nodded.

Guin looked confused.

"You know, you have a few drinks, you start talking about deals you're working on, which client's a pain in the ass…. That kind of thing," explained Murph.

"Ah," said Guin.

"Didn't occur to me that Rick would go after that deal," said Murph, again looking down into his beer.

"I don't know about you all, but I could use another beer," said Art.

Joe and Murph agreed.

"I'm good," said Guin, who had barely drunk hers.

"Be right back," said Art, going over to the bar to get more beer.

"And what about you, Joe?" asked Guin, eyeing the younger man.

Joe sighed. "My story's actually a lot like Murph's. I got a call from Rick a little while back. He said he was in town visiting relatives and could we go out for a drink? I didn't know him very well, but I figured it would be rude to say no. So we got together at a bar near my place. Rick was very good natured and insisted on buying the beer, even though I told him I should be paying as he was visiting."

Joe took a sip of his beer, then continued.

"Like Murph, I probably had a little too much to drink and maybe wanted to impress him a bit. So I told him about a couple of big deals I was working on, how I was counting on them to help pay for my honeymoon. What a chump I was."

He let out a hoarse laugh, and Murph patted him on the back.

"Go on," said Guin, trying to sound sympathetic.

"Rick was very encouraging. Asked me a whole bunch of questions about the deals. I had been having issues with one of them. This one guy was giving me a hard time about pricing. I told Rick about it, and he asked me the guy's name. And like an idiot, I gave it to him."

Joe looked down into his beer.

"Sorry, kid," said Art, giving him a sympathetic look. "No way you could have known."

"I was going to use the money from that deal to help pay for our honeymoon," Joe repeated. "I had it all planned out. I was going to pop the question to Josie, my girl, at this party her family holds over July Fourth, then take her to Paris over Christmas, when we both had time off."

"Sounds very romantic," said Guin.

"I know, right?" said Joe. He took a swig of his beer. "But I nearly lost that deal because of Rick."

"Nearly?" asked Guin, confused. "You mean he didn't get the deal after all?"

"Oh, he got the deal," said Joe. "But with his no longer being able to close it, Alan asked me to step in. It should have been my deal anyway," said Joe, making a face.

"So you'll get the credit and the commission?" asked Guin.

"Yeah," said Joe. "Funny, isn't it?"

"Same for you, Murph?" asked Guin, looking over at him.

"Yeah, I assume so," said Murph. "Deal should have been mine anyway."

The four of them sat in silence for several minutes.

"I don't know about the rest of you," Guin said, breaking the silence, but I could use some food.

"I recommend the peel 'n' eat shrimp," said Murph.

"Fine by me," said Art. "That work for you, Guin?"

"Fine by me," said Guin.

Art signaled for a server, who came over a minute later, and they gave him their order.

"And an order of Buffalo wings," added Murph.

"Anything else?" asked the server.

Art looked around the table. "Nope. We're good."

"Okay then," said the server. "That'll be an order of peel 'n' eat shrimp and some Buffalo wings."

"That'll do it," said Art.

"And some water, please!" said Guin.

"I'll send some right over," said the server.

"So," said Guin, looking from Murph to Joe, "you didn't find out about Rick taking your deals until the conference?"

They exchanged a brief look. "No," they said in unison. Though something about their expressions made Guin not quite believe them.

Guin turned to Art. "Surely Alan must have known about the deals. Why didn't he say or do something? I thought poaching was a big no-no."

"I've been trying to work that out myself," said Art. "But when I tried to bring it up with Alan, he changed the subject."

"Yeah, I asked him about it too," said Murph. "He told me that Rick had told him the deal had been dead, that I hadn't been able to close it—which was a lie, by the way—and it was only because of him that it had gone through."

"And you, Joe?"

"Same story."

"Mr. Tomlinson seems like quite the sweet talker," said Guin.

"Oh yeah," said Murph. "He had more blarney in him that I do," he added, taking another swig of his beer.

The server returned with the appetizers and placed them on the table.

"Thanks," said Guin. "Oh, and can we get some extra plates, please?"

"Be right back!" said the server.

"Go ahead and have a shrimp," Art said to Guin.

"I'll wait for the plates," said Guin.

"Well, I'm hungry," said Murph, grabbing a shrimp.

Guin smiled.

A minute later the server returned with four plates and a pitcher of water.

"Thanks," said Guin.

The four of them dug into the food and talk of Rick ceased. When they were done, though, Guin had more questions.

"So you two had no idea, before the conference, about Rick stealing those deals?"

"Nope," said Murph, polishing off the last chicken wing.

"So when exactly did you find out?"

"I can't remember the exact moment," said Joe, somewhat evasively.

"Murph?"

Guin regarded Murph, who was looking down into his almost empty beer mug.

"I don't recall."

"Were you angry when you found out?" Guin asked the two of them.

"Of course I was angry," said Murph. "Wouldn't you be if you found out someone stole your million-dollar deal?"

Guin whistled.

"How much was your deal worth, Joe?" Guin asked.

Joe was quiet.

"Go ahead, Joe, tell her," said Art.

"Over a million," said Joe, not looking at Guin.

"And now that Rick's dead, you'll both get the credit?" she asked.

"I suppose so," said Joe.

"I'm definitely taking credit," said Murph. "If it hadn't been for me, there would be no deal."

"And you had no idea about Rick before Alan informed you?"

Again, Joe and Murph exchanged a glance.

"I had my suspicions," said Murph, reluctantly.

"Me too," said Joe.

Art looked at Guin, who was looking at Joe and Murph. He knew where this was going.

"Hey, if you think we had anything to do with Rick's death, you're dead wrong!" said Murph, his face turning a bright red.

"I'm not saying anything," said Guin. "I'm just trying to ferret out the facts."

Just then the server returned, asking if they wanted anything else. "Maybe a piece of key lime pie?"

He glanced around the table, but the mood had become sullen.

"No thanks," said Joe. "I should get back to the hotel. I have some calls to make."

"Me too," said Murph.

"Just the check," said Art.

The server departed.

"We still on for golf tomorrow?" Art asked Joe and Murph, trying to lighten the mood.

"Sure," said Murph.

"Pick me up at nine?"

Murph nodded.

"Alan still playing with us?"

"As far as I know," said Murph.

"Good," said Art. "I have a few questions to ask him."

CHAPTER 31

The next morning Guin got up early, determined to go for a walk on the beach and hopefully add a few more shells to her collection. She hurriedly got dressed and pulled her hair into a ponytail. Then she walked into the kitchen, not stopping to fix herself some coffee. She just gave the cats some food and fresh water, poured herself half a glass of water, which she swiftly drank, and left a note for Art letting him know she'd be back by nine. Then she grabbed her keys and her beach bag and left.

Outside the front door she texted her friend Lenny, letting him know she was headed over to Blind Pass beach. It was before seven, but she knew Lenny was an early riser. She then ran down the stairs, opened the garage, and hopped into her Mini.

It was a beautiful morning—perfect for a beach walk. It had rained overnight, and the water was a little choppy, with the wind coming from the Northwest, so Guin hoped there would be lots of shells. She quickly checked her phone, to see if there was a text from Lenny, but there wasn't. So she placed her phone in her pocket and started walking eastward.

She walked along the shoreline, looking down to see what the current had washed up. She saw Florida fighting conchs and cockles and some lightning whelks, all of which she had plenty of, as well as piles of coquinas, arks, clams, and pen shells, which also did not interest her. She spied a rather large lettered olive, its glossy brown shell making it stand out in the water. She used her Sand Dipper to scoop it up and put it in her shelling bag.

As she walked farther east, she picked through piles of shells, finding apple and lace murexes, as well as some banded tulips and bright orange scallops.

There were very few people on the beach and Guin loved the quiet. She saw some brown pelicans diving for fish and stopped to watch them. She closed her eyes and stretched her arms up to the sky, feeling the sun's first rays wash over her. There was no place on earth she'd rather be at that moment.

Suddenly she felt her phone vibrating in her pocket. She pulled it out and saw she had a text message. It was from Lenny.

"Thanks for the invite. Can't make it this morning."

While Guin was disappointed not to see her friend, she was fine being alone on the beach.

"No worries," she wrote him back. "Another time."

She continued walking, gazing down at the sand or into the water in search of shells. She reached the end of the beach, where a bunch of trees and the tide made it difficult to continue. She stared out at the horizon. A flock of birds, probably gulls or brown pelicans, soared overhead in the distance. She watched as they flew toward Captiva. She smiled, then headed that way herself, back to her car.

As she meandered back down the beach, she pulled out her phone to check the time. It was a little before eight. Still no word from the detective. So she sent him a text.

"Any update?" she asked. "Will swing by later this a.m."

She smiled as she sent it. If the mountain won't come to Mohammed, she thought, then Mohammed will go to the mountain. She put her phone back in her pocket and continued walking.

It was nearly eight-thirty when she got off the beach, and she was starting to get hungry. Instead of driving straight home, she stopped in at the Sunset Grill and picked up a couple of muffins. Then she drove back to the condo.

She walked into the kitchen to find coffee in the coffee maker and a note from Art.

"Gone running. Be back later."

It was dated "7:55 a.m." Knowing Art, he'd run at least a few miles, maybe more. But he was pretty fast, so he'd probably be back soon.

She poured herself a cup of coffee and placed one of the muffins on a plate, leaving the other muffin in the bag next to the coffee maker. As she was about to head to the dining area, she heard the front door, and a few seconds later a very sweaty Art made his way into the kitchen.

"Good morning," Guin said. "How many miles did you run?"

"I'm not sure, maybe five?"

"Don't you have a golf game this morning?"

"I do," said Art, "and if I don't get into the shower, I'm going to be late."

"I got you a muffin," said Guin, looking over at the counter.

"Thanks," said Art. "I'll eat it in the car. Right now I've got to get ready."

"Don't let me stop you," said Guin.

Art headed toward the guest room, then stopped.

"If the guys get here before I'm ready, can you let them know I'll be down in a few? I told them to buzz the intercom when they got here, if they didn't see me."

"No problem," said Guin. "Now go!"

"Okay, okay," he said. "If I'm a few minutes late, no big deal."

Guin watched as he headed off to the guest room, staring, despite herself, at his lean, muscular physique. She sighed.

A little while later Art emerged, freshly showered and shaved, in his golf togs.

"I texted Murph and told him I might be a few minutes late. Gotta roll."

Guin looked him over.

"You are *not* going to wear those pants, are you?"

Art looked down at his pants, which were embroidered with sea turtles.

"What's wrong with them?"

"There are sea turtles on those pants."

"I know," said Art, smiling. "I think they're rather cute, don't you?"

"Adorable," said Guin. "But they don't belong on pants. Don't come complaining to me if the guys make fun of you."

"I doubt they will. You should see some of Murph's pants," said Art, smiling. "Well, gotta go," he said. "I'll text you later."

"Fine," said Guin. "Just take your keys—and remember to ask Alan about those deals," she called.

"I'll try," he called back. "Bye!"

Guin finished her muffin and her coffee and debated whether it was too early to go over to the Sanibel Police Department. Then again, she knew the detective liked to get in early, before everyone else got there.

She walked into the bathroom and checked her hair. She made a face. No matter what she did, it always looked frizzy.

She reached into a drawer and pulled out a ponytail holder. Well, that's a bit better, she thought, turning her head from side to side. She headed to her closet and regarded herself in the full-length mirror. Should she change? Screw it, she thought. Good enough.

Then she headed out the door.

When she arrived at the police department a little before ten, Officer Rodriguez, a petite (yet muscular) woman who Guin knew, was at the front desk.

"Hi Officer!" said Guin, cheerily.

"Hi Ms. Jones," said Officer Rodriguez. "What brings you here?"

Guin smiled. "Guess."

The officer, who was about Guin's height, with dark wavy hair pulled back in a bun, smiled back at her. "You here to see the detective?"

"Ding ding ding!" said Guin.

"I'll just ring him for you," said Officer Rodriguez.

"Thanks," said Guin.

Guin leaned against the wall as Officer Rodriguez turned away to call the detective's extension. She could see her talking, but she couldn't make out what she was saying. A minute later, the officer turned around and went back over to the window.

"He's kind of busy right now, Ms. Jones."

"Call him back and tell him I'm not leaving until I speak with him," said Guin.

"He had a feeling you would say that," said the officer, smiling at Guin.

"And?" asked Guin.

"He said if you refused to leave, to call him back and let him know."

"Well then, you'd better call him back," said Guin, crossing her arms in front of her chest.

Officer Rodriguez dialed the detective's extension again, or Guin assumed that was what she was doing. A few seconds later she was back at the window.

"He said to give him ten minutes—and that it better be important."

"Thank you. I'll just be outside," said Guin. "But if he's not out in ten minutes, I'm coming back in and going straight to his office."

Officer Rodriguez gave her a look that said, 'don't mess with me.'

"Don't make me do anything we'd both regret, Ms. Jones."

"Don't worry," said Guin, smiling. "Just make sure the detective comes and gets me."

"I'll do my best, but you know the detective," she said.

"I do," said Guin, suddenly realizing that she really didn't know him.

She exited and went to stand on the walkway, by the benches. She got out her phone and scrolled through her messages. Nothing critical. Then she pulled up the paper on her browser.

A few minutes later, Officer Rodriguez poked her head out the door.

"Ms. Jones? The detective will see you now."

"Thank you!" said Guin, walking quickly to the door.

Officer Rodriguez buzzed her into the back and was about to go with her when Guin stopped her.

"Thanks, but I know the way," she said, making her way down the hall.

The detective's door was ajar, so Guin let herself in.

"Ms. Jones," said the detective, not getting up from his chair. "To what do I owe the pleasure?"

"Well, you haven't been returning my calls or texts, so I decided to pay you a little visit."

The detective, a huge Boston Red Sox fan whose office was decorated with Red Sox paraphernalia, tossed a baseball between his hands.

"That's because I've been busy."

"So, any news about the case?" said Guin, taking a seat.

"And by 'case,' I am assuming you are referring to the matter of Richard Tomlinson's untimely demise?"

"Yes," said Guin. "I know that you saw that footage taken from the camera over at Ding Darling and that Rick had been poaching."

"Poaching?" asked the detective. "Did Mr. Tomlinson try to steal a manatee?"

"Ha ha, very funny," said Guin. "You know what I mean."

The detective smiled, or it could have been a smirk. Guin could never tell.

"So, any progress?" Guin asked. "Any idea who killed Rick?"

The detective sighed and put the baseball on his desk.

"We are still investigating."

"But have you made any progress? You can't possibly still think Art did it, not with all the new evidence," said Guin, leaning forward.

"He is still a suspect," said the detective, looking directly at her.

"I could name several other people who had as good a motive as Art," said Guin, staring back at him.

The detective regarded Guin.

"Are you at least close to solving it?" asked Guin. "My offer to help still stands, you know. Have you checked out where Murph—Bob Murphy—and Joe Walton were Saturday evening?"

The detective continued to regard Guin.

"What?" she said, becoming frustrated.

The detective picked up his baseball.

"Ms. Jones, need I remind that this is a murder investigation? Stop playing Nancy Drew and leave the detective work to the professionals."

Guin could feel the steam coming out of her ears. She leaned further forward and looked the detective in the eyes.

"And need I remind you, detective, that as an investigative reporter, it is my job to uncover the truth? And if you don't solve this case soon, and get Art out of my condo, you may have another murder on your hands."

The detective snorted and grinned at Guin.

"Trouble in paradise?" said the detective.

"It was paradise until Art got here. Why on earth you agreed to let him stay at my place, I'll never know," said Guin, huffily.

The detective looked at Guin.

"If you must know, I was against the idea. But that lawyer and your husband—"

"*Ex*-husband," interrupted Guin.

"Ex-husband," continued the detective, "assured me that it was for the best, that you would make sure he didn't get into any trouble."

Guin made a face. So it had been Art's idea. Why wasn't she surprised?

"Well, just hurry up and solve this case so I can get him out of there. He's made himself altogether too comfortable."

The detective tossed the baseball between his hands, continuing to eye Guin.

"What?" she said, becoming slightly annoyed. But the detective continued to just sit there, tossing his baseball back and forth.

"So, you find out how the ibuprofen got into Rick's system?"

"Someone laced his drink with it," said the detective.

Guin waited for the detective to continue.

"They found trace amounts of it left in the glass. It had been ground into a powder and then placed in his drink. There was a fair amount of it in his system, at least a few tablets worth, along with a fair amount of alcohol. They also found trace amounts of a sedative."

Guin raised her eyebrows.

"Sounds like someone was taking no chances," she said.

"The combination probably wouldn't have killed a person ordinarily, but with Mr. Tomlinson's ibuprofen allergy…."

"So you think the killer knew he couldn't take ibuprofen."

"That would be the logical conclusion," said the detective.

"How very Spock-like of you," said Guin. "So, what's our next step?"

The detective stopped tossing the baseball and leaned forward, looking directly at Guin.

"*Your* next step is to go back to writing about restaurant openings and summer activities for kids and leave the detective work to us," replied the detective.

Guin made a face.

"Fine. If you don't want us to work together to solve the case, I'll find the answers on my own," she said, getting up.

The detective sighed and watched Guin move to the door, not bothering to get up.

"Just try to stay out of trouble, Ms. Jones. I can't always be there to rescue you."

Guin was about to reply, in a very unladylike way, but she stopped herself. Instead, she turned and smiled sweetly at the detective.

"I can take care of myself, detective," she said.

"If you say so," replied the detective.

Guin opened the door. "Good day, detective. I'll be in touch."

"Oh, Ms. Jones," called the detective, as she was leaving.

"Yes?" Guin replied, thinking he might relent and give her a little piece of information she could use.

"Please close the door. I have work to do and don't want to be disturbed."

Guin gritted her teeth, narrowed her eyes, then slammed the door shut. She then marched back down the hall, into the foyer, and out the door, not even stopping to say goodbye to Officer Rodriguez.

CHAPTER 32

As the police department was just down the road from the Sanibel Public Library, Guin decided to walk over and check out some books before she headed home. As she made her way along the path, she replayed the footage from the Ding Darling video camera in her head. Rick, or the man she assumed was Rick, was shown swimming (or moving) toward the shore and the nature preserve. But then what? Where did he go when he made it back to dry land? And how did he get there?

If he had gone back to the hotel, wouldn't someone from the conference or the hotel staff have seen him? Then again, thought Guin, the resort was pretty big, and he could have snuck back to his room without being observed. But if he had gone back to his room, which was on the same floor as several of the other sales guys', surely someone would have seen him. Though he could have snuck back to his room, laid low, and ordered in room service.

Suddenly, she had a thought. "That's it!" she said aloud. Then she looked around to see if anyone was looking at her.

She had reached the entrance to the library, but instead of going in she turned around and headed back to her car.

She got in and drove as fast as she could to the San Ybel Resort & Spa, which wasn't very fast at all, as the speed limit was 35 mph and she knew there were cops just waiting to ticket speeders. Less than fifteen minutes later, though it had felt like an eternity, she was there. She parked in front and handed her keys to the valet. Then she made her way to the front desk.

"Excuse me," she said to the young man at the desk, smiling at him. "My name is Guinivere Jones. I'm with the *San-Cap Sun-Times*. I'm doing a big story that involves the resort, and I need to speak with whoever is in charge of room service."

The young man looked at Guin.

"So, you're a reporter?"

Guin sighed inwardly, but she continued to smile.

"Yes. As I said, I'm doing a piece that involves the resort," she said, trying to be as vague as possible, "and I'd like to speak with the head of room service," she repeated.

"Oh, is it one of those customer service pieces, about how we take such good care of our guests?" asked the young man, whose name was Henry, according to his badge.

Guin debated whether to tell the young man the truth, but she decided a little white lie, in this case, might be better.

"Yes it is, Henry. But please don't tell anyone." She leaned in closer and lowered her voice. "We don't want anyone to know we're reviewing the resort, do we?"

Henry smiled down at her. "Got it," he said. "Just give me a minute and I'll call Hermione for you. She's in charge of room service."

"Thank you," said Guin, giving him another smile.

She moved to the side of the desk, so as not to block it, and watched and listened as Henry placed a call.

"Hey, Hermione, it's Henry at the front desk. There's a reporter here to see you, a Ms. Jones. Could you please come down when you have a minute?"

Guin waited.

"Okay, I'll tell her," said Henry. "Thanks."

He hung up and looked over at Guin.

"She'll be down in a few minutes. Please, have a seat," said Henry, gesturing toward some couches.

"Thank you," said Guin.

She walked over to the nearest couch and plunked herself down. Then she pulled her phone from her bag. There was a message from Shelly.

"Hey, Shell," she replied. "Can't talk right now. Can I call or text you in a bit?"

"What's up?" Shelly replied.

Guin sighed. "Can't talk," she typed. "Busy. TTYS."

She then put the phone back in her bag and looked around. She was too anxious to sit, so she got up and walked around the sitting area. It was a lovely hotel, she thought, as she gazed out the floor-to-ceiling windows.

"Ms. Jones?" called out a female voice with a British accent.

Guin turned to see a woman, probably around her age, her light brown hair tied back in a neat ponytail, wearing a pair of chinos and a button-down shirt.

"Yes?" said Guin.

"I'm Hermione Potter—and before you say anything, yes, I know. But my mother named me long before the Harry Potter books came out, and I seriously thought of keeping my maiden name when I got married. And no, my husband's name is not Harry," she added.

Guin smiled and held out her hand. Clearly, Hermione was a bit self-conscious about her name.

"Guinivere Jones," she said. "And I wouldn't have said a thing. When your name is Guinivere, your brother's name is Lancelot, and your husband's name is Arthur, you don't make fun of other people's names."

Hermione gave her a big smile and shook her head. "Oh dear."

"Yeah, mom was a big fan of Arthurian legends. And believe me, I thought twice about marrying Art."

Hermione laughed.

"So, Ms. Jones, how can I help you?"

"Well," she said, glancing around, to make sure no one could overhear them. "I'm a reporter with the *San-Cap Sun-Times*, and I'm covering the death of Richard Tomlinson, who was a guest of the hotel. He was attending the sales conference."

"Oh yes," said Hermione. "Awful that."

"Indeed," said Guin. "I'm sure you know that he was found dead in one of the cabanas last Saturday, but he had disappeared during a charter fishing trip a couple of days before, and we—Detective O'Loughlin and I," she added, to help boost her cause, "have been trying to determine what happened to Mr. Tomlinson between the time he disappeared and when he was found. And we thought maybe he had returned to the hotel."

"I see," said Hermione, looking at Guin.

Guin took a breath.

"His colleagues claim to have not seen him in between, but I thought it was possible Mr. Tomlinson could have snuck back to his room and laid low. Of course, he would need food, and perhaps other things, so he would need—"

"Room service," said Hermione, interrupting Guin, a conspiratorial smile on her face.

"Exactly," said Guin, smiling back at her. "So could you ask your staff if they brought anything to his room between Thursday and Saturday?" Guin gave her the room number. "Also, it's possible he may have changed rooms and used a different name," she added, recalling the mystery woman she saw with Rick.

Guin dug out her phone from her bag and opened her photos.

"Here are a couple of pictures of Rick," she said, handing the phone to Hermione. "I can send them to you, and you can share them with your staff. If anyone's seen him, please let me know."

Hermione looked down at the photos. "I can't say I recognize him, but I spend most of my time in my office. But I'll ask the staff."

She handed Guin her card.

"You can email or text me the photos, whichever is easier."

"Thank you," said Guin. She dug into her bag again, withdrawing her card case. "And here's my card," she said, handing one to Hermione. "It has my mobile and my email. Text or message me whenever, or call, whichever is easier."

Hermione looked at the card.

"Will do," she said. "So, you work with the police?" she asked, looking at Guin.

Guin could feel her face color slightly.

"On occasion, yes," she said. It wasn't a lie, she told herself.

"That must be exciting," said Hermione.

"It has its moments," Guin replied.

They stood there a bit awkwardly for a few seconds, then Guin thanked the director of room service for her help and departed, waiving to Henry as she passed by the front desk. He waved back at her and winked. She stepped outside and pulled out her phone. It was a little before noon. She decided to text Shelly.

"Hey, you want to grab some lunch?"

"Sure!" Shelly wrote back. "What time and where?"

"Gramma Dot's in 15?"

"Go grab a table," Shelly texted back. "I'll get there as soon as I can."

Guin smiled. "OK. C u soon," she wrote.

he handed the valet her ticket and waited for her car. A minutes later, she was motoring over to the marina.

Guin arrived a few minutes later at Gramma Dot's and got a table outside. She sat down and ordered an Arnold Palmer while she waited for Shelly. It was warm, but not too warm, outside, and for several minutes Guin stared at the boats docked at the marina, imagining herself and Ris cruising the Caribbean in one. She smiled at the thought and pulled out her phone to text him.

"Miss you," she wrote. "When can I see you?"

"How about this weekend?" he wrote back.

"It's a date!" typed Guin.

"I'll make dinner," texted Ris.

"What are you smiling about?" asked Shelly, whom Guin hadn't noticed standing there.

"Oh, I didn't see you!" said Guin, blushing slightly. "I was just texting with Ris."

"Texting, or sexting?" said Shelly, a wicked expression on her face.

"Texting," said Guin, firmly.

"Uh-huh," said Shelly, taking the seat opposite Guin. "Well, don't let me stop you."

"Hey, gotta go," Guin wrote to Ris. "I'm at lunch with Shelly."

"Tell her I say hi," replied Ris.

"Will do," Guin typed back. "TTYL. xo"

Guin put her phone down. "Ris says hi."

"Tell him I say 'hi' back," said Shelly.

The server came over with Guin's Arnold Palmer and placed it on the table.

"I'll have one of those," said Shelly.

"I'll be right back," said the young woman.

"So how's the case going?" asked Shelly. "Does the detective know who did it yet?"

"Unfortunately, no. But at least he hasn't arrested Art."

"Though would that really be so bad?" asked Shelly.

"Hey, Art's no saint, but he's not a killer."

"If you say so," said Shelly, not convinced.

"I do," she replied. "So do you know what you're going to have?"

"Give me a sec," said Shelly, examining the menu. "What are you going to have?"

"The coconut curried lobster salad," said Guin.

"Hmm…" said Shelly, scanning the menu. "That does sound good. Though so does the mahi-mahi sandwich."

The server returned with Shelly's drink.

"You ladies ready to order?"

"I'll have the coconut curried lobster salad," said Guin.

"Make that two," said Shelly, laying down her menu.

"Very good," said the server. "I'll have that out to you in just a few minutes."

She smiled, picked up the menus, and headed back inside the restaurant.

"So…?" asked Shelly.

Guin sighed. "I'm afraid there isn't that much to report. It appears Rick was poisoned, by ibuprofen of all things."

"Death by Advil? Is that really a thing?" asked Shelly.

"Apparently, it is. He was allergic to the drug, which clearly someone knew. The detective suspects someone spiked his drink with it," Guin explained. "The combination of the alcohol and the ibuprofen caused his heart to fail."

"Wow," said Shelly. "So who knew Rick was allergic to ibuprofen?"

"Lots of people," said Guin. "He wore one of those medical alert bracelets, though it was missing when they found his body."

"Do you think the killer took it?"

"Possibly," said Guin. "If you didn't know Rick had an allergy to ibuprofen, it could have looked like he had died of natural causes. Bad heart or something like that. Even though he was relatively young, it happens. And he did drink a lot."

"But why kill him?" asked Shelly.

"Well, it turns out he was about to close a couple of big deals in two other guys' territories," Guin started to explain.

"Yeah, but you don't kill a guy over that, do you?"

"You don't know sales guys," said Guin. "Though I agree, it seems a bit extreme."

"Were the deals really big?" asked Shelly.

"Worth potentially millions," said Guin.

Shelly whistled.

"Yeah," said Guin. "And one of the guys Rick stole from had been counting on the money he made from that deal to take his fiancée on a honeymoon to Paris and put a down payment on a house."

"So did he do it?" asked Shelly. "I'd be pretty pissed off if I found out someone stole the money I had been counting on for my honeymoon and a new house!" Though, I don't think he would want to spend his honeymoon in jail," she said as an afterthought.

"True," said Guin. "But I can't count him out."

"What about the other guy?"

"The other guy…" Guin trailed off. She didn't really know Murph, but he seemed too good natured to be the killer, though you never know. "Like I said, it was a pretty big deal. Maybe he was counting on that money for something special, or he just didn't like the idea of Rick deceiving him and taking his deal."

"And what about Art?"

"What about him?" asked Guin.

"Is he still a suspect?" asked Shelly.

"He is. He and Rick were competing for the same promotion, and Rick had picked a fight with Art the day of their boat trip, to make Art look bad in front of their boss."

Shelly whistled again. "So where do you go from here?"

"I keep investigating," said Guin. "And try to eliminate suspects."

"What about the detective?" asked Shelly. "Are you working with him?"

Guin rolled her eyes. "He's been as helpful as usual."

Shelly laughed. "Which means not helpful at all."

"Exactly," said Guin, smiling.

"Two coconut curried lobster salads," said their server, depositing their plates on the table. "Is there anything else I can get you, ladies?"

"Just some water," said Guin.

"Will do!" said the server. "Enjoy!"

"So, what's up in Shelly World?" asked Guin. "How's business? Steve? The kids?"

Shelly spent the next fifteen minutes regaling Guin with stories about her family—her daughter Lizzy's new job, her son Justin and his girlfriend (whom Shelly still wasn't crazy about), and Steve's back (which was acting up again).

"And have you made any new jewelry?" Guin asked.

"I'm always making jewelry. It's my therapy. Well, that and shelling," said Shelly. "I have to make it now through the fall as I get too busy once Thanksgiving and Christmas roll around. And then it's the season."

Guin was actually wearing a bracelet Shelly had given her. She looked down at it as Shelly spoke.

"And how are things with you and Harry Heartthrob?"

Guin sighed. "You know he hates to be called that, Shell."

Shelly grinned. "I know, but he isn't here, and he is quite a dish."

"He is, isn't he?" said Guin, smiling conspiratorially.

"So…?" said Shelly, leaning forward.

"So, not a lot to tell. He still wants to give me a key to his place, though he's backed off slightly. And I've barely seen him since Art's been here."

"And how does he feel about you and Art shacking up?" said Shelly.

"We are NOT shacking up, Shelly!" Guin practically shouted.

Several people at nearby tables turned to look at her. Guin blushed and lowered her voice.

"Art is only staying with me because he concocted some stupid excuse with that lawyer, and the detective agreed to it. But as soon as he's cleared, I'm kicking him out."

Shelly regarded her friend.

"What?" said Guin, with a growl.

"Nothing," said Shelly. "Though you can understand why your boyfriend might be a bit uncomfortable with your ex bunking with you."

"I do," said Guin. "And believe me, the sooner Art is gone, the happier we'll all be. But there's nothing I can do about it, except to help solve this case."

"You're not going to see Ris this weekend?"

"Oh no. I'm not letting Art completely destroy my love life. As a matter of fact, I just made plans to see Ris this Saturday," said Guin.

"But what about Art? Aren't you supposed to be hubby-sitting him?"

"I think I deserve a night off," huffed Guin. "And maybe this whole thing will be wrapped up by then."

"But Saturday is just a couple of days away, and I thought you said the detective didn't know who did it," said Shelly.

"Yes, but we've narrowed it down to a handful of suspects. And with me and Craig helping…"

"Well, let me know if there is anything I can do to help," said Shelly.

Guin smiled. "I will."

"You ladies all done here?" asked the server.

"We are," said Guin, looking down at her and Shelly's nearly empty plates.

"Anything else I can get for you?"

Guin looked at Shelly.

"I'm good," said Shelly. "I've got to go back home and make some more jewelry."

"Just the check, please," said Guin.

The server took their plates and left. She returned a minute later with the check. "Whenever you're ready," she said, with a smile.

Guin picked up the check. "Shall we split it?"

"Well, we did have the same thing, so…" said Shelly.

They took out their wallets and put some money on the table.

"Keep the change," said Guin, as the server picked up the check.

"Thanks," said the server. "You ladies have a nice rest of your day."

They got up and walked to the parking lot.

"I know you said you were getting together with Ris this weekend, but Steve and I are having one of our barbeque bashes Sunday," said Shelly. "And we'd love for you and Ris to attend."

"I'll ask him," said Guin.

They hugged and then got into their respective cars.

Before driving off, Guin checked her phone. There was a text from Art.

"Emily was just taken to the hospital," it read. "Heading over there now. Can you meet me?"

He had sent the text just a few minutes before and had included a link to the hospital.

"Oh my God!" Guin said aloud.

She opened her map app and entered the name of the hospital. If she didn't hit traffic, she could be there in around fifteen minutes.

CHAPTER 33

Guin arrived at the hospital and hurried to the front desk.

"I'm looking for Emily Fielding," she told the receptionist. "She was brought in a little while ago."

The receptionist typed something into her computer and looked at her monitor. Then she looked over at Guin.

"I'm sorry, Ms.?"

"Ms. Jones. My husband, actually ex-husband, texted me that she was on her way here."

"I'm afraid I can't help you, Ms. Jones."

"Can you at least tell me if she's okay?"

"I'm sorry, Ms. Jones," said the receptionist.

Guin was about to argue with her but thought better of it. Instead she stepped aside, pulled out her phone, and texted Art.

"Where are you?" she typed.

"At the hospital," Art replied.

"I know that," Guin typed back. "WHERE? I'm at the front desk, but they won't tell me anything."

"I'll come get you," wrote Art.

Guin put her phone back in her bag and began to pace around the lobby. What had happened to Emily? Was she okay? And where was Alan? Was he with her?

"Guin!"

Guin jumped.

"Sorry," said Art.

"Where's Emily? What happened?"

"Let's go outside," said Art, gently taking Guin's elbow and steering her toward the door.

"Is she okay?" asked Guin, looking up at him.

Art ushered her through the revolving door and outside.

"You're scaring me," said Guin.

"Sorry," said Art. He removed his hand from Guin's elbow and ran it through his hair, his tell for when he was upset or worried about something.

"We were out playing golf and were about to sit down to lunch when Alan got a call from the hotel. Apparently the cleaning woman found Emily passed out on her bed. At first she thought Emily might be sleeping, but then when Emily didn't respond…"

"Oh my God," said Guin.

"I'm not clear on all the details, but they called 911 and an ambulance came and got her and brought her here. Alan and I drove like maniacs to get here. It's amazing we didn't get stopped by the cops."

"Oh my God," Guin said again. "Is she going to be all right?" She looked up at Art. "What happened?"

"I don't know," said Art.

"I saw her just the other day and she seemed a bit sad and distracted. You don't think she tried to kill herself, do you?"

Art ran his hand through his hair.

"Can I go see her?" asked Guin.

"I don't know. They brought her to the Emergency department just a little while ago. Let's go find Alan."

Guin followed Art back into the building and to the elevator bank.

"So Alan's with her?" she asked, as they rode up in the elevator.

"He's in the waiting room. Murph's with him. I thought it would be a good idea to have him here since he knows the place."

The elevator doors opened and Art guided Guin to the waiting area. Alan and Murph were both on their phones. Art waved to him and Alan held up a finger, indicating to give him a minute. A minute later he had put the phone back in his pocket and walked over to greet them.

"Guin, how good of you to come," said Alan, smiling as he took her hands in his. "I'm sure Emily will appreciate you being here."

"Of course," said Guin. "How is she? Is she going to be okay?"

"I'm still waiting to see the doctor," said Alan. "The paramedics suspected it was a drug overdose. I was just speaking with Em's sister."

They stood there in silence for several seconds, not sure what to say.

"Mr. Fielding?"

The group all turned their heads to see a doctor coming toward them.

"I'm Alan Fielding," said Alan taking a step forward.

"Dr. Espinosa," said the doctor, extending his hand.

Alan shook it.

"Is my wife going to be okay?"

"She is," said the doctor, "but we want to keep her here overnight."

"What happened?" asked Alan. "Did she take too many Xanax? I warned her those things were not candy."

The doctor frowned. "Your wife suffers from anxiety?"

"Yes, though what woman doesn't?" said Alan, giving a nervous chuckle.

The doctor did not look amused.

"Well, as it happens, we did find Xanax, and alcohol, in

her system. It's a good thing you got her to the hospital when you did."

"But you said she was going to be okay," said Alan, no longer chuckling.

"She should be. Like I said, she got here just in time. We'd like to keep her here overnight and have her speak with one of the psychiatrists on staff in the morning."

"Is that really necessary?" asked Alan. "I'm sure it was just the stress of being stuck on Sanibel. She'll be fine as soon as we get back to Connecticut."

Guin shot Art a look. He silently shook his head, warning her not to say anything.

The doctor regarded Alan.

"Mr. Fielding, your wife just overdosed on prescription medication. It is my professional opinion that she stay here overnight and be examined by a psychiatrist."

Alan glanced over at Guin and Art. Guin was looking daggers at him. Alan looked down at the carpet and then back up at the doctor.

"Whatever you think is best."

The doctor smiled. "Excellent. We will monitor her condition overnight and arrange for her to see a psychiatrist in the morning, when she's feeling a bit better."

"May I go see her?" asked Alan.

"She's still very groggy," said the doctor. "We're going to move her to a private room. Then you can go see her."

"Are we talking an hour from now, two hours?"

"I'm afraid I can't tell you. Hopefully, it won't take very long. In the meantime, if you could fill out some paperwork," said the doctor, gesturing toward the desk. "Then, as soon as your wife has been admitted, you can go see her."

Alan followed the doctor to the desk and spoke with the attendant there, who handed him a clipboard with some papers. As he was filling them out, Art, Guin, and Murph talked quietly amongst themselves.

"Did you hear that?" asked Murph.

"Hard not to," said Art. "Poor guy."

"Poor *guy*?" said Guin, staring at them. "Poor *guy*? What about poor Emily? She nearly died!"

Art and Murph both had the sense to look sheepish.

"Really?!" said Guin, looking from one to the other.

They both looked down at the floor.

Guin walked over to the desk and stood next to Alan.

"Would it be okay with you if I hung around and saw Emily as soon as it was okay?"

Alan looked up at her and smiled.

"I think Emily would like that. You sure you don't mind?"

"Hey, I offered," said Guin.

Alan looked over at Murph and Art. "They don't have to hang around, though."

"You can go tell them that yourself," said Guin. "But they'll probably insist on staying too," she added, smiling kindly at him.

Alan signed the last piece of paper and handed the clipboard back to the attendant.

"You'll let me know as soon as I can go see her?" he asked the woman.

"Yes, Mr. Fielding. It shouldn't be very long now."

"Thank you," said Alan. He walked with Guin to where Art and Murph were standing. When he got there, Murph put a hand on his back. "It's going to be okay."

"I hope so," said Alan, who suddenly looked very tired.

"You want to have a seat?" said Art, gesturing over to some chairs.

"Probably a good idea," said Alan. "Though I could really use some fresh air."

"Go ahead and go outside for a few," said Guin. "Murph, why don't you go with him? Art and I will stay here, and we'll text you as soon as we hear anything."

Art looked down at Guin, then over at Alan and Murph. "Yeah, you two get some air. We'll text you the minute we hear anything about Emily."

Alan glanced over at the desk, trying to decide what to do.

"Go," said Art. He made a shooing motion with his hands and Alan and Murph headed to the elevator bank.

Guin watched them go, then turned to Art.

"So, what did you find out?"

"We're in a hospital, Guin!" Art said in a stage whisper.

"So?" said Guin. "No one's going to pay attention to us, and Alan isn't here. Spill. What did Alan say about those deals?"

Art sighed. "We were playing golf, Guin."

"So?" said Guin. "I thought guys talked all the time on the golf course."

"They do, but they don't go accusing one another of foul play."

Guin smiled. "Ooh, 'foul play.' You made a pun!"

"I didn't mean to."

"Does that mean you didn't ask him?"

Art frowned. "No, I asked him what he knew about those two deals, when Murph and Joe couldn't overhear, which wasn't easy. He claimed he didn't know about them."

"How could he not know?" asked Guin, her eyes wide with disbelief.

"He said he's been really busy and hadn't been checking the sales reports."

"I find that hard to believe," said Guin.

"I know, but it happens," said Art.

Guin looked skeptical. "So, you're telling me that no one noticed that Rick was about to close two very big deals outside his territory?"

"It's possible he waited until the last minute to enter them into the CRM system," said Art. "He probably only entered them to get credit—and didn't include a whole lot of details. A lot of guys aren't good about entering information. But they can't get paid unless the deal is in the system."

"Huh," said Guin, thinking. "So it's possible that Joe and Murph, and Alan, didn't find out about the deals until after Rick died?"

"That's what I'm saying," said Art.

"I still find that very hard to believe," said Guin, giving him a skeptical look. "Maybe Joe and Murph didn't know, but Alan surely had to."

Art sighed. There was no use arguing with Guin. He knew his ex-wife well, and once she got an idea in her head there was no dissuading her.

Just then the woman from the desk came over.

"Mrs. Fielding was just moved to a private room," she said.

Guin and Art immediately stood up.

"Thank you," said Guin. "What's the room number?"

The attendant gave Guin the room number and instructions on how to get there while Art texted Alan. Then she and Art headed to the elevator.

CHAPTER 34

As Guin stood by Emily's bed and looked from her to Alan, to Murph, and then to Art, she was suddenly reminded of the scene at the end of the *Wizard of Oz*, when Dorothy wakes up in her bed back in Kansas, to find her aunt and uncle and the farm hands all gathered around her. Guin could easily imagine Emily as Dorothy. She glanced again at Alan, Murph, and Art, trying to figure out which one would be the Scarecrow, the Tin Man, and the Cowardly Lion. That made her smile.

Emily opened her eyes.

"Guin," she said, weakly, looking up at her.

Guin shook off thoughts of the *Wizard of Oz* and looked down at Emily, taking Emily's hand in hers.

"Hey, you," said Guin, smiling down at her. "You gave us quite a scare."

"Sorry," said Emily.

Alan was standing at the head of the bed, right next to Emily.

"Em..." he began, but he was unable to speak, seemingly overcome with emotion.

"Would you like us to leave?" asked Art.

"No, that's okay," said Alan. "Unless you want them to go, Em?"

Emily smiled weakly. "The more, the merrier."

"Well, I should probably get going," said Murph, who looked a bit uncomfortable. "But if you two need anything, just holler."

Alan put a hand on Murph's shoulder. "Thanks, Murph."

"We should probably get going, too," said Art, looking at Guin, who was still holding Emily's other hand.

Emily squeezed Guin's hand. "Can I have a word with Guin?"

Alan and Art exchanged looks.

"Of course," said Alan.

"Alone," said Emily, looking at her husband.

"Oh," said Alan. "Okay. We'll just be outside."

He and Art left the room and stood out in the hall. When she was sure they couldn't hear, Emily pulled Guin closer. Guin bent down.

"I need to talk to you," said Emily.

"I'm listening, but you need rest, Em. We can talk when you're feeling better."

"No, I need to tell you now. I—"

She was interrupted by a coughing fit. Guin handed her a glass of water, which Emily sipped.

"Thank you," she said.

"Really, Em, it can wait until the morning, when you're feeling better."

"No, it can't," said Emily.

"Okay then, tell me," said Guin.

"I lied to you about Rick," said Emily, her brown eyes looking right into Guin's blue ones. She darted her eyes over to the door, to make sure it was closed.

Guin waited.

"We were… friends."

Guin continued to hold Emily's hand and didn't say anything. From the way Emily had said the word *friends*, Guin guessed they were more than that.

"I was lonely, and he… he made feel a little less lonely," she finally said, again glancing at the door.

"They can't hear us," said Guin.

"He—"

Emily started to cough again. Guin quickly refilled her water cup.

"Throat's… dry," she croaked. "Hurts… to talk."

"Drink some water, Em," said Guin, holding up the cup. "You can tell me the rest later. Don't strain yourself."

Emily started to object, but Guin stopped her.

"Save your breath. I'll come back in the morning. We'll talk then."

Emily flopped back against her pillow, giving in. Just then the door opened and a nurse walked in, followed by Alan and Art.

"Visiting hours are almost over," said the nurse.

"You two have a good little chat?" asked Alan, looking from Emily, who didn't seem very happy, to Guin, who was still holding Emily's hand and looking down at her.

"We should go, Guin," said Art, placing a hand on her shoulder.

Guin nodded and let go of Emily's hand. "I'll be here first thing tomorrow, or whenever they allow visitors back in. Okay?"

Emily gave her a weak smile, then Art steered her out of the room, leaving Emily and Alan and the nurse alone in the room.

"You want me to drive?" Art asked when they got to the Mini.

"No, I'm fine. I just feel so bad for Emily. She looked so fragile…" She trailed off.

"Emily is going to be fine. She's tougher than you think," said Art.

Guin unlocked the doors. "I'm not so sure about that," she said, getting in.

"You mind if I turn on some music?" Art asked, as they left the hospital.

"Go right ahead," said Guin.

Art flipped through Guin's presets and stopped at Sirius XM channel 33, First Wave. "You always did like eighties New Wave music," he said, smiling.

"You got a problem with that?" asked Guin, glancing over at him.

Art held up his hands. "Nope! I'm fine with some eighties techno pop."

"Good," said Guin.

They spent the rest of the drive back to Sanibel listening to the radio and barely speaking, which was fine by Guin.

When they got upstairs, Guin announced she needed to do some work.

"Me too," said Art.

"Okay then," said Guin. "Shall we reconvene around seven for dinner?"

"What are you making?" said Art.

Guin paused. She hadn't really thought about dinner. She walked into the kitchen and opened the fridge. Not a lot to work with. And she didn't want to go back out to get groceries.

Art had followed her into the kitchen and saw the barren refrigerator.

"Why don't I go pick up something?" he suggested.

Guin closed the door to the refrigerator and turned to face him.

"Would you? That would be great."

"What's your poison?" asked Art.

Guin gave him a look.

"Oops. Bad choice of words," he said. "What can I get?"

Guin thought for a minute. "We could get a pizza from the Great White Grill or some fried chicken from the Pecking Order," she suggested. "We could also get stuff from the Sunset Grill."

"No health food restaurants on the island?" asked Art.

"There's the Sanibel Sprout, but I don't think it's open for dinner. And while their food is great, it takes forever."

As Guin was talking, Art whipped out his phone.

"What are you doing?" Guin asked.

"I'm looking up the Sanibel Sprout," he said, not looking up from his screen.

Guin sighed and waited.

"It says they're open until seven. It's five-thirty now. How about we order at six-fifteen, and I'll go get it?"

"If you're willing to drive over there and wait, sure," said Guin.

"What do you want?" Art asked.

"I'll have the Classic Burger," said Guin. "You need some cash?"

"Why, do they not take credit cards?" asked Art.

"No, they take credit cards," said Guin. "I just didn't want you to think I expected you to pay."

Art stared at her. "Seriously, you think I would accept money from you, Guin? You've been putting me up in your home and taking care of me for days. I think I can treat you to some take out," he said, smiling.

"Well, when you put it that way…" she said.

"Consider it done. I'll call you when dinner's ready," Art replied.

"Okay," said Guin. "See you in a bit."

She walked into her bedroom/office, to be greeted by both cats asleep on her bed.

"You two move at all?" she asked them.

Neither responded.

Guin smiled and shook her head. Oh, to be a cat. She petted the two felines, then sat down at her desk and turned on her computer. A few seconds later Fauna was in her lap, purring. Guin stroked her as she loaded her email. As she was scanning her inbox, her phone started vibrating. It was a text from Craig.

"Got some interesting information. Call me when you can."

Guin immediately pressed Craig's number.

"What news?"

"And a good evening to you, too," said Craig, chuckling.

"Sorry," said Guin.

"Perfectly okay," said Craig.

"So…?"

"So, I spoke with Ben Johnson, he's the captain who took your husband and his friends out on the fishing trip."

"I remember," said Guin. "And?"

"He heard about Rick being found dead, and he's worried people might think he had something to do with it."

"Why would anyone think that?" asked Guin.

"Well, as it turns out, Rick had paid Ben to look the other way when he went over the side of the boat."

Guin whistled.

"So Big Ben knew Rick didn't drown?"

"According to Ben, Rick had planned the whole thing," Craig said. "He actually hired Ben to take him out the day before your husband's little fishing trip, telling him he was planning to play a practical joke on his friends and needed to know if it was possible to get back to shore without being seen."

Guin raised an eyebrow. "And did Ben tell him?

"He did. Ben said he explained to Rick that the waters

where he typically took guys fishing for tarpon weren't that deep, so it was possible a guy could swim or even walk to shore or to one of the little islands in the sound. Then he said Rick asked him exactly where they'd be going fishing the next day—and offered Ben a couple hundred bucks if he'd look the other way when Rick went overboard."

"Wow," said Guin, astonished. "And Big Ben agreed to this?"

"Not at first," said Craig. "But your friend Rick was very persuasive. Apparently, he had some dirt on Ben."

"Wow," said Guin, for the second time. "But why did Ben tell you all this? Why didn't he go to the police?"

"Like I said, he's been worried about somehow being implicated in Rick's murder."

"Yes, but why tell you and not the police or the detective?"

"These guys know me," said Craig. "And they know they can trust me. Ben's had a few run-ins with the law."

"Ah," said Guin. "But you need to tell O'Loughlin what Ben told you. Or, better yet, get Ben to tell him."

"I'm working on it," said Craig.

"Well, thanks for letting me know," said Guin.

"There was another thing that Ben said that's been bugging me."

"Oh?" said Guin.

"He made a comment like, 'What is it with these sales guys and their weird requests?'"

"And?" said Guin, intrigued.

"And I asked him what he meant. He tried to walk the comment back, but I pushed him. And he confessed that another one of the guys, he didn't say which one, had asked him about a private tour—and if anyone had ever drowned or been attacked by a shark, and if so, where."

"That is odd, and creepy," said Guin. "Did you find out

which guy it was?" (She hoped it wasn't Art. Just the thought of it made her shiver.)

"No. Ben clammed up when I started asking him questions."

Guin had a bad feeling, but she didn't say anything.

"So, any news on your end?" asked Craig.

"I was at the hospital this afternoon," said Guin.

"Is everything okay?" asked Craig, concerned.

"Oh, I'm fine. Just went to see a friend," said Guin. She wanted to tell Craig about Emily, but she hesitated.

"Well, I hope she's okay," said Craig.

"I hope so, too," said Guin. "So, you going to speak to Big Ben again?"

"Yeah, we said we'd talk tomorrow. I thought I'd go down to the marina and chat with him there. Maybe go out in his boat. See if I can get him to go speak to the detective."

"Okay, keep me posted."

They ended their call. Guin looked at the clock on her monitor. It was nearly six-thirty. She wondered if Art had left to go to the Sanibel Sprout. She got up and wandered into the living room.

"Art?" she called.

No sign of him. He probably went to pick up the food. Her stomach gurgled. Good thing he left, she thought, looking down at her stomach.

It was nearly seven o'clock, and Art had yet to return. She decided to call him. He picked up after a couple of rings.

"Where are you?" asked Guin.

"Driving home," said Art. "You're right, that place takes forever. I called the order in at six-fifteen, but when I got there at six-forty it wasn't ready."

"Sorry about that," said Guin. "Did you take the insulated bag, like I told you?"

"I did," said Art. "Got the food tucked in all nice and cozy."

Guin could tell Art was smiling as he said it. She smiled, too.

"All right. See you soon."

"See you soon," said Art.

They sat down to dinner at seven-twenty. Guin immediately dove into her black bean burger.

"I love watching you eat," said Art.

Guin made a face and then took another bite of her burger.

"I'm hungry," she said.

"Hey, fine by me!" said Art. He took a sip of his Emerald Island, a mix of cucumber, kale, celery, apple, and lemon juice. "So, I heard you talking on the phone to someone earlier. Anything to do with the case?"

"As a matter of fact, yes," said Guin. "Craig got a call from that captain you hired, Ben Johnson."

"Oh?" said Art.

"Apparently Rick had paid him to help him disappear, or to look the other way when he slipped into the water. Told Ben he wanted to play a practical joke on his friends, that it was all in good fun."

Art made a face.

"You don't look surprised," said Guin, eyeing him.

"Knowing what I know about Rick? I'm not surprised at all."

"Well, the joke's on him," said Guin, taking a sip of her carrot juice.

"Did Big Ben say anything else?" asked Art.

"Not really," said Guin. "Craig said he was going to go talk to Ben down at the marina tomorrow morning, try to convince him to go speak to Detective O'Loughlin."

"Good luck with that," said Art. "I didn't get the impression that Captain Ben was very fond of cops."

"Yeah, well…" said Guin.

They finished the rest of their meal in silence.

"Well, I've got some more work to do," said Art, getting up.

"That's fine. I can clean this up. Not much to clean," said Guin, looking down at the table. "Thanks for getting dinner."

"Sure, no problem," said Art. "I'll see you in the morning."

"Okay," said Guin, who was a bit surprised Art was retiring so early—and hadn't made any attempt to flirt with her all evening. "Have a good night. You know where to find me if you need anything," she called after him.

Guin fully expected Art to say something inappropriate or flirty, but he just held up a hand and headed to the guest room, Flora following him.

Odd, thought Guin. She shook her head and finished cleaning up. She opened the freezer to get herself some toasted coconut ice cream and found Fauna sitting at her feet.

"Meow," said the black cat.

"Let me guess, you want some ice cream," said Guin, looking down at the cat.

"Meow," said Fauna.

"Fine, you can lick my bowl when I'm done," said Guin.

She scooped some ice cream into a small bowl and leaned against the counter as she ate it. Fauna jumped up on the counter next to her and put her paw into the bowl.

"Hey! Stop that!" shouted Guin, turning away from the cat. "You'll get your turn in a minute."

"Meow," said Fauna.

"Too bad," said Guin.

Guin finished the ice cream, away from the counter, so Fauna couldn't get at it. When she was done, she placed the bowl on the floor. Fauna immediately jumped down and started licking the bowl.

"Who needs a dishwasher?" she said aloud, smiling.

When Fauna was done, Guin gave the bowl a quick rinse and put it into the dishwasher. Then she headed off to her bedroom.

CHAPTER 35

Guin had stayed up late, or late for her, reading a new mystery she had downloaded onto her Kindle. As a result, she didn't get up until nearly seven o'clock.

She stretched and thought about staying in bed. That would make the cats happy. But the beach beckoned. So she went to the bathroom, splashed some cold water on her face, pulled her hair into a ponytail, then went into her closet and pulled on a pair of shorts and a t-shirt. She headed into the kitchen to feed the cats and found the coffee maker on warm, the carafe half empty. Art must have gotten up early and made some coffee, she reasoned. She looked around but didn't see or hear him. She walked to the guest room and saw that the door was ajar. She poked her head in. The room was dark.

"Art?" she called. Nothing.

She turned on the light. The sheets were thrown back on the twin bed Art had been sleeping in, but there was no sign of Art.

Guess he was in a hurry, Guin mused. He was usually fastidious about making the bed. Said it made him feel like he had accomplished something first thing in the morning. She smiled at the recollection.

She went back into the kitchen looking for a note, but she didn't find one. Oh well, she thought. He has a key. I'll just let him know I've gone for a walk on Bowman's Beach and will be back by nine.

She grabbed a piece of paper from the notepad she kept by the fridge and wrote Art a note. Then she gave the cats some food and fresh water, grabbed her keys and her beach bag, and headed out the door.

She arrived at the Bowman's Beach parking lot less than ten minutes later, then headed down to the beach. She had thought about asking Shelly or Lenny to join her, but decided she'd rather shell alone. As she crossed the footbridge, she noticed some bubbles in the water and leaned over to look. Just as she did so, she saw a manatee snout and stopped to watch. It appeared that there were several manatees in the water below, and Guin was entranced. Manatees, also referred to as sea cows, were rather large but very shy. She stood there looking into the water for several minutes, watching the manatees (or their snouts) come up for air, then she continued down the path to the beach.

It was a beautiful morning and already getting hot, but Guin loved the feel of the sun on her face and back. There didn't appear to be a lot of shells this morning—the tide was on the high side—but it felt good to be outside and breathing in the fresh sea air. She closed her eyes and raised her hands above her head, feeling the sun's rays on her face. She took a few deep breaths, then opened her eyes and looked out at the water.

"Hey, Neptune! You got a junonia for me today?" she called.

She looked down at the shoreline, but she did not see a junonia, or an alphabet cone, or even a lettered olive.

"Maybe tomorrow then, okay?" she called to the sea.

No reply. But she hadn't really expected there would be. Guin smiled and continued her walk down the beach, stopping to chat with a couple walking their dogs. Although a devoted cat person, Guin had always liked dogs. She just didn't relish the thought of having to walk one three times a day, especially during New England winters.

Guin arrived back at her condo at nine and was greeted by both cats. She knelt to pet them.

"You miss me?" she asked them. Flora rubbed against her and purred.

Guin straightened up and listened for signs of Art, but she didn't hear him. She called his name. No response. That's odd, she thought. She walked toward the guest room, to see if maybe he was taking shower, but she didn't hear the water running. Though she noted that the bed was now made. Then she walked into the kitchen.

She immediately spied the empty coffee carafe in the drainboard, drying. So, clearly, he had been back to the condo. Then she saw the note on the fridge.

"Meeting up with the guys. Will text you later."

Whatever, thought Guin. She put the note in the recycling bin, then went to take a shower and change. She emerged a little while later, feeling refreshed and ready to take on the day. She picked up her phone and checked her messages, hoping to have received something from the detective. Nothing. She sighed.

On the positive side, there was a message from Ris confirming their dinner date the next night. There was also a text from her mother, asking why she hadn't heard from Guin in ages. Guin rolled her eyes and shot her mother a quick text: "Super busy. Will call you later." She then sent Ris a text letting him know they were absolutely still on for dinner Saturday, and she was looking forward to it—and added a smiley face for good measure.

She quickly scanned her emails. There was one from Ginny asking how her story was going, and if she could handle doing a couple of articles as they were a bit short-staffed the next couple of weeks, what with people on vacation. Guin wrote her back, saying she'd call her later and no problem doing the articles. Then she grabbed her bag and her car keys and headed to the hospital.

This time Guin knew where she was going and didn't even bother to check in at the front desk. She just went right upstairs to Emily's room. She was pleased to see Emily looking much better.

"Guin, you came!" said Emily, giving her a big smile.

"Of course," said Guin. "I said I would. So, how are you doing? You feeling better?"

"Much," said Emily. "I feel like such an idiot. Alan's always telling me to be careful about my meds. He's no doubt gloating about being right."

"I'm sure he's just concerned about you," said Guin. "So, when are they springing you?"

"Good question," said Emily. "I'm still waiting for a psychiatric evaluation. I think they're worried I might go kill myself, but I told the nurses I'm fine."

"Just a precaution, I'm sure," said Guin.

"Well, I will kill myself if they don't let me out of here—and I don't get back to Connecticut soon. I know you love it down here, Guin, but I miss Greenwich."

"I know you do, Em. And no offense taken," said Guin, smiling.

She looked around.

"Is Alan here?"

"No, not yet," said Emily. "He called to say he had some important business to attend to, but that he would make sure that I was out of here by lunchtime."

"He's probably with Art," said Guin. "Art left me a

somewhat cryptic note this morning, saying he'd gone off with the guys. Most likely they got a last-minute tee time somewhere and didn't want to tell us," Guin said, giving Emily a conspiratorial smile.

Emily made a face. "What is it with men and golf?"

"I think they like the challenge," said Guin.

Guin debated whether she should bring up Rick, considering Emily's condition. But as Emily seemed fine....

"So, Em, yesterday you said you needed to tell me something, something about you and Rick..." Guin began.

Emily looked nervous and began to fidget with her sheet. "I was probably just babbling," she said, not looking at Guin. "It was the stress."

"You told me that the two of you were *friends*," said Guin, putting an emphasis on the last word and looking directly at Emily.

"Did I?" said Emily, glancing up at Guin.

"Yes, you did," said Guin, looking at her.

"Well, you know Rick," she said, giving a forced laugh. "He was friendly with everyone."

Guin regarded Emily. A part of her wanted to push the issue, to find out what Emily really meant by "friend," but she didn't want to upset her. So she decided to change the topic, slightly.

"So, Em, do you know who Alan was planning on promoting?"

Emily looked down at the bed sheets.

"Art said that Rick said he had it all sewn up."

Emily looked up at Guin, a frown on her face. "You know I don't like office talk, Guin."

Guin didn't say anything, just looked at Emily.

Emily sighed.

"Alan did mention that the two of them were driving him crazy. That they were acting like a couple of school boys and needed to man up."

"But did he ever happen to mention if he was planning to give the promotion to Rick?"

Emily looked down again, avoiding Guin's gaze. "Not that I recall."

Guin was frustrated. She felt that Emily did know something but didn't want to tell her, for some reason.

"You should just ask Alan," said Emily.

"Okay, I may just do that," said Guin.

"Good," said Emily. She turned to look up at Guin. "Now, can we please talk about something other than Alan and the company? Tell me all about *you*. You didn't really tell me about your life down here the other day. Tell me what it is about Sanibel that you love so much."

Guin smiled. "How much time do you have?"

Emily smiled back at her. "Too much. Where is that stupid psychiatrist?" she said, leaning forward and looking at the door. "I was hoping he'd be here first thing."

"Well, while we wait, I will endeavor to entertain you with tales of Sanibel," said Guin, pulling up a chair.

Guin spent the next thirty minutes or so telling Emily all about her life on Sanibel, her job at the *San-Cap Sun-Times*, Ris—Emily laughed out loud at his nickname, "Harry Heartthrob," and demanded to see photos of him ("a total hunk," she pronounced, upon seeing him in one of his yoga poses)—and her seashell obsession. Finally, a nurse came in, letting them know that the psychiatrist would be there in just a few minutes to perform the psychiatric exam.

"Finally!" said Emily.

Guin got up to leave.

"Don't go," said Emily, reaching for Guin's hand.

"You'll be fine," said Guin, taking Emily's hand. "I should go. And I bet Alan will be here any minute."

Emily sighed. "I suppose you're right."

"I'll text you a little later. Just let me know when they've let you out of here," said Guin.

"Will do," said Emily. "Hopefully, right after this exam," she said.

Guin leaned down and gave Emily a kiss on the cheek. "Talk to you later."

"Bye!" Emily called as Guin walked out the door.

Guin headed down the corridor, lost in thought, and nearly collided with Alan.

"Oh, sorry," said Guin. "I didn't see you."

Alan smiled at her. "No worries. I take it you were just in with Emily."

"I was. She's doing much better."

"Excellent. Do you think they'll let her out of this place?"

"She's counting on it. The doctor's on his way now, to perform the psychiatric evaluation. Assuming she passes, they'll probably discharge her."

Alan looked momentarily worried.

"Everything okay?" Guin asked. "Where's Art?" she added, looking around.

"Art?" said Alan. "I haven't seen him since yesterday."

Guin looked confused. "But I thought he was with you and the rest of the guys."

"He may be with the rest of the guys, but I haven't seen him. I've been working all morning."

"Oh," said Guin. That's odd, she thought. "Well, be kind to Emily, she's had a rough go of it."

A look flashed across Alan's face. Was he annoyed? A moment later, though, his expression softened.

"As soon as she's out of here, I'm going to take her shopping," he announced. "I hear there's a big outlet mall near here, and you know how Emily loves to shop."

Guin didn't know about Emily's shopping habits, but the

outlet mall in nearby Estero did have a lot of nice stores.

"I'm sure she'll enjoy that," said Guin, smiling. "Well, goodbye. I'm sure I'll see you two around."

"Most definitely. We should all have dinner one night, before we head back to Connecticut."

"Any idea when that will be?" Guin asked.

"Soon, I hope. Very soon."

They said their goodbyes, then Guin watched as Alan entered Emily's room. Suddenly, she felt a slight chill. She glanced back at Emily's door, then turned and made her way to the elevators.

Guin leaned against her car and pulled out her phone.

"Where are you?" she texted Art.

Seconds after hitting 'send,' her phone started ringing. It was Craig.

"Hey, Craig, what's up?"

"You better get down to the marina, Guin."

"Uh, okay. What's up?"

"Captain Ben is dead. He's been shot, though it could have been suicide. They found his body this morning. And your ex is here, along with a couple of his sales guy friends."

Shit, thought Guin. "I'll be right there. I'm just leaving the hospital. Should take me fifteen, twenty minutes, if I don't hit traffic."

"Oh, and Detective O'Loughlin is here too," added Craig.

Oh, great, thought Guin.

"I'll be there just as soon as I can."

CHAPTER 36

Guin arrived at the marina twenty minutes later. She parked her car and walked quickly toward the Ships Store, where she could see a crowd gathered. She spied Craig talking to Detective O'Loughlin and made a beeline for them, squeezing between people.

"What happened?" asked Guin, looking from Craig to the detective.

"And a good morning to you too, Ms. Jones," said the detective.

Guin shot the detective a look, then turned to Craig. "Captain Ben is dead?"

"I got here this morning in hopes of catching Ben before he headed out," explained Craig. "None of the guys in the shop had seen him this morning. So I went over to his boat, which was docked in its usual spot. But something just seemed off.

"I didn't see Ben, so I climbed aboard. Then I noticed some blood on the deck. I followed it to the back of the boat, where Ben stored his gear, but there was no sign of Ben."

"You said he had been shot," said Guin.

"They found Captain Johnson's body a little way from here this morning," said the detective.

"You think he was murdered?" asked Guin, looking from Craig to the detective.

"Could have been suicide," said Craig.

Both the detective and Guin looked at Craig.

"You really think so?" asked Guin.

"Anything is possible," said Craig.

Guin looked at the detective.

Reading her mind, he replied. "We're checking it out. And no, we haven't found the gun. Probably fell into the sea."

"Or the murderer tossed it into the water after he shot Captain Ben," said Guin.

"Is that your theory, Nancy Drew?" said the detective.

Guin made a face.

"You don't seriously think a guy like Captain Ben shot himself, do you?" she said looking from Craig to the detective.

"He was pretty upset when I spoke to him on the phone yesterday," replied Craig.

Guin turned to the detective, but he was his usual stoic self. She looked around.

"You mentioned Art was here," said Guin.

"He's over there," said Craig, pointing toward the Ships Store.

"What was he doing here?"

Craig and the detective exchanged looks.

"Wait. You don't think Art shot him, do you?" she said. "That's crazy. Art doesn't even own a gun."

"It's easy to get a gun in Florida," said Craig.

"Seriously?" said Guin, color spreading across her face. "I don't believe it."

"Mr. Jones claims he got a call from Captain Johnson last night, saying he needed to talk to him, and to come to the marina early this morning," said the detective.

"Did Art say what Big Ben wanted to talk to him about?" asked Guin.

"He did not," said the detective.

"When did Art get here?" asked Guin.

"I saw him and his two buddies as I was leaving Ben's boat," replied Craig.

"And?" said Guin.

"They asked me if I knew where Big Ben was."

"Did you tell them?"

"I told them I didn't know," said Craig.

"And how did they react?" asked Guin.

"Confused. Annoyed," said Craig.

Guin looked at the detective. "I'm assuming you've already questioned them, yes?"

"You know what happens when you assume, Ms. Jones…" said the detective, his lips curling up into what passed for a smile on him.

"Yeah, yeah, yeah," said Guin. "So, did you speak with them? Can I go see them?"

"Be my guest," said the detective.

"Thank you," said Guin.

She walked over to where her ex-husband and his colleagues were standing, along with two officers.

"Good morning," she said to the two policemen.

They nodded politely to her. Guin then turned to Art and his coworkers.

"So what's going on?"

"I presume you know about Big Ben," said Art.

"Craig told me. Please tell me you had nothing to do with it."

"How could you even think such a thing?" said Art, running a hand through his wavy blond hair.

Guin eyed him.

"I swear to you, Guin, I had nothing to do with it!"

"So where were you this morning?" she asked.

"He was with us," said Murph. "We picked him up at

eight and went out for breakfast over at the Lighthouse Cafe."

"You went all the way out to the West End and then had breakfast at the Lighthouse Cafe?" asked Guin, staring at Murph.

"Yes," said Joe. "We were going to play a round at the Dunes, and as Art doesn't have a car…"

"How come you didn't tell me?" she asked Art.

"I thought I did," he said.

"So…?" she asked, looking from Art to Murph to Joe.

"We went to pick Art up, and he asked us if we would mind stopping by the marina after breakfast," said Murph.

"I got a call from Big Ben last night asking me to come down here this morning," said Art. "He said he had something important to tell me. I asked him why he couldn't just tell me over the phone, but he insisted on me coming here. And as the marina is close to the golf course, I figured we could just stop by after breakfast," explained Art.

"I see," said Guin, looking from one to the other.

"If you don't believe me, ask over at the Lighthouse Café. Our server's name was Peggy," said Art.

"I had the blueberry whole wheat hot cakes," said Joe. "They were great," he added, smiling at the memory.

"Good to know," said Guin.

"Then we drove over here, to the marina," said Murph.

"And we ran into your friend Craig leaving Big Ben's boat," said Art.

"So you didn't see Captain Ben?" asked Guin.

"No," said Art. "When we got here, we went to the shop. They made a crack about Ben being very popular this morning. They suggested we look over by the docks. So we walked onto the dock where Big Ben's boat is, and we ran into Craig."

"And you swear you are telling me the truth," said Guin, eyeing Art.

"I swear, Guin. Ask your friend, the detective. Ben was already dead when we got here."

Guin looked from Art to Murph to Joe.

"Like he said," said Murph.

Joe nodded in agreement.

Guin sighed. "So you have no idea what Big Ben wanted to speak to you about?" she asked Art.

"I assume it had something to do with Rick," said Art. "I mean, what else could it be?"

Guin was about to say something when her phone started buzzing. She took it out and looked at who was calling. It was someone from the San Ybel Resort & Spa.

"Excuse me," she said.

She quickly walked away and picked up the call.

"This is Guin."

"Hi, Ms. Jones. This is Hermione Potter from the San Ybel Resort & Spa."

"Oh, hi Hermione. And please, call me Guin. Did you find out anything?"

"That's why I'm calling," said Hermione. "I showed that picture you sent me, of that guy, Rick, to everyone, and I asked if anyone had seen him."

"And?" said Guin, covering the phone, so no one could hear her.

"And one of the young women on the staff, Amy, said she saw him. She remembers because he gave her a really big tip."

Typical, thought Guin.

"So, when did Amy see him, and where?"

"It was that Friday night," said Hermione. "In one of our private bungalows."

"Is Amy sure it was Rick?" asked Guin.

"Oh yes," said Hermione. "She says he asked her her name and then gave her a big tip when she was done setting everything up."

"Setting everything up? What did he order?" asked Guin.

"Our special romance package," said Hermione. "We strew rose petals on the bed and bring you Champagne and caviar and chocolate truffles."

"Sounds lovely," said Guin, imagining herself and Ris enjoying the romance package. "So, was there someone else in the room with him?"

"I asked Amy that," said Hermione. "She said she didn't see anyone, but the door to the bathroom was closed and she could hear the shower running."

"I see," said Guin. "So she didn't happen to get a look at the woman—I'm assuming it was a woman—who was there with Rick?"

"No," said Hermione. "She just saw Mr. Tomlinson, though that wasn't the name he used."

"What name did he use?" asked Guin.

"Arthur Jones," said Hermione.

Guin nearly dropped the phone.

"He used the name Arthur Jones?" asked Guin, incredulous.

"That's who the room was registered to," replied Hermione.

Guin tried to compose herself. No way could Art have rented that room, could he?

"Ms. Jones? Are you there?"

"Sorry," said Guin. "You're sure the bungalow was registered to Arthur Jones?"

"That was the name the gentleman gave when he placed the order. I asked Felippe, who took the order. He said the man clearly said, 'This is Arthur Jones in Bungalow 3. I'd like to have the romance package delivered to my room as soon as possible.'"

Guin made a face. "But you showed Amy the photo of Mr. Tomlinson, and she said that was the man in Bungalow 3."

"Like I said," said Hermione.

Guin's head hurt.

"Thank you for calling, Hermione. And please, thank Amy—and Felippe. They've been a big help."

"Any time," said Hermione. "Hope you catch the guy who did it."

"Me too," said Guin.

She hung up and walked back over to where Art was still standing.

"I need to talk to you, in private," Guin said, in a low voice, grabbing Art's arm.

Art looked at her, confused.

"Just take a few steps with me over there," she said, tugging him away from his colleagues and the police, who glanced over at her.

Guin smiled. "We'll just be a second," she said, cheerily.

"What's this about, Guin?" Art asked her.

"I just received a call from the woman in charge of room service for the San Ybel Resort & Spa. I had asked her to check with her staff and see if any of them had seen Rick since his disappearance last Thursday."

"Why on earth would Rick return to the hotel?" asked Art.

"I know," said Guin, "but you said the guy was very cocky, and I thought maybe he had taken a room in a different part of the hotel, under an assumed name."

"But surely someone would have seen him," said Art.

"It's a big resort," said Guin. "And he could always order in room service. Anyway, I sent Hermione, she's the head of room service, those photos of Rick you sent me, and she shared them with her staff, and this one young woman, Amy, says she saw Rick Friday night, in one of the private bungalows. Apparently, he ordered the romance package."

"Romance package?" asked Art, confused.

"They strew rose petals over the bed and bring you Champagne and caviar and chocolate truffles," said Guin.

"Ah," said Art. "Would you—?"

"No," said Guin, before Art could finish. She gave him a look. "As I was about to say," she continued, "Amy told Hermione that the guy she delivered the romance package to in Bungalow 3 was Rick. She remembers him because he chatted with her as she was arranging everything and then he gave her a big tip."

"That sounds like Rick," said Art. "So who was he with? Did Amy see the woman?"

"I asked Hermione. She said Amy didn't see anyone else, though she heard the shower running."

"Hmm," said Art.

"I know," said Guin. "Oh, and here's the kicker: When I asked Hermione whose name the room was registered to, guess what she told me?"

"I have no idea," said Art.

"Yours," said Guin, looking right into his eyes.

"What?!" said Art.

"Keep it down," said Guin, looking around and noticing people looking over at them.

"That little prick registered the room in my name? Why I'll—"

"You'll what? The guy is dead, remember?"

Art ran a hand through his hair. "Right. Sorry. I just can't believe… Actually, I totally believe it." He made a face.

"So from your reaction, I can safely assume you did not, in fact, reserve Bungalow 3?" asked Guin.

"No!" said Art, again raising his voice. "I mean, yes, I did not rent that room. Why should I?"

Guin cocked her head and gave him a look.

Art looked frustrated.

"Come on, Guin. I told you, I'm not interested in anyone else. I want *you*. And why would I rent a room at the hotel?"

Guin continued to eye him somewhat suspiciously.

"Considering your recent past with Debbie Does Dallas, it's not ridiculous for me to think that you may have hooked up with someone."

Art was about to argue with Guin, but he stopped himself. He had, in fact, rented hotel rooms, albeit not ones at fancy resorts, when he was seeing Debbie. But he was a reformed man, he told himself.

"Uh-huh," said Guin, as if reading his mind.

"I swear to you, Guin, I did NOT rent that bungalow or any bungalow."

He ran his hand through his hair, and Guin could sense his frustration.

She sighed. "I believe you," she said.

"Thank you," said Art.

"Now I need to go speak with the detective," she said. "Try not to get into any trouble while I'm over there, okay?" she said.

He smiled, relieved she wasn't angry with him.

"I'll try," he replied.

Guin left Art with his colleagues and sought out the detective, who was chatting a little way away with a couple of marina workers. Guin stopped just shy of them and waited. However, she did not have to wait long as the detective stopped his conversation as soon as he saw her.

"Back so soon, Ms. Jones?" said the detective, eyeing her.

Guin felt her cheeks start to flush. Something about being around the detective made her feel self-conscious.

"Yes, I have important information I thought you'd like to know about," she said, trying to sound calm and professional.

"Would you excuse me?" the detective said to the marina workers.

They nodded at the detective.

"Shall we?" said the detective gesturing to an empty spot a few feet away.

Guin followed him, not saying a word.

"Yes?" said the detective, stopping and once again looking right at her, as though he could hear what she was thinking.

Guin felt herself coloring again and dug her nails into her palm to try to stop herself. She regarded the detective. In the bright sunlight, his hair looked coppery, and his eyes looked as though they had flecks of gold.

"You had something important to tell me?" repeated the detective.

Guin pulled herself to together and cleared her throat.

"Yes. I just got off the phone with the head of room service over at the San Ybel Resort & Spa."

The detective waited.

"I had sent her some photos of Rick, and I asked her to ask around and see if anyone on her staff had seen Rick since his disappearance."

Guin paused and waited for the detective to say something, but he continued to calmly regard her.

"It turns out one of the women there had."

Guin paused again and looked at the detective, waiting for him to jump in. When he didn't, she continued.

"This woman, the one who saw Rick, Amy is her name, delivered a romance package to Rick's room and—"

The detective interrupted.

"Romance package?" he said.

Guin could feel the color rising to her cheeks, again. Stop it, Guin! she ordered herself.

"It's something the hotel does for guests. They bring a

cart to your room, with Champagne and chocolate truffles and treats and place rose petals on the bed," Guin explained.

"Go on," said the detective, his mouth creasing into a slight grin.

"Yes, well, as I was saying, Amy delivered the romance package to Rick's room, only it wasn't his room, or the one he had been staying in before he disappeared. He was in one of their bungalows, Bungalow 3, and it seems he wasn't alone."

The detective raised an eyebrow.

"Unfortunately, Amy didn't see anyone else, though she says she heard the shower running," Guin explained.

"This young woman, Amy, she's sure that the man in the room was Rick?" asked the detective.

"She is," said Guin. "She apparently spent several minutes in the room, setting up the romance package, and Rick chatted with her—then gave her a big tip."

Guin waited for the detective to ask her another question, but he continued to stand there, quietly, regarding her.

"And here's the kicker," said Guin. "He used the name Arthur Jones to reserve the room. I asked Art if he had rented the bungalow, and he swears he didn't," she quickly added.

"I'll check it out," said the detective.

Guin waited for the detective to say something more.

"Is there something else, Ms. Jones?"

Guin felt a bit unsure and didn't know what to say.

"Don't you have something to share with me?" she asked.

"Is there something specific you'd like to know?" asked the detective, still looking intently at her.

Yes, thought Guin, looking at the detective's rugged face and quickly glancing at his solid upper body and arms.

The detective saw her looking at him and gave her one of his bemused grins.

Guin quickly looked down, clearing her mind, and then looked up at his face again, determined not to let herself be distracted.

"Do you know who killed Rick?"

Guin watched the detective's face closely, looking for some kind of reaction. But, as usual, his expression revealed nothing.

"Not yet," he replied. "But your information helps me with a theory I've been working on," he added.

Guin smiled. "So my information was helpful, eh?"

The detective smiled back. "Don't get too cocky, Nancy Drew."

"So you going to tell me about this theory of yours?" asked Guin.

"Not yet," said the detective.

"Can you at least give me a hint?" asked Guin.

"How's your friend Emily doing?" asked the detective, changing subjects.

"How do you know about Emily?" asked Guin, somewhat taken aback.

The detective gave her a look.

"Oh, right," said Guin. "You know everything." She made a face.

"Not everything, Ms. Jones," said the detective. His lips curled into a smile. "Just some things. I hear she's being discharged from the hospital."

"I'll call her later," said Guin, slightly confused as to why the detective had brought up Emily.

"Ask her where she was Friday evening," said the detective.

Guin regarded the detective. Clearly, he knew something.

"I will," she said. "So, any idea who killed Captain Ben?

Do you think it was the same person who killed Rick?"

"It's possible," said the detective. "But it's too early to say."

Though from the expression on the detective's face, or lack thereof, Guin guessed the detective knew or suspected more than he was letting on.

"Well, will you keep me posted?" asked Guin.

The detective looked at Guin.

"Please?" asked Guin.

The detective sighed.

"Do I have a choice? If I don't, you're just going to show up at the police department."

Guin grinned at him.

"Just let me know if you have a major break in the case. I'm on deadline."

"Deadline, Ms. Jones?" said the detective, glowering at her. "I have two murder cases to deal with, and I'm sorry if the Sanibel police force and I haven't worked them out in time for your precious deadline. Maybe you should go find the killer and tell him about your deadline."

Guin blushed. Clearly, she had upset the detective.

"If there isn't anything else, Ms. Jones…"

Guin shook her head, too embarrassed to say anything.

The detective turned and started to walk away, then stopped and turned around.

Guin waited.

"Just one thing," said the detective.

"Yes?" said Guin, a bit too eagerly.

The detective smiled, which immediately made Guin suspicious.

"You free for lunch Tuesday?"

Guin stood there, stunned.

"Well, Ms. Jones?" asked the detective.

"Uh…" said Guin, too surprised to speak.

The detective continued to smile at her.

"I'll take that as a yes."

Guin realized she was staring.

"Good day, Ms. Jones," said the detective. "I'll text you Tuesday morning with the time and place."

He turned back around and headed over to where the police officers were now speaking with some other people while Guin watched. She shook her head. Did the detective just smile at her and ask her out for lunch? She grinned. However, she had work to do. So she wiped the silly grin from her face and headed over to where Craig was chatting with some people.

CHAPTER 37

Guin chatted briefly with Craig, sharing with him what she had learned. Then she made her way over to where Art, Murph, and Joe were still standing.

"Is there a reason you're still here?" asked Guin. "Does the detective have more questions for you?"

"No, we're free to go," said Art.

"He was just waiting for you," said Murph, smiling.

"He was hoping you would give him a ride back to your place," said Joe.

"You guys not going to play golf?" asked Guin.

"Missed our tee time," said Murph. "So I'm going to take young Joe here over to Fort Myers Beach."

"And you don't want to go?" Guin asked Art.

"He'd rather hang out with you," said Murph, giving her a wink.

"They're going drinking," Art explained, "and I have work to do."

"Ah," said Guin. "Well, let's go," she said.

They headed to the parking lot, then stopped next to the Mini.

"Hey, do you mind if we stop by the paper?" Guin asked, as she unlocked the car. "It's on the way back, and Ginny, my boss, has been dying to meet you. I kind of blew her off the other night."

"Oh, so you've told your boss about me, eh?" said Art, smiling.

Guin rolled her eyes. "Don't flatter yourself. Just behave, okay?"

"Don't I always?" he said, still grinning.

Guin rolled her eyes again, then unlocked the car.

"Get in," she commanded.

They arrived at the offices of the *San-Cap Sun-Times* a few minutes later and were immediately greeted by Peanut, Jasmine's miniature labradoodle puppy. (Jasmine was in charge of laying out the paper.)

"Hello, Peanut!" said Guin, bending down to pet the puppy.

Peanut immediately tried to jump on Guin and lick her face.

"Down, Peanut!" called Jasmine. "Sorry, Guin. I'm still training him."

"That's okay," said Guin, laughing.

"And who is this you've brought with you?" said Jasmine, eyeing Art.

"Arthur Jones. I'm Guin's husband," announced Art, extending a hand.

Jasmine raised an eyebrow.

"*Ex*-husband," clarified Guin, standing up and giving Art a sharp look. "I'm still trying to train him," she added.

Jasmine let out a loud bark.

"Ginny's in the back, in her office. Just knock if the door is closed."

"Come along, Arthur," said Guin.

"Woof," said Art, with a smile, as he followed her down the hall.

Peanut immediately started barking.

"Shh, Peanut!" said Jasmine, bending down and shaking her head.

Ginny's door was, indeed, closed. So Guin knocked.

"Yes?" called Ginny from within.

"It's Guin. And I have a surprise for you!"

A few seconds later Ginny opened the door and immediately spied Art towering behind Guin.

"You must be the ex-husband," she said, looking Art over.

"That would be me," said Art, giving her his best salesman's smile. "Arthur Jones," he added, extending his hand.

Ginny eyed it, but she did not shake it. "At long last, the infamous Arthur Jones."

"Infamous, eh?" said Art.

"Come in, come in," said Ginny, ushering them into her small, cluttered office. "Excuse the mess," she added, moving piles of papers from one of the chairs so one of them could sit.

"We just stopped by to say hello," said Guin.

"Well, hello," said Ginny, taking a seat behind her desk. "How goes the murder investigation?" She looked over at Art. "So, just between us, did you do it?"

"Sorry to disappoint you, but no," he said, with a smile.

"Well, at least Guin's not harboring a killer."

"Thanks, Gin," said Guin, making a face at her boss.

"And what's this I hear about someone knocking off Big Ben Johnson?"

"Do you have a spy at the marina?" asked Guin.

Ginny smiled. "They're not spies, darling."

"Ginny knows everyone—and everything that goes on—on Sanibel," Guin informed Art.

"And on Captiva," added Ginny. "Speaking of which, I'm still waiting on that piece from you."

"I'm writing it this weekend," said Guin.

"And I want an update on the Tomlinson murder from you and Craig by Tuesday. Hopefully by then the detective will have solved the case."

"I'll talk to Craig. I'm sure he's on it. Anything else?"

"Yes, I want you to do a piece on Fourth of July happenings," said Ginny.

"No problem," said Guin. "So who's covering the Captain Ben murder, Craig?"

"Yes. As he was the one to discover Ben's body, it seemed appropriate."

"Poor Craig, all these murders are seriously cutting into his fishing time," said Guin.

"Personally, I think he's enjoying it," said Ginny. "I think he's missed crime reporting."

"I don't know," said Guin. "He seemed pretty happy to spend his days fishing—and getting paid to go and write about it."

Ginny turned to Art. "So, handsome, what do you think of our little island?"

"I can see why Guin loves it here," Art said, giving Ginny another big smile.

"Save the charm for someone who buys it," said Ginny. "I'm immune at this point."

Art chuckled. "I do quite like it here," he said. "As a matter of fact, I'm thinking I may need to get a place here myself."

Guin turned to Art with a look somewhere between confusion and terror.

"What?!" she said, staring at him. "You can't be serious."

"I'm quite serious," said Art. "I've come to love your little island in the short time I've been down here. I can play golf, go fishing—"

"You hate to fish, and what about work?" said Guin.

"Assuming I get that promotion, I'll be coming down here more often—and I'll have four weeks off."

"No," said Guin. "I won't allow it."

"I don't believe it's up to you to decide where I vacation or buy a place."

Ginny looked from one to the other.

"This is better than watching a tennis match!"

Guin blushed. "Sorry, Ginny. I don't know what's come over Art. We should go."

She glared at Art, who continued to smile.

"Don't leave on my account," said Ginny. "I'm quite enjoying myself."

"See, Ginny thinks it's a great idea," said Art.

"Don't go putting words in my mouth, big fella," said Ginny.

"Let's go," said Guin, grabbing Art's elbow and moving towards the door. "I'll talk to you later, Ginny."

"Toodle-oo," called Ginny. "And get those two pieces to me by Tuesday!"

Guin marched Art down the hall and out the door, not even stopping to say goodbye to Jasmine and Peanut. When they got outside, Guin stopped and let go of Art's elbow.

"What the hell was that about?" said Guin, her hair springing up all around her.

"What was what about?" asked Art.

"Don't play the innocent with me, buster. That whole, 'I'm thinking of getting a place down here.'"

"Oh that," said Art, grinning at Guin. "Actually, I have been thinking about it."

"Oh no," said Guin. "You are not coming to Sanibel. No."

"I like it here," said Art. "And admit it, you like having me around," he said, taking a step closer and gently placing a hand on Guin's arm.

Guin felt herself growing warm. She hated that Art still had that effect on her.

Art tucked one of Guin's unruly curls behind her ear and then gently caressed her face.

"Admit it," he whispered in her ear.

Guin was finding it difficult to concentrate.

"Admit it," he said again, pinning her against the Mini and gently darting his tongue into her ear.

Guin closed her eyes as Art planted kisses along her neck. Then she abruptly opened her eyes and pushed him away.

"No! Stop!" she said, a little too loudly. "This is wrong."

"I'd say it was very right," said Art, moving his hand to caress Guin's face again.

She slapped it away.

"No, Art. I'll admit, I still have feelings for you."

Art smiled triumphantly.

"But we are NOT getting back together, and I do NOT want you getting a place on Sanibel or even visiting Sanibel again," she stated, feeling her confidence growing. "I have a new life down here, a life that doesn't include you. And as soon as the detective says it's okay for you to leave, I want you to get on a plane and go back to Connecticut and to not contact me again."

"But Guin——" said Art.

"No, 'but Guins.' I mean it, Art. As a matter of fact, I'm going to speak with the detective this afternoon about having you go back to the hotel or stay with Murph."

Art knew better than to argue with Guin when she was like this, so he held up his hands in surrender.

"I'm sorry. I thought you felt it, too," he said. "You don't have to send me back to the hotel or to Murph's. I'll behave. I promise."

Guin eyed him suspiciously.

"Give me another chance," he said, giving her that look

he used to give her when he knew he had screwed up.

Guin sighed. "Fine, but one pass, one stupid comment, and I'm kicking you out of the condo. I don't care what the detective says. He doesn't like it, you can go live with him."

Guin then unlocked the Mini and jerked open the door. "Get in," she said.

Art got in, and they drove back to the condo in silence.

CHAPTER 38

Guin was still in a foul mood when she walked in the door.

"I'm going to call Emily, see if she's back at the resort."

"I'm sure she'll appreciate that," said Art. "I'm going to go do some work."

"Fine," said Guin.

Guin went into her office/bedroom, followed by the cats.

"Not now, guys, I need to make a call and then do some work."

"Meow," said Fauna, looking up at her.

"Sorry, girl."

Flora started rubbing against Guin's legs. Guin sighed and bent down to pet her, stopping after a few seconds, much to the cat's dismay.

"Sorry, Flora. I'll pet you more later. Right now, I need to do some work."

As usual, both cats ignored her and continued to vie for her attention. Guin ignored them as best she could and took out her phone to call Emily. But before she could dial the resort, her phone started buzzing. It was Ris. She debated whether to pick it up, finally deciding to answer.

"Hey you, what's up?"

"Just calling to confirm our date tomorrow. We still on?"

"Absolutely!" said Guin. "I'm looking forward to it."

Though she suddenly realized she was not.

"Just one thing," said Ris.

"Yes?" asked Guin.

"Would it be okay if Fiona joined us?"

Fiona was Ris's daughter, who had just finished her freshman year of college.

"Of course!" said Guin. "Is something wrong?"

Fiona and her twin brother, John, usually stayed with their mother, though they had a room at Ris's cottage in Fort Myers Beach.

"Not really. She just got into another fight with her mother and asked if she could stay here this weekend. I hope you don't mind."

"She's your daughter, Ris! Of course I don't mind."

"Thanks for being so understanding."

"Hey, if you need some alone time with her, just say the word and we can go out next week," said Guin, part of her hoping he would cancel.

"No way am I cancelling our date," he replied. "I'm not even sure if she'll be around tomorrow night. You know teenagers. I just wanted to warn you," he said.

"Okay," said Guin. "I'd be fine ordering in a pizza and renting a movie."

Ris laughed. "If we stay in, I'm cooking something healthy. Gotta watch my weight."

Guin rolled her eyes. Ris had barely an ounce of body fat on him, a fact that irritated her.

"Well, let me know tomorrow what you want to do. I'm fine doing whatever."

"Is your ex still staying with you?"

"Yes," she replied, feeling slightly irritated.

"Any idea when he'll be leaving?"

"Hopefully, very soon. The detective won't divulge much, but I have a feeling he's very close to solving the case—and I'm pretty sure Art's in the clear," she added.

"Excellent. The sooner he goes, the sooner we can get on with our lives."

Guin didn't know how to reply.

"So how's your article coming?" Ris asked.

"There's actually been another murder," Guin answered.

"Another murder? And to think Sanibel used to be a sleepy little fishing village—until you came along," said Ris, chuckling.

"Ha ha," said Guin, not finding the comment amusing, especially as the murder rate had indeed gone up in her short time living on Sanibel.

"So who's the corpse this time?"

"A charter boat captain named Ben Johnson."

"Big Ben?"

"Yeah, you know him?" asked Guin.

"A bit," said Ris.

"Know anyone who'd want to kill him?" asked Guin.

"I didn't know him that well."

"Oh well," said Guin, wanting to end the call. "Well, ring me back or text me tomorrow and let me know what you and Fiona want to do."

"Will do," said Ris. "And Guin?"

"Yes?" said Guin.

"Thank you."

"For what?"

"For being so understanding," said Ris. "About this weekend and Fiona."

"Hey, if anyone's been understanding lately, it's you," said Guin.

"Yeah, well, I'm not sure how much longer I'm going to be so understanding," he said. "I feel like I've barely seen you the past couple of weeks."

"Well, you were away and…"

"You know what I mean," said Ris.

"Anyway, I'll see you tomorrow," said Guin.

"Okay. I'll text you in the morning."

"Good. Until tomorrow."

"Until tomorrow."

Guin ended the call. Then she immediately dialed the San Ybel Resort & Spa and asked for Emily's room.

"Hello?" said a female voice.

"Emily, it's Guin."

"How come you didn't call me on my mobile?"

"I wasn't thinking," said Guin. "Anyway, how are you?"

"I feel like an idiot, Guin."

"Don't," said Guin. "Hey, you want me to come by? We can go for a walk or something, if you're up to it."

"I'd love to," said Emily.

"Then it's a date."

Guin looked at her clock.

"How about I swing by a little after five?"

"Sounds good!" said Emily. "Hey, I know: Why don't you and Art join us for dinner tonight at the resort?"

"I don't know, Em," said Guin.

"Oh, come on. It will be like old times."

That was what Guin was afraid of. But she could hear the need in Emily's voice and decided to put her own feelings aside.

"Fine. Let me just go check with Art that he hasn't made any plans and I'll give you a call back in a few minutes, okay?"

"Okay. Just call me on my mobile. You need me to give you the number again?"

"Sure," said Guin, "though I should have it in my contacts."

Guin took down Emily's cell phone number and ended the call. Then she walked into the living area, where Art was glued to his laptop.

"Ahem," said Guin, trying to get his attention.

He looked up. "Yes?"

"Emily just invited us over for dinner. That okay with you?"

"Not like I've got other plans," said Art.

"Can you be ready by five-thirty? And would you be okay hanging out with Alan for a little while, while I went for a walk with Emily? I still have some questions for her, and maybe you can buy Alan a drink and do a little digging."

"I'll try," said Art. "But I have a feeling he's not going to tell me anything."

"Well, do your best," said Guin.

He smiled at her. "I always do."

Guin rolled her eyes. "Just be ready to go at five-thirty."

"Aye aye!" said Art, saluting her.

Guin turned and walked back into the bedroom.

She called Emily on her mobile and waited for her to pick up.

"So?"

"We're all set," said Guin. "We're going to leave here at five-thirty. So we should get to the resort around five forty-five. I told Art to entertain Alan, so you and I can go for a beach walk."

"Perfect!" said Emily.

"Could you make us a dinner reservation?"

"Sure, which restaurant do you want to go to?"

"You pick," said Guin. "I know the resort has good food."

"What time?" asked Emily.

"How about seven-thirty?"

"Sounds good. I'll ask Alan if he has a preference. And I'll see you here around five forty-five!"

"Do you want to meet me at the front desk?"

"Sure," said Emily.

"Great. See you soon," said Guin.

Guin ended the call and booted up her laptop. She had planned on spending the evening working, but now work would have to wait, again. Oh well. She wondered if it was even worth doing any work as she had to leave in an hour and decided to read the paper online instead. Before she knew it, it was nearly five-thirty, and she had yet to change. She dashed into her closet and threw on a dress. Then she went into the bathroom and examined her hair. Her strawberry blonde curls were frizzing, as usual. She spritzed them with a little water and worked a little mousse into them, to get rid of the frizz. She turned her head from side to side and sighed. It would have to do. She quickly applied a little mascara and some lip gloss, then made her way to the living room.

"You ready?" she asked Art, who she swore hadn't moved since she last saw him.

"Yup," he said, staring at the screen on his laptop.

"You going to wear that?" Guin asked, looking at his polo shirt and board shorts.

"You got a problem with it?" asked Art, glancing her way.

"Could you at least put on some pants?"

"For you? Sure," said Art, smiling at her.

"Go!" said Guin, pointing toward the guest room. "I told Emily we'd be there around five forty-five."

"So what if we're a few minutes late? I'm sure they won't care," said Art.

"Just put on a pair of pants, okay?"

Art smiled, stood, and saluted her (again). Then he took his laptop and headed off toward the guest room.

Guin sighed and walked into the kitchen. She gave the cats some food and some fresh water. A few minutes later, Art emerged from the guest room, wearing a pair of chinos and a collarless button-down shirt.

"You look very nice," said Guin, giving him a smile. Though Art always looked good.

Art smiled down at her. "Shall we?" he said.

"Let's," said Guin.

"Goodbye, cats!" she called from the doorway. "No throwing up while we're gone, please!"

A few minutes later, they were in the Mini, heading to the resort.

CHAPTER 39

They arrived at the San Ybel Resort & Spa a little before six. Guin handed the keys to the valet, and she and Art walked into the lobby. They immediately spied Alan and Emily and exchanged greetings.

"So, you boys okay grabbing a drink while Emily and I go for a walk?" asked Guin.

"I think I can choke one down," said Alan. "How about you, Arthur?"

"I think I can manage a beer, or two," he said, smiling.

"Just don't get smashed," said Guin, giving him a warning look.

Art gave her that 'who me?' look. Guin made a face.

"We'll meet you at La Mer at seven-thirty," Emily called, as she guided Guin toward the patio and the path that wound its way down to the beach.

"La Mer?" asked Guin.

"That's the new French place here. It's supposed to be very good."

"Sounds great," said Guin.

They walked in silence for a few minutes.

"This path goes down by the pool and then along the beach," Emily explained.

"Sounds good," said Guin. "I wore my comfy sandals, so it's okay if I get a little sand in them."

"If it's okay with you, I think I'd prefer to stay on the path," said Emily, looking down at her elegant, definitely not beach ready, sandals.

They continued walking, past the main pool and the smaller pool. Then Guin stopped.

"Are those the private cabanas?" Guin asked, pointing to a group of cabanas around the smaller pool.

"I believe so. Why?" asked Emily.

Guin walked over to them.

"This is where they found Rick."

She turned and saw that Emily hadn't followed her toward the cabanas and was staring at them.

"Are you okay, Em?"

"I'm fine," she replied. "Just still a little weak, I guess."

Guin eyed her. She did not look fine. But Guin decided to ask her the question anyway.

"Emily, was there something between you and Rick?"

Guin could tell from Emily's body language and expression that she was struggling.

"I know you've had a miserable couple of days," said Guin, apologetically.

"Make that a miserable couple of weeks, no months," said Emily, clenching her hands.

Guin gave her a sympathetic look.

"You want to talk about it?"

"Not really," said Emily. "But I have a feeling you won't leave me alone until I do," she said, a half-resigned, half-amused expression on her face. "You promise not to tell anyone, not even Art?"

Guin hesitated, then said, "I promise." Though she was tempted to cross her fingers behind her back.

Emily took a deep breath and unclenched her hands.

"Rick and I were more than friends."

She looked at Guin, waiting for her to say something, but

Guin just waited for her to go on.

"It started at the Christmas party," she continued. "I know, what a cliché, right? Alan was chatting up everyone, and I was pretty miserable and probably had too much to drink. Rick came over to me and started chatting with me. At first I kind of ignored him, but Rick could be pretty persistent."

She smiled at the memory. Then looked at Guin, expecting her to say something. But Guin continued to stand there quietly, looking at Emily.

"I wish I could have a drink," Emily said. The doctor had told her alcohol was off limits. "Anyway, Rick and I wound up chatting for a while. I don't even remember what about. At some point he suggested we get out of there, go have a drink someplace else. I told him I couldn't, that I was the boss's wife and was expected to stay and be sociable, even though I loathed the office Christmas party. And he said, 'I won't tell Alan if you won't,' and that made me laugh."

She smiled again at the memory.

"I really didn't plan on leaving the party with him," she said. "But then I saw Alan chatting up the new head of Marketing. You should see her, Guin. She was wearing this blouse that was unbuttoned practically down to her belly button. Alan called her 'sex on a stick.'"

She made a face.

Guin gave her a sympathetic look.

"But you know what men can be like, especially when they've been drinking," said Emily. "Anyway, I kind of snapped. And I told Rick, sure, let's get out of here. And we left. I didn't even tell Alan I was leaving. Not like he even noticed. He was too busy with Miss Cleavage."

Emily made a face.

"So then what happened?" asked Guin.

"What do you think happened?" asked Emily. "We went

back to Rick's hotel and had a couple of drinks at the bar there. I know some of the guys have issues with Rick, but he can be very charming, and he kept telling me that Alan didn't deserve me, what a jerk Alan was."

Emily glanced out at the ocean and was silent for several seconds. Guin waited.

"I hadn't had a lot to eat, or really anything, and I was feeling kind of woozy, and Rick suggested I go lie down in his room. I know in retrospect that was stupid, but at the time it seemed like a good idea."

"So you went up to his room?" asked Guin.

Emily sighed. "I did. But nothing happened. I swear," she said, looking at Guin. "He was a total gentleman. Frankly, I was a little surprised and hurt that he didn't come onto me. We just hung out on his bed, watching TV, and he ordered up some room service. It was actually really nice. Then I took a car service back to our place."

"Does Alan know?"

"I don't think so," said Emily.

"So did you see Rick again?" asked Guin, looking at Emily.

Emily looked down, then back up at Guin.

"I did. I didn't mean for it to happen, Guin. And I don't think Rick did either."

Guin could believe the part about Emily not wanting to have an affair with one of her husband's underlings, but she doubted Rick's innocence. From what she knew of Rick, he never did anything without a good reason.

"Go on," said Guin.

"Well," said Emily, looking a little uncomfortable. "You swear you won't say anything about this to Art?"

"I swear," said Guin, though this time she did cross her fingers behind her back.

"So Alan was supposedly called away at the last minute

on New Year's Eve, though I had a feeling he was sneaking off to see Miss Cleavage. And I got a call from Rick, who somehow knew Alan would be out and invited me to some party he was going to in the City. I begged off, saying I would be happy to just stay home by myself. But he wouldn't take no for an answer, and the party did sound like fun."

"So you went? Did you have a place to stay in the City?"

"My cousin, Dot, has a place. She's always inviting me to crash there. So I emailed her to see if it was okay to stay over there New Year's Eve, and she said she was out of town, but to go ahead. She'd leave instructions for the doorman to let me in."

"How very nice of cousin Dot," said Guin.

Emily smiled. "Yeah, she's great. She's a lot older than I am, more like my aunt than my cousin. She travels a lot, so I don't get to see her as often as I'd like. Anyway, I texted Rick back to let him know I'd go to the party, and he said he'd meet me there."

"So you went?"

"I did," said Emily, smiling. "I felt so rebellious!"

"And how was the party?" asked Guin.

"A lot of fun. I was sort of surprised. Rick's friends were great. So not like Alan's crew. No one talked about sales or P and L statements."

Guin smiled.

"And there was a lot of booze, as you might expect."

Emily paused, and Guin waited for her to continue.

"Then, suddenly, it was almost midnight, and we all gathered in the living room to do the countdown with Ryan Seacrest. And the next thing I knew, it was midnight and Rick was kissing me, and I was kissing him back."

Emily blushed at the memory.

"Did you make it to cousin Dot's?" asked Guin.

"I did, with Rick," said Emily. "Oh Guin, he was

amazing. With Alan, it was, like, one, two, three; in, out, and done. But with Rick… He made me feel things I hadn't felt with Alan in years."

Guin could feel herself blushing.

"Did you continue to see Rick afterward?"

"I did, but he traveled a lot for work. So we didn't get together that often, but he would call or text me from the road."

"And Alan has no idea?" asked Guin.

"I don't think so, no," said Emily. "He's been so absorbed in work, he hardly notices me anymore."

"Oh, I doubt that," said Guin.

"You know, I thought when Peter [their son] went off to boarding school, our sex life would improve, but it's like Alan completely lost interest. It was always work, or golf, or…"

"Miss Cleavage?" said Guin.

"Yes," said Emily.

"So did you and Rick get together here on Sanibel?"

Emily glanced off into the distance, then back at Guin. "Yes," she said quietly.

"Did you see him after he disappeared?" asked Guin, looking right at her.

Emily looked at Guin. Guin could tell she was debating what to tell her, if anything.

"Emily…" said Guin, softly. "Did you see Rick after he disappeared?"

"Yes," said Emily, very softly—so softly Guin could barely hear her.

"Sorry? I couldn't hear you," said Guin.

"I said *yes*!" said Emily. "I didn't know about him disappearing. Not at first. I only found out about it that Friday evening."

"Alan didn't mention anything to you?" Guin found that hard to believe.

"No. Like I said, Alan barely talks to me. I was asleep, I think, when he finally got back to the room Thursday, and he left early Friday."

"So he didn't tell you until Friday night?"

Emily blushed slightly.

"Ah," said Guin, suddenly understanding.

"Rick and I met up at Doc Ford's, on Captiva," explained Emily. "He had left a message for me. I had no idea about him leaving the boat. I just assumed he was busy with conference stuff. And we wanted to make sure no one saw us together."

"So it was you with Rick at Doc Ford's!" said Guin, suddenly putting two and two together.

Emily looked confused.

"I was having drinks with friends at Doc Ford's over on Captiva, and I saw this guy who looked familiar having dinner with some brunette who also looked familiar. I realized later it was Rick. So that must have been you."

Emily grimaced. "So much for no one spotting us."

"And you really didn't know he was missing?"

"No!" said Emily. "I swear to you, Guin. I had no idea. I told you, Alan doesn't talk about work, and I've barely seen him since we've been down here. He's either working, or fishing, or out playing golf, or hanging with the guys."

"So how did you find out?"

"Rick told me, over drinks. He said he was playing a practical joke on the guys and not to tell anyone I'd seen him."

"Then what happened?" asked Guin.

"Then we went back to his place," said Emily, smiling again.

"His place?"

"Rick had rented one of those bungalows, at the other end of the property," Emily explained.

"And let me guess, he ordered the romance package from room service."

Emily's eyes got wide. "How did you know?"

"Lucky guess," said Guin. "So did you stay overnight in Rick's room?"

"Oh no!" said Emily. "I'm not that crazy. I was back in my room by ten-thirty. Alan wasn't even there when I got back."

"And what about that Saturday? Did you see Rick then, too?"

"Briefly, that afternoon."

"Where did you two meet?"

"In his bungalow," said Emily.

"Did he happen to mention anything about his little practical joke, or seeing any of the guys?" Guin asked.

"He just reminded me not to tell anyone that I had seen him. I felt a little uncomfortable. I knew by then that everyone was looking for Rick, and I didn't like lying."

Guin gave her a look.

"I know. I know," said Emily. "I'm a hypocrite. But you know what I mean. Lying about having an affair is one thing. Lying about someone not being dead is another."

"Go on," said Guin.

Emily took a deep breath, then exhaled.

"I told Rick I was uncomfortable lying about not knowing his whereabouts, and he said I wouldn't have to for much longer."

"Did he explain what he meant?" asked Guin.

"Not really. I asked him how much longer, and he said 'tonight.' I started to ask him more questions, but he pulled me into an embrace and…"

Emily blushed, and Guin could guess the rest.

"So you didn't see Rick again that Saturday?"

"No," said Emily, suddenly looking sad.

"Where did you go after you left Rick's bungalow?" Guin asked.

"I went for a walk."

"And Alan had no idea you were secretly meeting with Rick?" Guin asked, looking directly at Emily.

Emily looked back at Guin.

"I don't think so," she said.

"But you're not sure?"

"No," said Emily. "When I got back to the room, Alan was there, having a drink from the mini bar. He was clearly in a mood. He was murmuring to himself, something about 'that son of a bitch,' so I tried to avoid him. But as soon as he saw me, he asked me where I had been. I told him I had been out for a walk, but from the look on his face, I'm not sure he believed me. I told him I had a headache and went into the bathroom to take a shower. When I got out, Alan was gone."

"Do you know where he went?" asked Guin.

"I have no idea," said Emily.

"When did he come back?" asked Guin.

"A little after six, maybe?" replied Emily. "We got into an argument about the dinner. I told him I still had a headache and was not going. He eventually gave up arguing with me and left."

They looked at each other for a few seconds, then turned to look out at the sea. Eventually Guin turned back to face Emily.

"Thank you," she said.

"For what?" asked Emily, turning to face Guin.

"For telling me about you and Rick. But Em…"

Emily looked hesitant.

"You should really tell Detective O'Loughlin what you told me. You don't have to tell him all of it, but it will help with the murder investigation," said Guin. "You do want to find out who killed Rick, don't you?"

"You don't believe it was an accident?" said Emily.

"Doubtful," said Guin. "I'm pretty sure someone slipped some ground up ibuprofen into Rick's drink, knowing it could kill him."

The wind picked up and Emily wrapped her arms around herself.

"Okay," she said, "I'll tell him, but can it wait until tomorrow Guin? Please?"

Guin looked at Emily and felt unable to argue with her, though she was itching to tell the detective herself as soon as she could slip away.

"Fine," she said. "Just please, Em, call him first thing tomorrow. Now we should probably go meet up with the boys."

Emily sighed. "If we must."

"Come on," said Guin.

They made their way back down the path, to the restaurant.

CHAPTER 40

"I thought dinner went well," said Art, as they drove back to the condo in Guin's Mini Cooper. "The food was certainly good, as was the service."

Guin didn't say anything. She was still thinking about what Emily had told her and wondering if she would indeed contact the detective in the morning and tell him about her and Rick.

"Penny for your thoughts," said Art.

"Sorry, I've got a lot on my mind."

"I can tell," said Art. "You're thinking about the murders, aren't you?"

Guin shot him a quick look. "How did you know?"

"I was married to you, as you may recall," replied Art with a grin. "And I know that face, even in the dark. It means you're plotting something."

Guin laughed. "There goes my professional poker career."

"So, did you find out anything from Emily?"

Guin was silent. She had promised Emily she wouldn't tell anyone what she had told her, not even Art, especially Art.

"Just that she's been unhappy," she finally said. "I don't think things are good at home. You learn anything from Alan?"

"Not much. He kept changing the subject whenever I asked him about Rick. I have a feeling the two of them weren't as tight as I thought they were."

"Oh?" said Guin, trying to keep her eyes on the road.

"Yeah," said Art. "Like I said, Alan didn't say much, and he got really annoyed when I kept bringing up Rick. He said, 'I told you, I don't want to talk about that lying son of a bitch.' Though he immediately apologized and said one shouldn't speak ill of the dead."

Guin was about to say something when her phone started ringing.

"You going to answer it?" Art asked.

"Not while I'm driving," said Guin.

"You want me to get it?"

"No!" said Guin.

"Afraid to let me speak with your boyfriend?"

Guin glared at Art.

"We'll be back at the condo in five minutes. If it's important, they'll leave a message."

As soon as they walked in the door, Guin checked her phone. There was a voicemail and a text message from Craig. That's odd, she thought. She opened the text message first. "Call me as soon as you get this" it read. Guin didn't bother to check her voicemail. Instead, she walked into her bedroom, closed the door, and immediately called Craig back. He picked up after the second ring.

"I got your text. What's up?" Guin asked.

"Did you listen to my voicemail message?"

"No," said Guin, "not yet. I called as soon as I got your text. Art and I were having dinner with Alan and Emily and just got home."

There was silence at the other end of the line.

"Craig?" asked Guin, a feeling of dread welling up inside her.

There was silence on the other end of the line for a few seconds, then Craig spoke again.

"So, I was just at my regular Friday night fish fry and poker game. And a couple of the guys got to talking about Big Ben. We had all had a bunch of beers at this point, and everyone there had heard about Ben. And one of the guys, Danny, his boat is docked near Ben's, mentioned that a guy had been looking for Ben."

"So?" said Guin. "I imagine lots of guys go looking for Ben."

"Yeah, but not at six o'clock in the morning," said Craig.

"Maybe the guy had scheduled an early morning fishing trip," said Guin.

"You going to let me finish or what?" asked Craig.

"Sorry," said Guin. "Go on."

"So this guy comes up to Danny, who happened to be at the marina early and was one of the only people there, and asks where Big Ben's boat is. And Danny asks him why he wants to know, it being so early, though Ben's been known to head out pretty early in the summer time, if the tide's not too low. Anyway, the guy tells Danny he has an appointment with Ben. Danny didn't quite believe him, but like I said, Ben kept unconventional hours."

"Did Danny tell the guy where Ben's boat was?"

"I was just getting to that," said Craig. "He did, but he told the guy he hadn't seen Ben yet. The guy thanked Danny and said he'd wait. Danny said, 'suit yourself,' and then headed out in his boat a few minutes later."

"So who was the guy who was talking to Danny?" asked Guin, though she feared she already knew the answer.

"Danny only saw the guy for a few minutes, but he has a pretty good memory for details, and he said he hadn't seen the guy before, that he wasn't a local."

"So do you know who the guy was?" Guin asked again,

impatiently. "Do you think he's the person who killed Big Ben?"

"I wondered about that, so I asked Danny to describe the guy, and something about the description rang a bell. I pulled up that photo of Art and his buddies on my phone, the one that was taken just before their fishing trip, and I had Danny take a look at it and see if he recognized the guy."

"And?" asked Guin, clutching the phone tightly.

"And he said 'that one there, the guy in the middle. That's him.'"

Guin racked her brain, trying to recall the photo, worried about disconnecting Craig if she went to look at it on her phone. She tried to picture the photo, and suddenly it came to her.

"Alan?" said Guin, momentarily stunned. "He pointed to Alan Fielding? But why would Alan kill Captain Ben?"

"That's what I was wondering," said Craig. "So I asked the guys if Ben had said something to them, something that might connect Ben and Alan, and my buddy, Jimbo—"

"Wait, there are really people named Jimbo?" asked Guin, interrupting Craig.

"Yes, there are. And you'd know that if you watched college football."

He paused for a few seconds, then continued.

"So Jimbo says, 'I wasn't going to say anything, but as Ben is dead, I guess it doesn't matter.'"

"What doesn't matter?" asked Guin, unable to contain herself. She realized she was interrupting again and quickly apologized. "Sorry," she said. "Go on."

"So Jimbo explains that he and Ben were out drinking a couple of nights before Ben got whacked. Ben had had a lot to drink, which was par for the course with Ben. And they see some cops come in, and Ben kind of freaks out. Jimbo asks him, half-jokingly, 'What's up, Ben? You in trouble with the law again?'"

"Again?" asked Guin.

"Yeah, Ben had a bit of a record. Nothing serious. Just some minor violations. Anyway," he continued, "it turns out Ben had helped Rick disappear. He told Jimbo the whole story. Like I said, he had had a lot to drink, and he thought the cops were there to arrest him."

"Why would they arrest him? Did he kill Rick?"

"No," said Craig. "Jimbo said Ben told him the whole thing was a practical joke, or that's what Rick had told him. Just a bunch of guys pranking each other, something Ben understood. But when Rick was found dead a couple of days later…"

"Why didn't Ben just go to the police, tell them what happened?"

"Like I said, Ben's had some run-ins with the authorities and was worried that they'd arrest him."

"So did Ben say anything else to Jimbo, anything that could connect him and Alan?"

"I asked Jimbo that. He had to think a minute. He had also had a lot to drink that night and didn't remember a whole lot, but he did say that Ben told him that 'those sales guys are all crazy. Just the other day another one of them offered me double my rate if I would take him and his wife out.'"

"That seems odd, but not criminal," said Guin. "Was there more to it?"

"I asked Jimbo to try to remember if Ben said anything else about the guy."

"And?" said Guin, growing impatient.

"He said Ben told him there was something fishy about the guy, that he had asked him if he could take them someplace really secluded, where there wouldn't be other boats or people, and that he would make it worth Ben's while."

"Do you know if Ben agreed?" asked Guin.

"According to Jimbo, Ben initially turned him down. He had another booking the morning the guy wanted to take his wife out. Then the guy offered to pay him double his rate."

Guin raised her eyebrows. "Which morning did he want to take his wife out on the boat?"

"The morning they found Ben dead."

"Did Jimbo say if Ben took the booking?"

"According to Jimbo, Ben said he had agreed, but he was having second thoughts and was going to call the guy and cancel."

"And you think Alan was the guy who had hired Ben to take him and his wife out to a secluded spot?"

"I do," said Craig.

"And you think Alan was going to do something to Emily?" asked Guin.

"I don't know for sure, but the whole thing didn't sound good," said Craig.

Suddenly, the pieces of the puzzle started to click together in Guin's mind.

"Have you told the detective all of this?" she asked.

"I called and left a message at the police department. I'm waiting to hear back," Craig replied.

"Why don't you call his mobile?" suggested Guin.

"Because I respect the guy's privacy," said Craig.

Guin felt her face growing hot.

"I told the officer in charge it was urgent," he continued. "And he said he would get in touch with Detective O'Loughlin right away."

"I need to warn Emily," said Guin.

"Just be careful, Guin," cautioned Craig.

"I will, but Emily could be in serious danger."

Guin was itching to tell Craig about Rick and Emily having an affair, and her suspicion that Alan knew about it, but she had promised Emily she wouldn't say anything to anyone. Instead she asked him to call or text her the minute he heard from the detective and to ask the detective to call her immediately. In light of what she just learned, she wanted to persuade Emily to speak with the detective immediately, not wait until the morning. But if Emily refused, she would tell the detective herself, even if it meant breaking her promise to Em.

"I've got to go," Guin said to Craig. "Thanks for the call. And remember, if the detective calls you, have him call me afterward."

They said their goodbyes and hung up. Then Guin immediately called Emily's mobile. No answer. She paced her bedroom and tried Emily's number again, but it went directly to voicemail. She opened the door and went into the living room, where she found Art on his computer.

"I'm worried about Emily," she said.

Art looked up. "We just saw Emily."

"I know," said Guin, "but she's not answering her phone."

"Maybe she's asleep," suggested Art.

"I guess it's possible, but…"

Art could tell from Guin's expression that something was wrong.

"What aren't you telling me?"

Guin bit her lip.

"Craig thinks Alan may have killed Captain Ben," she blurted out.

"Alan?" said Art.

"Yes, Alan," said Guin. "I don't have time to explain, but I think he's going to try to kill Emily too."

"You drunk?" asked Art.

"No, I am not drunk," said Guin, indignant. "You were with me at dinner. I barely drank."

"So what do you want me to do?" asked Art.

"I want to drive back over to the resort and make sure Emily's okay."

"Why don't you call over there first?" suggested Art.

"I already called her mobile. She didn't answer. Went straight to voicemail."

"Why don't you call the main switchboard and have them ring Emily's room?"

Guin huffed. "Fine. But if no one picks up, we're heading over there."

"Fine," said Art.

Guin turned her back to Art and called over to the resort.

"Emily Fielding's room, please," she told the operator, when she picked up.

She waited for the call to go through, but the extension just rang and rang, and then the voicemail picked up.

"Em? This is Guin. Call me as soon as you get this. Thanks."

"She wasn't there?" asked Art. "You know, she could be asleep and have turned the phone off. She's had a pretty taxing couple of days."

"I'm going over there," Guin announced. "Are you coming with me or not?"

Art closed his laptop. "I'm coming with you. You sure you're okay to drive?"

Guin thought about it. She grabbed the key to the Mini and flipped it to Art.

"No, you drive. Now let's go."

As they headed over to the resort, Guin decided not to wait for the detective to call her. Instead she pulled her phone out of her bag and sent him a text, despite the late hour.

"URGENT:" she typed. "Call me as soon as you get this."

A few seconds later her phone rang. It was the detective.

"This better be good," he said.

"Have you spoken with Craig?" Guin asked.

"I was about to call him when I got your urgent text," replied the detective. "What's this all about?"

Ignoring the fact that Art was in the car, she summarized what Craig had told her—and told the detective that Rick and Emily had been having an affair and she suspected that Alan had found out about it.

"Rick and Emily were having an affair?!" said Art, swerving slightly.

"Watch where you're going," hissed Guin. "You weren't supposed to know."

Art turned and looked straight ahead, the speedometer climbing past 45 mph.

"Hello?" said the detective. "Anybody there? Don't tell me you're driving."

"No, Art's driving," Guin replied. "We're on our way over to the resort, to warn Emily."

"You are to do no such thing," said the detective.

"Too late," said Guin, "we're pulling in."

"Under no circumstances are you to go looking for your friend this evening, Ms. Jones."

"Gotta go, detective," said Guin, getting out of the car.

"I'm serious, Guin," said the detective. But Guin had already hung up.

CHAPTER 41

Guin made a beeline for the lobby, not waiting for Art.

"Hey, wait up!" called Art.

"I need to make sure Emily is okay," Guin called over her shoulder, practically running towards the stairs.

Art followed her up to the second floor, then down the hallway to where Alan and Emily were staying. When she got there, she banged on the door.

"Emily? Are you in there? Emily?"

No reply.

"We need to find someone to let us into that room!" said Guin.

Just then Art spied a maid leaving a nearby room.

"Excuse me," said Art, giving her a sheepish smile. "I locked myself out of my room, and my wife here is about to kill me," he said, looking over at Guin, who did look quite upset.

The maid looked from Art to Guin.

"Please?" said Art, mustering his powers of persuasion. "I feel like an idiot. And she really needs to pee. I promise it won't happen again."

The maid sighed and used her passkey to open the door.

"Thank you," said Art. He held the door open for Guin, then waved to the maid. "Good night!"

The room was dark and quiet. Art switched on the light.

"Is that wise?" asked Guin.

"Clearly no one is here," said Art, glancing around.

Guin looked around the room. The beds were still made up and nothing looked disturbed.

"Where could they be?" asked Guin.

"Maybe they went out dancing or for a nightcap," suggested Art.

"On Sanibel? After nine o'clock? Highly unlikely."

"Well, we should check the bar, just to be sure," he said.

Guin walked around the room, looking for anything suspicious.

"What are you hoping to find?" asked Art.

"I don't know. Something."

She looked in the closet. Everything seemed to be in order. Then she looked under the bed.

"What are you looking for, the bogeyman?" asked Art.

"No," said Guin.

Suddenly she heard music.

"You hear that?" she asked.

"Hear what?" asked Art.

"I could have sworn I heard music." She stood still and listened. She heard it again.

"Sounds like someone's ringtone," said Art.

"It must be Emily's phone! Help me find it."

They waited for the music to play again, but it didn't.

"Why don't you call her mobile?" suggested Art.

"Good idea," said Guin.

She dialed Emily's number and the music started playing again.

"I think it's coming from that drawer," said Art, pointing to one of the nightstands.

Guin hung up and walked over to the nightstand, pulling the drawer open. Emily's phone was inside. She sat down on the bed and placed the phone in her lap.

"This isn't good," she said, looking up at Art.

"It doesn't mean anything, Guin," said Art, trying to calm her. "They could just be down at the bar."

"Fine. Let's go down to the bar and see. But I have a very bad feeling…"

They left the room and headed down to the bar, Emily's phone tucked into Guin's bag.

There was barely anyone at the bar.

"Hey, what are you two doing here?" came a familiar voice.

Art and Guin turned and saw Joe.

"What are you doing here?" Art asked.

"Drowning my sorrows," said Joe, raising his nearly empty glass to him.

"Hey, Joe, you see Alan or Emily, by any chance?"

"Haven't seen them, sorry."

Art patted Joe on the shoulder. "Can I buy you another drink?"

"We don't have time," said Guin, impatiently.

"What's up?" asked Joe, looking from one to the other.

"Guin's worried that Alan's going to harm Emily," Art explained to Joe.

"Why would he hurt Emily?" asked Joe, confused.

"Come on, Art, we need to find Alan and Emily," said Guin, pulling on Art's arm.

"Can I tag along?" asked Joe. "I could use a distraction. If I sit here thinking about Josie any longer, I'll go insane."

Guin sighed. "Fine. Just, let's go."

"Where exactly are we going?" asked Joe, following Guin out of the bar.

"I have a funny feeling I know where they may be," said Guin, heading toward the path that led down to the pool and the private cabanas.

"Shouldn't we call the cops?" asked Joe, trying to keep up with Guin, who was practically running toward the private cabanas.

"No time," said Guin.

"I just hope she knows what she's doing," Joe said, in a stage whisper, to Art.

"I heard that," Guin snapped. "If you're worried, you can go back to the hotel."

"Prickly, isn't she?" said Joe.

"You don't know the half of it," said Art.

"Can you two please keep it down?" retorted Guin. "I'm trying to keep my ears open for any strange noises."

"Like what?" asked Joe.

Art shrugged.

"Stop and be quiet," Guin hissed.

They were standing a few feet away from Cabana 5, where Rick was found dead.

Guin stepped closer to the cabana and leaned an ear toward the door.

"Do you hear anything?" asked Joe, whispering.

Guin shook her head. With the wind blowing and the waves lapping nearby, it was hard to hear anything, inside or out.

"We should call the cops," said Joe.

"Shh!" admonished Guin.

Joe and Art exchanged looks.

"Well, if you don't want to call them, I will," said Joe.

"Just do it over there, where they can't hear you," hissed Guin.

"Don't I want the police to hear me?" asked Joe, confused.

"Not the police," said Guin, exasperated, "Alan and Emily!"

"Assuming they're in there," said Art.

Joe walked a few steps away.

Guin turned back to the cabana.

"I think we should go in," she said to Art.

"And I think we should wait for the police to get here," said Art.

"Emily could be dead by then!" said Guin. "She may be dead already!"

Art strode over to the door of the cabana and knocked.

"What the hell are you doing?" asked Guin.

"Room service!" called Art.

"Are you effing kidding me?" snapped Guin.

Art put a finger to his lips, indicating for her to be quiet.

Art knocked again.

"I have your order, sir. Do you just want me to leave it outside?"

Guin watched, half in horror, half curious.

"We didn't order room service," came a male voice from inside.

Guin and Art exchanged looks.

Just then Joe came over.

"The police are on their way."

"What did you tell them?" asked Art.

"That a woman was missing, and we feared she was in serious danger, and to come to the San Ybel Resort & Spa, where she was last seen."

"Good thinking," said Art.

"Thanks," said Joe.

Guin glared at the two of them.

"What?" said Joe. "Did I say something wrong?"

"No," said Guin. "Art here decided to play room service and knocked on the door of the cabana."

Joe looked at Art.

"Well, it worked, didn't it?" said Art.

"Be quiet!" said Guin, in a loud stage whisper.

"We still don't know it's them," said Art. "We only know someone is inside."

"Then let's find out, shall we?" said Art, walking back to the cabana and knocking loudly.

"Are you crazy?" Guin said, again in a stage whisper, glaring at Art.

"I told you, we didn't order room service!" came the man's voice again.

Just then the door opened and a head popped out.

"Good evening, Alan," said Art.

Alan whipped his head around.

"Art, what are you doing here?"

"I think the better question is, what are you doing here, Alan?"

"Where's Emily?" interjected Guin.

"Lying down," said Alan.

Guin raised an eyebrow.

"I'm coming in," she said, taking a step forward.

"I don't think so," said Alan, blocking the way.

"Good evening, Mr. Fielding," Joe called out, waving at him.

Alan turned to see who was calling him. As he did, Art rammed his fist into Alan's solar plexus, causing him to bend over.

Guin stared at Art in disbelief.

"Guess I won't be getting that promotion," said Art, looking down at Alan in disgust.

Guin smiled, despite herself.

Art shoved Alan aside and opened the door. Guin quickly scooted in, followed by Joe. The room was dimly lit, and it took a moment for Guin to spy Emily, seemingly asleep on the day bed. She rushed over.

"Emily?"

No response.

"Emily?" she said again, shaking her gently.

She looked up at Art and Joe.

"See if she has a pulse," said Joe.

"Right," said Guin. "I should have thought of that."

She grabbed Emily's left wrist and felt for a pulse. It was there, but very weak.

"We need to get her to the hospital," said Guin, looking down at Emily's inert form.

Suddenly, Guin heard a loud thump behind her. She turned her head to see Art crumple to the floor. Alan was standing over him, holding a broken bottle in his hand.

Joe took a step toward Alan.

"I wouldn't do that if I were you, Joseph," Alan said, tossing the broken bottle aside and removing a gun from behind his back.

"Where the hell did you get that?" asked Joe, wide eyed.

"It is amazingly easy to get a gun here in Florida," Alan calmly replied.

"Are you going to shoot us?" asked Guin, looking over at Alan, trying desperately to remain calm.

"That depends," said Alan.

"On what?" asked Joe.

Alan sighed.

"You really are hopelessly naïve," he replied.

"I may be from a small town in the Midwest, but I'm not naïve," Joe retorted. "And I know how to use a gun," he added.

Alan looked at Joe, an amused expression on his face.

"What did you do to Emily, Alan?" Guin asked.

"She took one too many Xanax again," Alan replied. "Terrible shame."

"I don't believe you," said Guin.

"Well, that's too bad," said Alan.

"Why did you kill Rick?" Guin suddenly asked, looking

up at him.

Alan didn't seem at all surprised by the question.

"He was blackmailing me," he answered.

"Blackmailing you?" asked Joe.

Alan sighed.

"He found out I had given myself, shall we say, an early bonus, and he threatened to tell upper management."

"So you killed him over a bonus?" asked Joe, confused.

Alan sighed again. "And to think I had high hopes for you. Mr. Tomlinson also had some other information, information that didn't concern him, that I did not want made public."

"Like the fact that you were having an affair with the new head of Marketing and charging the company for your little dalliances?" said Guin, a note of disgust in her voice.

Alan glared at Guin.

"But why harm your wife?" asked Joe, still confused.

"Because the little bitch was having an affair with the scumbag," said Alan, vehemently, waving the gun toward where Emily was lying unconscious.

"You forced her to take those pills, didn't you?" asked Guin, glaring at Alan.

"She took them willingly," said Alan.

"With the help of your little friend there," said Guin, looking at the gun in Alan's hand.

"But how did you kill Rick?" asked Joe.

"That was easy," said Alan. "I knew Rick had a severe allergy to ibuprofen—that's the generic term for Advil," he explained to Joe, who replied that he knew what ibuprofen was. "Emily kept a bottle in her bag, for when she got one of her headaches."

"But how did you get him to swallow the pills? Surely he couldn't have done it willingly?" asked Joe.

Alan smiled.

"Simple, really. I ground a few pills into a powder and put the powder into an envelope. Then I slipped the powder into his beer when he went to relieve himself. He had had a couple by then, and I doubt he noticed, until it was too late."

"So, you knew Rick was alive and hiding out at the hotel?" asked Guin.

"Not at first. I only discovered his deception when I followed Emily that Friday and discovered their little love nest. At least I had the sense to conduct my affairs away from home."

"But how did Rick wind up here?" asked Guin.

"Ah yes," said Alan, smiling. "When I discovered where he was hiding out, I had a message delivered, asking him to meet me in the company cabana that evening."

"How did Art fit into your little scheme?" asked Guin.

"Ah Arthur," said Alan, a sad look momentarily crossing his face. "I am a bit sorry about that. I rather liked Art. Good salesman. Was planning on promoting him. But it was just too easy."

"Too easy?" asked Joe, not following.

Guin made a face.

"Alan here set Art up to take the fall for Rick's death," Guin explained. "It was you who sent Art the note, posing as Rick, asking him to meet at the cabana just before the dinner, wasn't it?"

Alan smiled.

"Very clever of you, Guinivere. I always thought Arthur was stupid, leaving you for that hairdresser, though I could see her charms," he said, leering.

Guin made another face.

"And what about Captain Ben?" she asked.

"What about him?" asked Alan.

Was it Guin's imagination or was Alan enjoying himself?

"Did you kill him?" asked Guin.

"I don't think I'll answer that," said Alan, smiling down at Guin.

"And what about Emily?" said Guin, looking down at her friend.

"That little slut? She—"

Guin suddenly heard a gunshot and turned around to see Art wrestling with Alan, the gun having fallen to the floor.

"Joe!" called Guin. But Joe was already ahead of her, diving for the gun. He grabbed it and stood, pointing it at Alan.

"Hold it right there, Mr. Fielding," said Joe, leveling the gun at Alan's heart.

Just then the door to the cabana flew open.

"Nobody move!" shouted a familiar voice. O'Loughlin.

Guin looked over to see the detective and two armed police officers, their guns pointed.

"Drop the weapon," the detective ordered Joe.

Joe immediately lowered the weapon, putting it on the nearby table. One of the officers came forward and bagged it.

"That's Alan's gun," said Guin. "Joe saved us. Alan hit Art over the head with a bottle, then held that gun on us. Art came to and disarmed him, and Joe grabbed the gun."

The detective looked from Guin to Art to Joe.

"I'm telling you the truth, detective," Guin said.

The detective nodded.

"I'll need you all to give a statement," he said.

"Fine, whatever," said Guin. "But right now, we need to get Emily to the hospital. She swallowed a bunch of Xanax. I don't know how many."

Detective O'Loughlin looked over at Emily's prostrate form.

"Officer Pettit, get Mrs. Fielding to the hospital. Officer Getty and I have this."

"Yes, sir," said Officer Pettit.

"Do you need a hand?" asked Joe.

The officer looked over at the detective, who nodded his okay.

"I'll just need to speak to you later," said the detective. "So don't make any plans."

"Hey, if I haven't bolted yet…" said Joe.

He and Officer Pettit then gingerly carried Emily, who was still unconscious, to the patrol car. Guin prayed that they'd get her to the hospital in time.

"All right you three, let's go," said the detective.

He and Officer Getty then escorted Guin, Art, and Alan to his car, which was parked a little way away.

Guin noticed Art wince as he got in and looked over at him. There was blood all over the top of his right shoulder.

"You're hurt," she said to him.

"It's just a superficial wound," he replied.

"Detective!" called Guin, holding the door to the backseat open.

The detective stopped and peered in.

"Art's been hurt. He's bleeding."

The detective eyed Art's shoulder.

"He'll live," he said, closing the door.

He and Officer Getty then got in the front.

CHAPTER 42

It was very late when Guin, Art, and Joe emerged from the Sanibel Police Department, and all three were exhausted. Joe had been cleared of any wrongdoing, and Art had been cleared of any involvement in Rick's death, but the detective had told him not to leave the island just yet, in case the police had additional questions. Guin was relieved the whole thing was over, or nearly over, and just wanted to go back to the condo and crawl into bed, though she was eager to tell Craig everything that had happened and write the final draft of their article. But that could wait until morning.

Guin's Mini was still at the resort, and Joe was still staying there, so the detective had an officer drive them back over. When they got there, Joe wished them a good evening, or morning, and headed up to his room. Then Guin found the valet, who had been taking a nap, and gave him her ticket.

Guin yawned as the valet pulled the car around.

"You okay to drive?" asked Art.

"I'll be fine," said Guin, stifling another yawn. "Not like anyone's on the road at this hour. And besides," she said, looking at Art's bandaged arm and imagining the cuts and bruises on the back of his head, "you're in no shape to drive."

They drove back to the condo in silence, too tired to say

anything. When they got there, the cats were by the front door, waiting.

"They're probably hungry," said Guin, looking down at the two felines. "I'll give them some food, then I'm going to bed."

Art yawned.

"I'm going to try to get some shut-eye, too" he said.

"I'll see you in the morning," said Guin. "Or later this morning."

Art waved with his good arm and departed to the guest room. Guin went into the pantry, grabbed the bag of cat food, and filled up the cats' bowls. She yawned again.

"Goodnight, you guys," she said to the cats. "Try to keep it down."

She then made her way to the bedroom, threw off her clothes, and pulled on her nightshirt. She thought about climbing right into bed, skipping brushing her teeth this one time, but her need for routine won out. A few minutes later, teeth brushed, she was fast asleep.

Later that morning, after she had some coffee and a shower, Guin went to see Emily at the hospital.

"I'm getting a sense of deja vu," said Guin, upon entering Emily's room and seeing her in a hospital gown, propped up in bed.

Emily smiled. "Tell me about it. At least you didn't have to have your stomach pumped, twice, in one week."

"Ugh," said Guin. "You okay?"

"Surprisingly, yeah," said Emily.

Guin wanted to ask her if she had heard about Alan, but she wasn't sure what to say.

"I know about Alan," Emily said, as if reading Guin's mind. "And I hope they put the bastard in jail and throw away the key."

"Sounds like you may get your wish," said Guin. "Though what about Peter?"

Emily looked sad. Despite her feelings toward her husband and his many absences, he had been a decent father to their son, Peter.

"I don't know. He's spending the summer on the Vineyard, with a couple of his friends from school. He got a job there, and I've barely spoken with him. He's always too busy. Funny how that happens," she said, wistfully.

"Someone needs to tell him," said Guin.

Emily sighed. "I know. Though Alan may have spoken to him already. God only knows what he told him."

"All the more reason for you to speak to him," said Guin, gently.

"I know," said Emily. "I'm just so tired. This whole trip has been a nightmare."

"I know," said Guin. "But you'll be going home soon." She paused.

"Will you be going back to Greenwich?" Guin asked.

"Initially," said Emily.

"It will no doubt be strange to be there without Alan."

"Not really," said Emily. "He was rarely there."

"So..." said Guin, not sure what to say.

"I was thinking I might go up to the Vineyard for a bit, see Peter. Then maybe go with my cousin Dot on one of her trips."

"Sounds like a plan," said Guin. "Well, I should let you get some rest. Let me know if you need anything."

"I'm hoping they'll discharge me later this morning. The doctor said I should be fine, to just take it easy for a few days. But I just want to go home. It feels like it's been ages."

Guin looked out the window. For her home was now Sanibel, and she couldn't imagine going back to Connecticut.

"Well, like I said, if you need anything, call or text me," said Guin.

"What about you and Art?" asked Emily.

"What about me and Art?" she asked.

Emily smiled.

"You two getting back together? He's crazy about you, you know."

"I'm sorry to disappoint you, Emily, but no, we are not getting back together. You of all people can understand why."

"Hey, it's not like Art killed someone."

Guin laughed out loud.

"Sorry," she said.

Emily dismissed the apology with a wave of her hand.

"No, he didn't kill anyone, at least as far as I know," said Guin. "But he did break my heart, Em, and I've moved on."

"That marine biologist?"

"Yes… maybe…" said Guin, pausing.

Emily regarded her.

"You don't seem so sure."

"Well, I'm sure I'm not getting back with Art," said Guin.

"Well, good luck to you, Guin. And please look me up if you are ever back in Connecticut."

"Thanks, Em. Will do," said Guin.

Guin left the room and headed down the hall, her mind several miles away.

Guin got back to the condo to find Art on his laptop.

"How's Emily?" he asked her, looking up.

"Surprisingly okay," said Guin.

"That's good, isn't it?"

"Yes," said Guin. "I guess. I just wasn't expecting her to be so calm."

Art looked thoughtful.

"Yes?" said Guin. "I recognize that look. What's up?"

"I was just trying to picture what it must have been like for you, after I left, being alone in our house."

"Technically, it was my house, and as you recall, I sold it."

"You know what I mean," said Art.

Guin sighed.

"How about we leave the past in the past?"

"Fine by me," said Art. "Though…"

He got up and moved toward Guin, taking her hands in his.

Guin looked down at their hands then up into Art's brown eyes.

"Guin…"

"Yes?" said Guin.

"Guin, I want us to get back together."

Guin opened her mouth to protest but Art interrupted.

"Please, just hear me out. I know I was a jerk…"

He paused.

"Go on," said Guin, smiling. "Don't let me stop you."

Art smiled back at her.

"I know what I did was wrong, and I hurt you. I was an idiot. I get that. But if you take me back, I swear to you, I'll never cheat again."

Guin looked dubious. She glanced at Art's face and knew, in that moment, that he truly meant what he said. But she also knew that once he got back to work, things would go back to being the way they were, and she didn't want that life anymore.

"I'm sorry, Art, but no."

"Won't you just think about it?"

"I have, and the answer is no. I have a new life here. Sanibel makes me happy, and I realize I wasn't happy in

Connecticut. Here I have friends, a job I like, and people who share my passions."

"You mean that marine biologist," said Art, making a face. "What do people call him, Dr. Heartthrob?"

Guin pulled her hands away from Art's.

"His name is Harrison Hartwick, and yes, there's him too."

"What if I was willing to move down here—"

"No!" Guin practically shouted, interrupting him.

Art smiled, but it was a sad smile.

"Then I guess I should book my flight home."

"Did the detective say you were allowed to go?" asked Guin.

"Ah, I guess you didn't receive the message. We're wanted back at the Sanibel Police Department this afternoon at two."

Guin had been so preoccupied, she hadn't checked her phone.

"We can go together," she said.

"Can I at least buy you lunch?"

Just then Guin's stomach let out a loud noise.

"I'll take that as a 'yes,'" said Art, smiling.

"Fine," said Guin. "We can go out for lunch on the way. But right now, I really need to speak to Craig and Ginny."

Guin retreated to her bedroom/office and spent the better part of the next hour speaking with Craig and then Ginny, telling them everything that had happened over the last 24 hours.

Ginny whistled. "That's quite a story. It will be on the front page of all the papers."

"But it will be on our website first," said Guin.

"Well, you and Craig better get going then," said Ginny.

"I already spoke with Craig," Guin said. "We're going to get together later."

"Think you two can get me something tomorrow?"

"We'll do our best," said Guin.

"Well, off you go," said Ginny. "See you Tuesday, as usual? I have a bunch of stories I've been saving for you."

"See you Tuesday," said Guin. "Bye!"

Their visit to the police department was shorter than Guin had thought it would be. The detective just needed Art and Guin to answer a few more questions. Then they were free to go.

"So I'm free to leave Sanibel?" asked Art.

The detective eyed him. "I thought you were thinking of moving here."

Art looked over at Guin. "I've been led to believe that wouldn't be a good idea."

The detective looked at Guin and raised an eyebrow. Guin could feel herself blush under the detective's gaze.

"Well, if you two are done," said Art, puncturing the silence. "I need to go make myself an airline reservation."

They left and drove back to the condo in silence. When they got there, Art immediately got on his computer.

"When do you think you'll go?" Guin asked, looking over at him.

"As soon as I can get a flight out of here," said Art, not looking at her.

"You're welcome to stay here a couple more days," said Guin.

"Thanks, but I'd like to get back to Connecticut," he said, continuing to stare at the screen.

"Well, just let me know when your flight is, and if you need a lift to the airport."

Art ignored her, focusing all his attention on his computer.

Guin went into her room and texted Craig, letting him know she was available.

"How's 4?" he typed back.

"Good," she wrote. "C u then."

She had briefly texted with Ris earlier, confirming their date that evening. Ris's daughter was going out with some friends, so it would just be the two of them, and Ris had suggested they have dinner at the Beach House, their favorite place in Fort Myers Beach. As Craig's house was close to the Causeway, she figured she would head over to Ris's from there.

She sat down at her computer and typed up her notes. Then she printed them out, so she could better share and discuss them with Craig. That done, she walked into her closet to get changed, wishing her friend Shelly was there. Just then her phone started vibrating. She pulled it out of her back pocket. It was Shelly.

"Hey you! Do you have ESP?"

"No, why?" asked Shelly.

"I was just thinking about you," said Guin. "It feels like forever since I've seen you."

"That's why I'm calling," said Shelly. "You coming to our barbecue tomorrow? You can even bring that ex-husband of yours, if you want," she added.

Guin smiled. "Thanks, but Art's probably going to be headed home, back to Connecticut."

"Oh?" said Shelly. "Do tell."

Guin had so much to tell Shelly, but it would have to wait.

"Hey, Shell, I need to get dressed and go meet Ris for dinner. Can I call you in the morning? What time is the barbecue?"

"Remember when we used to have brunch every Sunday?" said Shelly, wistfully.

"Yeah, well, I've been kind of busy," said Guin.

"I've been busy, too," said Shelly. "I just miss them."

"We'll do Sunday brunch again soon, Shell. But right now, I've really got to go."

"Okay, okay," said Shelly. "The barbecue starts at six tomorrow, but we probably won't eat until at least six-thirty or seven."

"Great. Okay, bye Shelly. Talk to you in the morning."

"Yeah, yeah," said Shelly, knowing Guin was distracted. "See you tomorrow."

Guin ended the call, then pulled out a sundress and changed.

"I'm heading out," Guin called down the hall.

A few seconds later, Art appeared with his suitcase.

"Where are you going?" asked Guin.

"To Murph's," said Art.

"Oh?" said Guin.

"I have a cab coming to take me there."

"Okay," said Guin, slowly.

"Your keys are on the counter," he said, pointing.

"When's your flight to CT?" Guin asked.

"Tomorrow afternoon. Murph's going to give me a lift to the airport."

"Well, then…" said Guin, not sure what to say.

They stood there by the front door, looking at each other. Sensing something was up, both cats came trotting over, rubbing themselves against Art's legs. He bent down and petted each of them.

"Goodbye, you two. It's been fun. Take good care of your mom."

He rubbed their ears, then stood up.

"Shall we?" said Art, opening the door.

Guin stepped through, and together they headed downstairs.

CHAPTER 43

A sudden feeling of sadness, or loss, came over Guin as she drove to Ris's cottage in Fort Myers Beach. Could it be that she missed Art? She shook her head at the thought. It would never have worked. He would have been miserable on Sanibel, and no way was she going back to Connecticut. Besides, she was over him, she told herself. She had Ris now, and her friends. But the thought of spending the evening with Ris did not make her feel better.

She arrived at Ris's beach cottage and rang the doorbell. He appeared a few seconds later, looking handsome and relaxed in a pair of drawstring pants and a form-fitting polo shirt. Guin smiled.

"Hey there," she said.

"Hey yourself," he said, pulling her to him.

He lifted her chin and proceeded to kiss her.

"What was that for?" asked Guin, a bit dazed after they finally broke off.

"Do I need a reason to kiss you?" he asked.

"No, of course not. It just felt…" she searched for the right word.

"I've missed you," he said, though Guin had a feeling he was jealous of the time she had been spending with Art and wanted to make sure she knew how much he cared about her.

"He's gone, you know," she said, stepping into the house.

"Who?" Ris asked, innocently.

"You know who, Art. He left this afternoon. He's staying at his buddy Murph's overnight, then flying back to Connecticut tomorrow."

"Do you miss him?" Ris asked, looking at her.

"No," said Guin, honestly. "For a minute, I thought I did. But no, I don't. That life is in the past."

Ris smiled. "Good! So are you ready for some dinner? I made us a reservation for seven o'clock."

"You know me," said Guin, smiling. "I'm always ready to eat."

"Then let's go. We can have a drink at the bar if our table's not ready."

They turned around and headed to the garage, where Ris kept his vintage red Alfa Romeo convertible. He opened the passenger side door for Guin, then walked around to the driver's side and got in.

It was a beautiful evening, and Guin loved the feel of the wind whipping through her hair as they drove.

They arrived at the Beach House, and Ris parked the car—not allowing the valet to touch it. Then they jogged up the steps to the restaurant.

They were greeted at the door by Simone, the hostess.

"We'll have a table by the window for you in just a few minutes," she said, flashing them a big smile. "That couple is just finishing their coffee."

"No rush," said Ris. "We'll go sit at the bar."

They found two seats at the driftwood bar and ordered drinks, a beer for Ris and a margarita, no salt, for Guin.

"So tell me about your week," said Ris, as they sat there.

"Where to begin?" said Guin. "Why don't you tell me about yours."

And he did. Guin smiled politely and sipped her margarita as Ris regaled her with tales of his daughter's love life, work, and how he had decided to compete in an Ironman race in November.

"Wow," said Guin. She knew Ris was an athlete, but an Ironman was serious business. "You're going to be busy."

"I know, but it's something I've always wanted to do, and I'm not getting any younger," he said with a smile.

Just then Simone came over.

"You're table's ready. Sorry for the wait."

"No worries," said Guin.

They followed Simone across the room to a table overlooking the Gulf of Mexico. There were half a dozen boats in the water, either parked or going by the restaurant.

"It's so lovely here," Guin said, looking out.

"Your server will be right over," said Simone, leaving them to go back to her post.

A couple of minutes later a young man with "Dave" on his nametag came over and handed them menus.

"Can I get you a drink while you're deciding?" Dave asked.

"I'm good," said Guin. "Just some water."

"Me too," said Ris.

"Very good," said Dave. Then he disappeared.

Over dinner, Guin told Ris a bit about Rick and Alan, leaving out the part about Emily and Rick having an affair. When she was done, Ris whistled.

"You could have been killed, Guin."

"But I wasn't," she replied.

"Still, you should be more careful."

Guin made a face.

They finished their decaf cappuccinos, then Ris asked for the check.

"Why don't you stay overnight at my place," he

suggested, as they were walking out.

"I'd love to," said Guin, "but I'm awfully tired. I didn't get a whole lot of sleep last night."

"You could sleep at my place," he said.

Guin smiled. "I think you and I both know there wouldn't be a whole lot of sleeping."

Ris smiled back at her. "Well, why don't you hang out for a little while and we can play it by ear?"

Guin agreed to stay for a little while, but she was already yawning by the time they got back to the cottage.

"I should really go home," she said, trying to stifle another yawn.

"I'd offer you coffee, but I know you don't drink the real stuff at night."

Guin smiled.

"Just stay for a few minutes," he said, softly, resting his hands on her shoulders and looking into her eyes. "Come sit with me on the lanai. We can look up at the stars."

She followed him out to the lanai and they sat on the rattan sofa.

As they gazed up at the heavens, Ris pointed out different stars and constellations. Guin tried to pay attention, but she kept nodding off.

"You sure you won't stay over, sleepy head?" said Ris, gently nudging her.

Guin gave him a sleepy smile.

"The cats wouldn't like it," she said.

"They'll survive," he said.

Guin yawned again.

"That does it. You're staying here," he said. "And I won't take 'no' for an answer."

Guin was so tired she didn't have the energy to disagree.

"I'll grab one of Fiona's big concert tees. She probably won't even notice."

He then gently led her into the bedroom, seating her at the foot of his bed.

"I'll be right back," he said.

Guin was so tired, she could barely sit up straight.

A couple of minutes later, Ris returned with a Walk the Moon t-shirt.

"Here, put this on. Though…" he said, eyeing her and giving her a lascivious smile.

Guin laughed.

"What if Fiona comes home and walks in? I'll go put on the tee."

She disappeared into the bathroom and brushed her teeth. Then she changed into the tee. Ris was still dressed when she reappeared.

"You not coming to bed?" she asked.

"I've got some work to do, and I'd like to wait up for Fiona."

"Okay," said Guin, somewhat disappointed. "Well, see you later."

She climbed into the bed and felt herself nodding off as soon as her head hit the pillow. Ris came over and planted a kiss on her forehead, then on her lips. Guin smiled.

"Good night," she said.

"Pleasant dreams," called Ris, as he turned off the lights and closed the door.

The next morning Guin got up to discover Ris was not in bed beside her. That's odd, she thought. She went to the bathroom, then into the main living area. She walked into the kitchen, prepared to make a pot of coffee, but the coffee maker was already on and the pot full. There was a note beside it.

"Gone running. Back by 8." It was signed "Ris."

He must have gotten up very early, thought Guin, as it was only 6:45. Then again, if he was training to compete in an Ironman.... She helped herself to some coffee and sat at the dining table. She realized she had forgotten to ask Ris if he wanted to go to the barbecue with her that evening. Oh well, I'll ask him later, she thought.

She sat at the table, drinking her coffee and reading the *New York Times* on her phone while she waited for Ris to return. He finally walked through the door, drenched with sweat, a few minutes after eight. He smiled at the sight of her, still in the Walk the Moon tee.

"You just get up?" he asked.

"Oh no," replied Guin. "I've been up for some time. I was just too lazy to get dressed."

Ris grinned.

"Oh no," said Guin, eyeing him. "You're all sweaty!"

"I'd be happy to take a shower. You're welcome to join me," he added, his dimples showing as his smile broadened.

Guin looked at Ris's toned, tan body, glistening in the doorway, and she felt her face grow warm.

"I should really get back to Sanibel. I have a big article to write, and it wouldn't be fair to Craig."

"Screw Craig," said Ris, moving toward her.

Guin giggled and moved away.

"I'm afraid I'm going to have to take a rain check, much as I'd like to stay," she said, though a part of her didn't really feel like staying, which surprised her.

"Well, if you must," said Ris, removing his shirt.

Guin regarded his naked torso.

"I'm just going to get dressed and go," she said, getting up.

"Is there no way I can convince you to stay?" he asked, taking a step toward her.

She dodged him, giving him a smile, and then ran into

the bedroom, shutting the door behind her. A few minutes later she emerged, dressed and ready to go. She looked around the living area, but she didn't see him. Then she remembered, the outdoor shower.

She went out onto the lanai to where the shower was and heard the water running.

"I'm leaving!" she called over the water.

"Okay!" he called back. "I'll call you this week!"

"Okay!" she answered. "Please thank Fiona for the t-shirt!"

Then she left, realizing, as she drove back to Sanibel, that she hadn't invited him to the barbecue.

She got back to the condo and immediately got to work. As she typed, she kept thinking about the detective.

"The hell with it," she said out loud.

She reached into her drawer, pulled out her phone, and texted O'Loughlin.

"You want to go to a barbecue?"

She didn't expect him to write her back and chastised herself for even asking. He'll never go, she thought. Besides, we're having lunch on Tuesday. I was stupid to even ask. What an idiot. But a few seconds later she received a text back from him.

"When?"

She could feel her cheeks turning pink.

"Tonight at 6. It's at my friend Shelly's. Her husband Steve will be there too," she hastily added, though she wasn't sure why.

She waited for him to respond. It seemed like minutes, but it was only a few seconds.

"OK," he wrote.

Guin let out the breath she hadn't realized she was holding.

"Great!" she wrote.

She texted him the address and said she'd meet him there.

She put the phone down. She could feel herself blushing. What on earth had compelled her to invite the detective? And what would Shelly and Steve say? But what was done was done.

She told herself to stop obsessing and to get back to work—and spent the better part of the next six hours banging out her part of the article, so she could send it to Craig before she headed off to the barbecue.

At five-thirty she sent the article to Craig, along with some notes, and told him she was heading out but would be back later that evening. She then went into her closet to get changed. She stood there for several minutes, debating what to wear. She eyed her collection of sundresses, but she finally decided on her blue skinny jeans and a pretty floral peekaboo top. She then went into the bathroom and ran a comb through her hair, but as usual there was no taming her strawberry blonde curls. She sighed.

"It's useless," she said aloud.

Finally, she put on some mascara and lip gloss.

"Good enough," she said, giving herself a final once-over in the mirror.

She walked down the hall to the kitchen and opened the door to the pantry. The cats miraculously appeared as she did. Fauna meowed loudly.

"Yes, yes," said Guin, retrieving the bag of cat food. "I'm about to feed you."

Fauna gave her a look that implied 'That garbage again? Come on!'

"Too bad," said Guin aloud. "I'll give you the good stuff in the morning. I have to go."

Fauna gave her a look of reproach but dove into the bowl of dry food nonetheless. Flora followed suit.

"Be good, you two!" Guin called, grabbing her purse and her keys.

She slipped on a pair of heeled sandals, then left.

She arrived at Shelly and Steve's a few minutes early and sat in her Mini, her heart pounding. Why am I so nervous? she thought. A couple of minutes later she saw the detective's car pull up. She got out of the Mini and headed toward it.

The detective smiled when he saw her.

"You look nice," he said, coming around the car to meet her.

"Thank you," she said, a smile on her face.

The detective, as usual, was dressed in chinos and a button-down shirt, albeit one with short sleeves. And he was carrying a six-pack of beer. Guin eyed it.

"Figured I shouldn't show up empty-handed," he said.

"I'm sure Steve will appreciate it," said Guin, still smiling.

The detective smiled back at her.

He's actually rather handsome when he smiles, Guin thought, gazing at the detective's slightly weathered, freckled face, with its strong jaw and tawny eyes that matched his hair.

"Shall we?" he said, gesturing toward the door.

"I guess so," said Guin, taking a breath.

She walked with the detective to the front door and rang the bell.

"Coming!" called a female voice.

A minute later the door was opened by Shelly.

"Well, hello, you two!" she said, a smile spreading across her face. "It's about time."

Epilogue

The rest of the summer on Sanibel seemed to fly by for Guin. Much to her surprise, and delight, her brother Lance and his husband, Owen, showed up at the end of July, just as they had threatened, and stayed for several days, continuing on to Miami afterward. It had been great to see Lance, and Guin promised to visit him in Brooklyn in the fall.

She had also attended a couple of baseball games with the detective. She had initially been surprised when he had invited her to go see the Red Sox play the Tampa Bay Rays, but she had agreed to the day trip with the proviso that he go with her to see the Mets play the Miami Marlins a couple of weeks later, which he had agreed to.

As for Ris, he had been so busy with his Ironman training, teaching a summer course at Florida Gulf Coast University, and working at the Shell Museum, that Guin had barely seen him. But part of her was glad for a little time off.

Guin had also come to a decision. She would start looking for a house on Sanibel. Nothing big or fancy. Just a nice little beach cottage, kind of like Ris's, but close enough to the beach so that she could walk there in under 15 minutes. Just the thought of owning her own place on the island filled her with joy.

Then, at the end of August, she received an email from

Art. She had heard from him a couple of times since he had left. The first time was to thank her for all she had done for him while he had been down on Sanibel. The second email, a couple of weeks later, was to inform her that he had been promoted to Alan's job, after Alan had been let go by the company upon being charged with first-degree murder.

The subject line on the third email was "I thought you should know," which peaked Guin's curiosity. She opened the email and read.

"Dear Guin," it began. "I hope this email finds you well. I have something to tell you, and I don't know how you'll react, but I hope you'll be okay with it. I've been seeing Emily. I know, I know. First, I got Alan's job, now his wife, but it's not as creepy as it sounds. I felt bad for Emily while we were down on Sanibel and looked her up shortly after we got back, just to see how she was doing. She thanked me for my email, and we wound up writing to each other pretty regularly. She had gone to the Vineyard and then went to the South of France with her cousin Dot for a couple of weeks. She's actually pretty funny, and I found myself looking forward to her emails describing her adventures. Her cousin Dot sounds like quite a character.

"Anyway," he continued, "one thing led to another, and when she got back to Greenwich a couple of weeks ago, we got together, and, well, things just seemed to click. We're actually talking about moving in together. I know it might seem kind of sudden, but…. Apparently, the fact that I'm a workaholic doesn't concern her too much. Though the funny thing is, since my time on Sanibel, I've come to realize that work isn't everything, and I've been thinking that maybe I'd get out of sales. I know, I know. You're probably rolling your eyes." And, in fact, Guin was. "But I'm not getting any younger, and I'd like to travel and do things other than work all the time, sooo…

"Don't worry, I'm not going to quit my job anytime soon, or next week," he continued. "Not that you care. I just wanted you to know. And wanted you to know about me and Emily.

"Hope you are well," he concluded. "Best always, Art"

Guin sat staring at her monitor.

Well, what do you know? She had, like Art, received emails from Emily, but Emily had said nothing to her about Art. She grabbed her phone and sent Emily a text.

"Just received an interesting email from Art," she wrote.

A few seconds later, her phone rang.

"I was going to tell you myself," Emily said, not bothering to say hello. "Are you angry?"

"No, I'm not angry," said Guin. And truly, she wasn't. "I was just a bit surprised, that's all."

"You sure you're okay with it, us?" asked Emily.

Guin felt a slight pang.

"I'm happy for you, Em, really," she said. "Just don't let him work all the time and ignore you!"

Emily laughed.

"Well, good luck to you," said Guin.

"Thanks, Guin," Emily replied. "How are things with you and that hunky marine biologist?"

"Okay," said Guin.

"Just okay?" asked Emily.

"He's been very busy. He's training to do an Ironman race and has been working a lot."

"Ah," said Emily. "Well, I have to go. I just wanted to ring you to make sure you were okay with all of this."

"I'm fine with it, Emily. And I wish you and Art the best."

She got off the phone and noticed she had a new text. It was from Ris. His ears must have been burning, Guin thought, smiling.

"Dinner tonight?"

"Sure," Guin wrote back, adding a smiley face.

"Great!" he replied. "How about my place at 7?"

"Sounds perfect," she texted back. "C u then."

To be continued…

Look for Book Three in the Sanibel Island Mystery Series, *In the Market for Murder*, on Amazon and on Sanibel December 2018.

Acknowledgments

First, my thanks to everyone who bought a copy of *A Shell of a Problem*, the first book in the Sanibel Island Mystery series, especially to those of you who left kind comments on the Sanibel Island Mysteries Facebook page and on Amazon and Goodreads. Your support means everything.

I also want to thank all the stores on Sanibel that took a flyer on me and *A Shell of a Problem*. Thank you, Rebecca, Cate, Marcy, and the rest of the crew at MacIntosh Books and Paper of Sanibel, my home away from home. You guys have been terrific. Thanks for hosting all those book signings, and for the sweet treats (especially the cake). And I love your latest acquisition, Brady the rescue cat. Black cats rule.

Similarly, thank you Gretchen and the staff at the Bailey-Matthews National Shell Museum and Melissa and everyone at Bailey's General Store. I appreciate you carrying my books.

For help with the fishing and boating scenes in *Something Fishy*, I owe a debt of gratitude to Paul Primeaux, aka Captain Paul, who patiently answered all my questions about tarpon fishing off Sanibel and took me out on his boat and showed me around Pine Island Sound. You're the best, Paul. And thanks for telling all your shelling tours about *A Shell of a Problem*. I still owe you that beer, probably a six-pack's worth at this point.

And for making sure the characters and plot were consistent, and hunting down typos, thank you Diane Thomas and Amanda Walter. You are good friends and loyal readers, and *Something Fishy* is a better book because of the two of you.

Speaking of hunting down typos, I am indebted to Sue and John de Cuevas (aka Mom and John), who copyedited *Something Fishy*. I am very fortunate to have two former Harvard writing instructors as parents, and I appreciate your edits and comments. The latter often had me smiling or laughing out loud. Thank you for your love and support. (And if there are any errors in the Acknowledgments, it's because I didn't have them copyedit it.)

Thanks, too, to my wonderful cover designer, Kristin Bryant. You make me look good, and everyone loves your covers—and the promos you did. I look forward to working with you on book three. Similarly, thank you Polgarus Studio (Marina and Jason) for making the inside of the book look as good as the outside.

As anyone who is a writer knows, writing is a very solitary and often frustrating profession. So it's important to have someone who will listen to you moan and groan and tell you can do it when you think you can't. For me that person has been my husband, Kenny. He never once doubted I could write a book, even when I did, and he has patiently listened to me worry about this and that since I started this adventure—and has cooked me dinner nearly every night, so I would have one less thing to worry about. Bless you, Kenny.

I would thank my two cats, Flora and Felix, who have stood (or, more accurately, napped) by my side throughout this process, but they can't read—and I'm still mad at them for puking all over the carpet and the sofa.

About the author

Jennifer Lonoff Schiff is the bestselling author of *A Shell of a Problem*, the first book in the Sanibel Island Mystery series, and a writer whose work has appeared in numerous publications. A cat lover, bird watcher, shell collector, and avid cozy mystery reader, she and her husband and two cats divide their time between New England and Sanibel Island, Florida.

About the Sanibel Island Mystery series

To learn more about the Sanibel Island Mystery series, visit the website at http://www.SanibelIslandMysteries.com or like the Sanibel Island Mysteries Facebook page at https://www.facebook.com/SanibelIslandMysteries/.

Made in the USA
Lexington, KY
13 December 2019

58544445R00212